DeathWalker

DeathWalker

A Vampires Vengeance

Edwin F. Becker

AuthorHouse™
1663 Liberty Drive
Bloomington, IN 47403
www.authorhouse.com
Phone: 1-800-839-8640

© 2011 by Edwin F. Becker. All rights reserved.

No part of this book may be reproduced, stored in a retrieval system, or transmitted by any means without the written permission of the author.

First published by AuthorHouse   10/26/2011

ISBN: 978-1-4670-6260-2 (sc)
ISBN: 978-1-4670-6259-6 (hc)
ISBN: 978-1-4670-6258-9 (ebk)

Library of Congress Control Number: 2011918628

Printed in the United States of America

Any people depicted in stock imagery provided by Thinkstock are models, and such images are being used for illustrative purposes only.
Certain stock imagery © Thinkstock.

This book is printed on acid-free paper.

Because of the dynamic nature of the Internet, any web addresses or links contained in this book may have changed since publication and may no longer be valid. The views expressed in this work are solely those of the author and do not necessarily reflect the views of the publisher, and the publisher hereby disclaims any responsibility for them.

Other Titles by this author,

A TRIP BACK IN TIME

BANISHED

A Demon, an Exorcist, and a Battle of Faith

TRUE HAUNTING

13 CHILLING TALES

ELEVENTH COMMANDMENT

Let He Who Harms the Children Be Struck Down

VISIT THE AUTHOR AT

www.EdwinBecker.com

To my wife, Marsha,
who inspired me to write this story, and to my
daughter, Katherine, who helped me
turn it into reality.

Foreword

ampires may very well exist! We are led to believe that complete **exsanguination** (complete bleeding out) of a body is the only sign of a vampire. In reality, the body does not have to be completely drained of blood. Common **hypovolemia or hypovolaemia** is all that is necessary to kill a human being and stop their heart. This translates to '*massive blood loss*.' Now think, how many times have you heard that term? The official numbers keep growing every year, but hundreds of thousands of people go missing in the United States, never to be seen again. It is a valid number established by our FBI annually. Do vampires exist? Could vampires exist? Do you really wish to know? Enjoy!

Edwin F. Becker

Chapter One

As she ran along the road, the only sounds were the rhythm of her soft jogging shoes hitting the black tar pavement and the sound of her heart pounding a steady beat. Every morning found her training at 3 A.M. for the marathon races that she loved so much. This day, she was pushing herself, and instead of the normal ten mile run she would do sixteen. She ran without the characteristic ear-buds and MP3 player, so to be aware of every sound as she moved along the road. There was no traffic at this time of the morning and the only illumination was the circles of brightness every quarter mile provided by the highway lights. She made it a game of turning her exercise into a race, from one highway light to the next, all the while maintaining a steady rhythm as she ran.

From the sky, the runner was easily spotted, as vampires can see the glow of warm blooded beings moving across the cold dark ground as easily as you or I can see each other in broad daylight. This vampire could not resist the temptation of a meal that had literally delivered itself to her. It only took a moment for her to land and wait anxiously a half-mile ahead.

As the runner left the circle of brightness and entered the darkness between the highway lights, a silhouette in the distance broke her concentration. She wiped her eyes, making certain that her mind wasn't playing tricks on her. There, standing under the street light ahead, appeared to be a woman watching her approach. She looked about for a car, thinking one must have broken down, leaving the poor woman stranded . . . but saw none and thought the car must be further up the road.

As she jogged closer, she noticed that the woman had taken an offensive position, much like a teacher who was waiting to admonish a student. The woman was facing her with arms folded and legs spread apart, just glaring in her direction. It was at that moment that the little hairs on the back of her neck began to stand on their own and a feeling in her gut told her to turn and run in the opposite direction. Having already ran twelve miles, she ignored her body's warning signals, thinking that this run had taken its toll on her mind and was playing games with her. She ignored the little voice in her head warning her of danger.

Only when she was close enough did she witness the eyes of this woman glowing bright red, and suddenly felt a sense of fear. With no one but the two of them on this deserted road, calling for help was futile, so she turned and changed her rhythmic run to a full sprint in the opposite direction. She knew her physical limitations at this point and could keep this fast pace for at least a mile before collapsing in exhaustion. As she ran, she only hoped a mile at this pace would be enough to distance herself from whatever it was that she thought she had seen.

When she felt something brush against her back from behind, she panicked and turned off the road toward the shelter of the trees and bushes of the countryside. Leaving the black tar surface for the soft moist ground slowed her down a bit, but fear and adrenaline were kicking in and it was like turning on a booster rocket. She was running as fast as she could and never looked behind, as her only thoughts were of increasing the distance and finding a place to hide.

She heard herself scream as she felt two hands grab her from behind and lift her completely into the air. She struggled to stay on the ground as her feet lifted off and then touched back on the solid surface as she bounced back and forth between the earth and the air.

"Let me go!" she screamed. "Dear God, let me go! Please!"

Suddenly there was a sensation of cold breath on the back of her neck, then the shocking pain of having flesh torn away, her blood flowing freely. Hearing her own skin being torn, combined with the pain, put her into instant shock. The pain, exhaustion, and blood loss prevailed, as she blacked out into an inevitable deathly sleep.

The female vampire drank the blood with enthusiasm and enjoyment as a commanding voice pierced the silence.

"Anne, I told you not to take risks," he scolded.

"But I needed it. Christian, I was so hungry, I couldn't help it. She was alone and there were no witnesses," she explained as she licked the blood from her fingertips.

He paced back and forth. "Well, what's done is done. I'll disguise the kill." She had drained the body, so Christian began dragging it further into the brush, leaving a clear trail. With his razor sharp claws, he tore at it, much the way a wild animal would do, until the body was completely

DeathWalker

mutilated. He knew that it was likely that the real animals would tear at it long before the body was ever found, making it appear clearly as an animal attack.

"Anne, it will soon be daylight. We must go."

Satisfied that their presence would not be detected, they lifted their arms and floated effortlessly, disappearing into the night sky.

*   *   *

The body was literally torn apart. As he viewed the photographs of the death scene, he wondered, "Where's the blood?" He turned to his friend, a detective, asking that exact question.

"Mike, where is the blood? This girl was torn to shreds?" Mike Evans was a ten-year veteran of the Minneapolis police and had seen these types of tragedies before.

"Teddy, when an animal attacks a human, it will typically drag them to another location, especially if they're hungry and intend on feeding. She could have been killed a mile from where her body was actually found."

Ted Scott was a writer. He was visiting his good buddy, hoping to find the subject for his next book.

"What kind of animal was said to have done this?" Ted thumbed through a whole series of pictures.

"A bear . . . or possibly wolves," Mike answered. "The county examiner hasn't confirmed it yet, but they think it's a bear. It's really a tough call, because the body was at least a few days old. The forest rangers are out there tracking it down as we speak."

Ted didn't agree with that answer, but would say nothing. He had grown up in the North Woods and a real bear attack was rare. Minnesota was primarily Black Bear country, with a lesser population of Brown Bear. He had hunted when he was growing up and knew that these bears kept to themselves; they are not exactly in the same category as the Grizzly. The only way to force an attack is to approach a cub, and then any mother bear would surely become aggressive. Other than that, bears were pretty hard to find, even for the experienced hunter. At this time of the year, food was plentiful, so it was not likely that this bear was hungry. So why would a bear attack a jogger? It was possible, but not likely.

Ted turned to Mike. "So? You said that you had a good story for me. A bear attack doesn't make for a whole book; an article, maybe."

Mike turned away from the file cabinet and tossed another stack of pictures on the table. "So far, we have had three attacks in this region of the state. Three bodies found in less than three months. Check these out . . ." Mike stood in anticipation of Ted's reaction. Mike looked the part of a cop; tall, muscular, dark haired, with an air of authority about him.

"I didn't hear about three . . . three, in three months? Nothing was on the news or in the papers?" Ted was puzzled.

"Yes, it was. The problem was how it was treated. Three different counties, actually, have found remains of bodies." Mike replied.

"Where have I been?" Ted responded.

Mike smiled. "I got these from the Hennepin County investigators, as you know, and they're right in this same building. These other two happenings really weren't considered all that newsworthy. One was identified as a homeless man; the other wasn't because they didn't find all that much to identify. Both had been savagely ripped apart by an animal. Because of the condition of the bodies, the coroners could only guess at the cause of death. Now, is this a story?" Mike really wasn't sure if this was what Ted was looking for to use as a basis for his book.

"I'm not sure. I'd like to speak with the county coroner first." Ted stated.

"Sure, I can arrange it for you. I'll call him and introduce you. He'll show you one of the bodies, it's still on ice." Mike smiled, thinking Ted would be reluctant. Writing about ghastly events was one thing, viewing the actual carnage was another.

"You don't have to introduce me, he's my cousin. I can stop by tomorrow and get the inside information about all this. I don't know if this is a story or not, but I'll work on it." Ted continued to flip through the pictures, with a look of disinterest on his face.

"What the hell do you want for Minneapolis? It's not like we're New York or Chicago. We have our share of crime, but nothing compared to big cities." Mike saw his job and the crimes as routine. "I just thought that as a writer, you might find this interesting, but what do I know?" Mike felt he had wasted Ted's time and what he had presented was likely not at all that compelling.

DeathWalker

"No, don't apologize. I might be able to build a good story out of this. Thanks—really." Ted was sincere and Mike knew it. "Can I buy you a drink?" Ted asked, anticipating the response.

"Naaah. Not tonight. It's my anniversary. I have to be home on time or all hell will break loose. But you wouldn't know about that, being single, would you?" Mike was kidding.

"I'm out of here. If I don't get home to my dog, all hell will break loose." Ted laughed, for his dog was his only commitment. "See you, and thanks."

Ted left the City Jail Building perplexed about what he had just seen. As he drove home, it seemed more and more improbable that an animal had done this. He knew the animals of the North Woods. Attacks were rare and near impossible at this time of the year. It was summer and food was bountiful. Bears had a full diet available with no need to be aggressive. Minnesota has the largest Timber Wolf population next to Alaska, so wolves could be a remote possibility, but a pack wouldn't have left anything but a few bones after feeding. A big cat wouldn't attack something that was larger than itself, unless cornered or threatened. A wounded bear maybe, but over three months? Not likely. Over a three month period, the wounded bear would have certainly healed or died. Ted laughed to himself. "We ARE the gopher state . . . maybe it's a 200 pound mutant gopher?"

Ted drove only a mile or so southwest of downtown before turning toward his condominium building. Passing the opulent residences in his Loring Park neighborhood, he crept only a few blocks north and he was at his 10th Street address. He pulled his car into the underground garage and parked. As he rode the elevator to the tenth floor, he was in a trance-like state. His mind was playing back the photographs that he had seen of the human bodies torn apart in almost an unrecognizable condition. He unlocked the door to his condo and Brutus came running. Brutus was a four pound Yorkshire terrier, and Ted's only constant companion and roommate. Ted scooped up Brutus and flopped his six foot frame on the couch. Grabbing the remote, he switched on the television. He sat, petting Brutus as he watched the national news.

As a feature, there was a special report on rescue dogs. Ted was looking to Brutus and mumbled, "Watch these guys, boy." Ted watched as the film captured the dogs in live footage of actual rescues. Then it showed a search near Winnipeg, in Manitoba, Canada, northwest of Minneapolis. A

5

tourist was missing and assumed lost in the dense woods. The rescue dogs eventually found the body, as the narrator explained; the tourist became the victim of a wild "bear attack". The words "bear attack" stunned Ted. He noticed the foliage in the film and again, it was a summer scene—not exactly a time when bears would be hungry or aggressive. It simply didn't make any sense.

Ted's father, Ray, lived to the northwest. His house was close to the Canadian border, near the town of Roseau, only a few miles away from Manitoba Province, Canada. A small town, Roseau's only claim to fame was that the snowmobile was actually invented there in 1953. Ted picked up the phone and dialed.

"Dad? It's Ted. How the hell are you?"

"Good to hear from you, son. How is it going? When are you going to visit your old man?"

"Dad, I'm fine. In fact, I may stop by in the near future, but I have a question to ask." Ted paused.

"Go ahead, son . . . shoot."

"Is there a bear problem this year? I mean, like, maybe with there being too many bears or them being overly aggressive?" Ted awaited his father's answer.

"Hell no! Aggressive? Jesus, we're not talking grizzlies here, they're brown and black bear. Most of the time, I can kick them in the ass when they mess up my garbage. As long as you don't mess with their cubs, they don't want much to do with you. Is that what you mean? Hell, son, you know that as well as I do. You grew up with them."

Ted knew his dad wasn't kidding. Although in his sixties, his father was a big man at 6' 3" and near 250 pounds. He probably would not hesitate kicking a bear in the ass.

"Yeah, I know, but I was wondering if ecologically anything has affected them. Like maybe their food supply has been affected or something." Ted continued probing.

"Food supply? You should see these fat old things. If they got any fatter, their butts wouldn't fit between the trees. No son, there is no problem with the bears, yet. I say yet, because they say this could be a bad year for berries, but time will tell. May I ask why you're asking?" Ted's dad was confused on his sudden preoccupation with the recent attitude of the local bear population.

DeathWalker

"Well, I'm kind of working on a story and noticed there have been a number of bear attacks this summer. We've had three down here and I just saw the report of a similar one in Winnipeg. I was just wondering if the balance of things had changed up in your neck of the woods."

"Bear attacks? Teddy, I only know of one legitimate bear attack in my forty years of living up here, and he was wounded. You know as well as I that if you dangle food in front of a hungry bear, anything can happen, but barring that, it don't sound right. Nope, don't sound right."

"Well, Dad, I'll let you go for now." Ted had satisfied his curiosity.

"Teddy, stop up and see your old dad. Bring me some of your stuff to read. Since your mother died, it's not the same up here. I'm talking to myself, for Christ's sake!"

"I will, Dad . . . I will bring you some stuff. Call you soon. I love you, Dad." Ted hung up.

Ted had tried to get his father to move in with him in Minneapolis after his mother had died two years ago, but his father refused. To Ted, Minneapolis, St. Paul, had everything a person could want. At his fingertips were sports teams, theater, symphonies and culture, not to mention the many fairs and gatherings that went on almost all year long. Why his dad chose to stay up in the northwest corner of the state was a mystery, but he knew his father valued the solitude and could never imagine socializing without his late mother. His father's house still had his mother's things scattered about, as if his father needed the warmth of the memories of days gone by.

Ted also felt that his dad didn't want to be a burden, as he was one stubborn old man, demanding his independence, even if he had to live in the wilderness to do it. Ted knew that is exactly how he would be at his father's age, for they were very much alike. He had his dad's thick brown hair and dark brown eyes, along with a heavy build. At 6' 2", 220 pounds, he looked more like a football player than a writer.

Ted, at age 29, was fairly successful. Finishing college with a degree in journalism from the University of Minnesota, he went right to work immediately for the Minneapolis Press. In only a few years, he would be writing his own column. This year, he quit. He became disillusioned with the press, as his subjects were dictated and many of his articles were censored. He found there was no longer a "free" press. Tired of the everyday routine and restrictions of production writing, he would try his hand at writing novels. His first manuscript, "A Good Day to Die," was a detective story and was soon to be published. This talent, he got from his mother. She was the creative one of the family. It was to her that he dedicated this first book.

His mother was a full blooded Anishanabe Indian, more commonly known as Chippewa. It was from her that he developed his imagination, as she would put him to sleep as child with her wonderful stories of Chippewa folklore. It was his first example of how mere words could make the night either frightening or wonderful, depending on how she crafted the story. The only outward sign of Indian blood in Ted was his perpetual reddish-tan appearance. Inside, he carried her heart, courage, and appreciation for nature.

He picked up Brutus and walked toward the door. "Come on, Brutus, time to drain the old dragon before bedtime." Brutus was wagging his tail. "Let's go walking, okay boy? You'll protect me from those mean old hungry bears, right fella?" Brutus just gazed up at him, wagging his stub of a tail.

The next morning, Ted was knocking on the door of the Hennepin County Coroner, located in the basement of Hennepin Medical Center, around the corner from the City Jail Building and Hennepin County Building. Paul Malone had been told that Ted would soon be there. Paul was about fifty, and an old pro at forensics. He appeared the part of a coroner, with the white lab coat, gray hair, and thick black glasses. If Ted didn't know him, he would have guessed him to be either a coroner or a science teacher.

Malone also was part Chippewa, and therefore considered a "cousin" in the sense, that a bloodline was shared between them. Ted had met Malone a number of times at ceremonial functions, and they were friends.

"Hey Cousin, I need some information relating to the bear attacks." They shook hands.

"So you know Mike?" Malone asked.

"Yeah, I once dated his sister. That's how we met. When I was with the Press, Mike helped me with information from time to time." Ted offered.

"Mike called, as if you and I had never met. Didn't you tell him that we're cousins?" Malone asked.

DeathWalker

"Yeah, I told him, but obviously he didn't hear me."

"So? What can I do for you today?" Malone questioned.

"I'd like your impression and professional opinion regarding these possible bear incidents. I'm doing research for a book."

"Well, they certainly are unusual. To be perfectly honest, we have not put these deaths under a microscope. No CSI here, as we don't have the budget. They are pretty cut and dry. There is no doubt it was a bear. There are a number of claw marks that could only be made by a large animal. The claw damage is much too massive for a mountain lion or wolf. In every case, we had evidence that a number of animals had violated the body, probably after the bear killed them. But only a bear could produce some of the tremendous damage we found." Paul almost sounded casual about his findings; after all, this was everyday business.

"What about blood?" Ted asked.

"You mean, total lack of blood, don't you?" Paul asked, and Ted nodded a very quick affirmative, anticipating his answer.

"This is not all that unusual. These people were killed by massive wounds. It is likely that the blood loss occurred at the location of the killings. Those bodies were then moved to the areas where we eventually found them. It's really very common. Forget animal killings; let's take a gang killing as an example. A gang member takes a .357 to the head or a shotgun blast to the chest, or has his throat cut. They take the body and throw it in the river. What do you think we find? Typically, we find a near-bloodless corpse. I'll show you one." Paul motioned for Ted to follow.

They walked from his office down the hallway and through a set of double doors, into a very chilly examination room. There, in the middle of the room, was a stainless steel table. On it was a body covered by a white sheet. Paul threw the sheet back and Ted cringed at the sight of a young man with a giant hole in the side of his head. The corpse was porcelain white, with a slight blue cast to the skin.

"You okay, Cousin?" Malone asked, seeing Ted's face go pale. Ted nodded. "We haven't worked on this one yet. See what I mean? Pretty much exsanguinated in appearance. Not much blood. However, we will always find some blood in the capillaries. There is a difference in hypovolemia, or bleeding out, and complete exsanguination. They found this guy in a dumpster. God knows where he was actually shot before they dumped the body there." Paul was simply proving his point. "His body had some blood present, but not enough to fill a small cup. What was left in the veins coagulated."

"How much analysis do you perform on each body, Paul?" Ted asked.

"It depends. First, let me ask you this: Are you here as a cousin, or as an investigative reporter? Because I have two answers I can give you. I have one for the record, and the other, between us. Which one do I give?" Paul looked to Ted before continuing.

"I'm not here investigating anything. I'm only asking to satisfy my curiosity and gather material for my novel. You can be off the record in your response." Ted awaited his answer.

"Well this is a job, like any other. In 90 percent of the cases, we're expected to have instant answers. With limited resources, we address the obvious in most of those cases. Like this guy here. I think we can easily judge that he's been shot in the head. We examine that wound and establish the manner in which he was shot and by what caliber bullet. We determine at what distance and at what exact angle. It's assumed that big hole in his head is the cause of death. Unless there is a strong reason and justification, we will not expend the time, effort, and financial resource looking very much beyond that surface. That's off the record." Paul looked to Ted for a reaction. "Like I said, it's not like CSI in real life."

"So, what you're saying is that this guy may have been poisoned, but you could care less?" Ted asked candidly.

"Right. It's not likely someone might poison a person and then blow his head off. Why waste the tax payer's money and time while on a limited budget? Toxicology is not only expensive, but it can take months, without reason; it's just not done . . . unless the person killed is a public or controversial figure, or the blood level of alcohol or narcotics is an absolute factor. Don't misunderstand, we do care; but it's not our job to spend the taxpayer's money chasing our tails. This guy was found in a dumpster. His wallet was intact and had $1000 in it. His rap sheet is long, and he has been in trouble all his life. Now he has a hole in his head; obviously, he was executed. Let me ask you, would you spend a small fortune analyzing every molecule on this man's body?" Paul rested his case.

Ted thought for a second. "No. I wouldn't spend the money. I guess you're right."

Paul continued. "I take my lead from the detectives. If they dump a body here, it's business as usual. If they are curious or have a suspicious

DeathWalker

feeling, we put it through the whole process. But let's get back to the mutilations. We found no evidence on the bodies that any human contact was made, relative to the cause of death. I spoke to the other coroners and we compared notes. The detectives found no evidence at the scenes leading anyone to believe that any human being was in the vicinity when these people died. Now, I say it's a bear that did the initial damage, based on the wounds. As you know, a large black male can easily weigh in at 500 pounds, but I did no extensive analysis to prove that it wasn't a 500 pound gopher."

Ted laughed, "Yeah, Gopher State, I get it." All the while thinking that he heard that somewhere before. "I hear you. Thanks, Cousin, for your time. I may be back with a few more questions. Not investigating, mind you . . . just doing a little research. Is that okay?"

"Anytime, Ted, anytime." Paul assured him.

Ted left, somewhat satisfied that an animal did the killings, but still unsatisfied that it was a bear. His next call would be to the forest rangers. He drove back to his condo, the only office he had, parking in front of his building. Coming out through the front entrance was Pat, the sixteen year old girl who he paid to walk Brutus twice a day.

"Did Brutus do his business?" Ted asked.

"He's a doll. If ever you want to give him away, I'll have him." Pat was smiling.

"Thanks, Pat, see you later." Ted rode the elevator up.

He made himself a quick sandwich, which he shared with Brutus, as was his habit. His curiosity was getting the best of him.

He remembered a story that his mother told him many times as a child. She said that a creature would sometimes visit the woods, and that the tribe would conduct ceremonies designed to frighten it away. It could never be killed, but could be driven to leave and haunt another tribe. Anyone with Chippewa blood had heard the stories of the "Windigo." As a child, Ted found the tales frightening, but as a young man, he decided that the "Windigo" was nothing more than an equivalent to the white man's "Bogey Man." Or was it?

Ted had this feeling in his gut that there was more to this than was on the surface. In reality, there are so many square miles of wilderness in northern Minnesota, who knows if there are other human remains to be discovered—or worse yet, never found? He had read the true accounts of a serial killer caught in Texas, who was tied to forty killings in his years, traveling as a hobo across the country while riding the rails. Then again, who would be traveling the wilderness of northern Minnesota?

He became obsessed that the bear theory did not make sense. The evidence on the surface seemed conclusive, but *too* conclusive. Or was it his creative imagination kicking in?

Chapter Two

Ted reached for his cell phone.

"Department of Forestry . . ." answered a friendly female voice.

Ted had decided to use his former newspaper credentials. "This is Ted Scott, Minneapolis Press. I'm doing a story on a possible bear attack. Could I get an appointment for an interview?" he asked her.

"Sure, Mr. Scott. Exactly what is it that you're concerned with?"

"Mainly bears, and their habits."

"Well, the top expert in the state is located up in Thief River Falls, near the Agassiz National Wildlife Refuge," she answered.

"How soon could I see him?" Ted asked.

"I'm sure you could see him at anytime, provided I contact him to let him know you're coming."

"How does tomorrow sound?"

"How about nine in the morning? That way we'll be sure the Captain will be in before he heads out for his rounds." She was more accommodating than he expected.

"That sounds fine. Thank you so much—I'll be there." He hung up, and then realized it was almost three hundred miles to his destination. "God, I have to be up at three in the morning and on the road before four . . ."

This also presented Ted with an opportunity to visit his dad. The office of the Forestry Department was only a stone's throw, or forty miles, from his dad's house and the town of Roseau. He immediately dialed his father.

"Dad, I'll be seeing you late tomorrow. I'll probably stay a few days. Wondered if you needed anything?" Ted asked.

"Naaah, just bring yourself and Brutus. I'll be glad to see you." He sounded happy.

"See you tomorrow, then, Dad." Ted felt pleased as put his phone away.

He turned to Brutus. "Hey, Brutmeister, want to go on a trip?" The Yorkie cocked his head and wagged his tail as if to say, 'Sure, let's go!'

*　*　*

It was at least a four-to-five hour drive from the city to the Department of Forestry, at Thief River Falls. As Ted drove, Brutus sat on the rear window ledge, watching the world go by. They arrived early. There, in the middle of the woods, was a red brick building. Ted got out of the car, calling for Brutus, and then stretched, taking deep breaths of the clean fresh air. He loved the woods and everything about them. He could smell the strong scent of wet marshes combined with the distinct odor of the cool, moist earth. Ted watched as Brutus immediately started chasing a chipmunk. Ted laughed as Brutus tried his best to catch up with his prey. 'Brutus: bear hunter.' Ted thought, and laughed again.

"Come here, Brutus, you fearless hunter!" Ted called. Brutus came running, and Ted was amused, because if dogs could smile, sure as heck, Brutus was grinning from ear to ear. He put Brutus into the car and proceeded into the building.

"Ted Scott, to see the Captain, please."

The receptionist smiled. "I'll tell him you're here." She walked to a nearby office and returned quickly. "Go right in," she announced, as she pointed to the office. Ted walked in, equipped only with his micro cassette recorder.

"Hi, I'm Ted Scott." He extended his hand.

"Captain Williams, Ted. How can I help you?" They shook hands.

Captain Williams was exactly what you would expect a forest ranger to look like. Kind of like a lumber jack, but in a green uniform. Reddish blonde hair with matching beard, he was six foot tall and about 240 pounds. His hands were huge, and solid as granite, which Ted noticed as they shook hands.

"Captain, I'm interested in these bear attacks. What can you tell me about them?" Ted decided he would sit back and play dumb.

The Captain smiled. "What is there to say? We obviously have a small problem. It seems that we likely have a renegade bear out there. We're

DeathWalker

guessing he's an old one, which is why he's attacking people. It might be that he's crippled or wounded, but for sure he's not your normal 'everyday' bear."

"Old bears do not attack people simply because they're old, Captain. They simply start raiding garbage cans and hanging around the dumps." Ted put him on the spot. "How many attacks have there been in this state?" Ted pretended not to know.

"Well, we know about one for sure, but there might have been two so far this year." The Captain wouldn't look Ted in the eyes.

"Captain, isn't it almost certain that there have been at least three?" Again, Ted was boxing him in.

"Three? No sir, that hasn't been proven. We don't know of three bear attacks." The Captain was now becoming very nervous.

"Captain, I'm not here for any other reason besides doing research. Honestly, this is not going into the paper. All I would like to know is whether it's possible, in your expert opinion, that three people have been killed by bears in three months."

"Mr. Scott, it's a fact that we have heard of three mauled bodies. It seems to be a bear. If so, it's the first time we've had such a problem in the fifteen years that I've been here. A bear is not the only animal in these parts capable of doing this kind of damage to a human body. But, if it's a bear, we'll find him. We've got the best hunter in this part of the country to track him down. He's also with the Department of Forestry. John Hall is his name. Hall is a specialist; he will observe the bears before acting. If he observes one acting abnormal or too aggressive, he'll make an expert judgment. I have faith in him. He'll be here this morning, in fact. Remember, we do have homeless types that actually die a natural death, and some from exposure. Those bodies don't sit around long before the predators set in."

Ted was satisfied with the Captain's answer, but had one more question to ask. "What if it's not a bear? What then?"

The Captain's face went blank as he scratched his thick red beard. "Frankly, I don't know. If it's not a bear, then I can only hope that it doesn't happen again. It's certainly not the wolves, and it's not likely to be a big cat. It's got to be a renegade bear. I mean, what the hell else could it possibly be?"

The Captain's secretary interrupted. "Mr. Hall is here."

"Send him in," the Captain responded.

15

Hall appeared more of a soldier of fortune than a forest ranger. John Hall was about six foot tall and slightly overweight, with a gut protruding over his belt. His hair was long and in need of grooming. He sported a three day growth of whiskers, and with his brown coloring, it made his face look dirty. He appeared as if he had just returned from the jungle, with his combat boots and camouflage outfit, complete with a large knife strapped to his thigh. He looked prepared for war.

"Good morning, Captain."

"Please, sit down Mr. Hall. This is Mr. Scott. He's with a Minneapolis paper." They all shook hands. Hall's grasp was solid and strong, as Ted would expect of such a 'soldier'.

The Captain continued. "I've explained our strategy to Mr. Scott. Maybe you'd like to explain to him how you operate."

Hall spoke in a whisper-like voice. "I'm going out to observe and terminate any bear that I find which isn't acting normal. I'll be out there day and night, until I find him. I truly expect to find him within a week or so. Once I do, I'll observe him for as long as it takes to make the proper determination. I assure you that I will not bring back a bear unless I can guarantee there will be no more attacks. If it takes me a month, then so be it." Hall sounded very confident.

Ted was curious. "How will you zero in on the exact bear, Mr. Hall?"

Hall reached in his pocket, pulling out a small map. "See these X's?" Ted nodded affirmative. Hall continued. "These are where the bodies were found." He drew a large circle encompassing that specific area. "This is where I'll start. I'll begin under the assumption that these were done by a single animal, and he's traveling in the direction indicated by the progression of X's. There is no doubt that this is very unusual, that a bear would drift as far south as Hennipin County and reverse, making his way back north . . . but it's possible."

Ted scratched his head. "Pretty big territory for one man to cover?"

Hall chuckled. "I'm not alone, for Pete's sake. I have a number of state employees that work with me. I prefer the Chippewa. It seems that Native Americans have an instinct for these things. Together, we'll find your bear—if he's out there."

Ted was satisfied that the action and method of solving the problem was logical and competent. He excused himself. "Thank you for your time, Captain. I have other business, so if you will excuse me, I must be on my way."

DeathWalker

Ted left for his father's place. As he drove, the words spoken by the hunter, John Hall, echoed in his mind. "Observe and terminate." Hall appeared more like an assassin than a hunter. Was he brought in because they are unsure of what they would find? If so, what were they really hunting, if not a bear? From a reporter's standpoint, Ted felt badly that the other deaths went unreported. He knew it wasn't unusual, for homeless people or vagrants were not that newsworthy, but never the less, they were people, too.

This was always one of the things that bothered him while he was a reporter. If a homeless person was found dead in some alley, who cared? Even in Minneapolis, where every death made the news, certain items didn't get the same coverage. Many times there wouldn't even be an obituary, for there was no one who would pay for it. This was a question that he needed to ask the coroner, just for curiosity sake. If a homeless person or vagrant was found dead, would there be a determination of death or autopsy? Or would they just put them in a pine box and dispose of them, without question? He guessed it would be a glance and a shrug before dumping them into a pine box and a pauper's grave, but Ted would eventually ask the question anyway on his next visit.

As he drove, he marveled at the beauty of the Northwest Territory. He looked at the basin as if it were an ocean of green. Valleys of marshes as far as the eye could see. Ted would spot an occasional hawk suspended in the air, searching for prey, as if defying gravity. He loved the woods and resented many of the modern threats to its existence. At one time, seventy percent of Minnesota soil was covered in woods. Today, it is barely thirty-five percent, with many of those trees being second growth. Ted wondered if the monument to Paul Bunyan at Bimidji, Minnesota, was really a tribute—or a solemn memorial to the raping of the woods.

Besides the damage created by forest fires, the harvesting of the trees and the rampant hunting were two items Ted wrote about when he was a reporter. Although Ted was known to hunt, he despised guns, except for protection. Ted felt it was not truly hunting if one used a gun.

Shooting a grazing animal by using a high powered rifle and a scope that allows you to see clearly at 100 to 200 yards was not hunting, for it was far too easy. It was more like harvesting, and not his definition of a hunt. It was almost like shooting stationary targets. Ted also didn't believe in "baiting," which was also a most popular method of "hunting" bears. Baiting is where a hunter would set up attractive bait, like a ham, and wait while sitting in a tree twenty feet above. When the unfortunate animal came there to feed, the hunter could shoot down from the tree, at literally a sitting target. Ted did not believe that just because you shot a living animal, that it was defined as hunting. Ted believed that hunting was far more than just killing an animal. He believed that various skills were necessary to hunt. Knowing your prey was first. He learned about the animals he had hunted and knew their habits.

He could track them through the woods, using skill to stay down wind. He had learned to sit motionless for long periods of time. Ted had learned to get close, beating the animal at his own game. Finally, Ted would only shoot an arrow if he was sure it would be quick and fatal. This took time, endurance, and skill. Guns were far too easy.

Ted was aware of other dangers relative to guns being used in the field for hunting. He was very much aware of the fact that bullets can travel far beyond the intended target. A .223 or 30.06 hunting bullet could kill a man at a half mile away, should the hunter miss his target and the bullet have a clear path to travel. No, Ted didn't approve of hunting with guns.

Ted grew to favor the crossbow. It was a lot easier to carry through the thick woods and marshes, and both powerful and accurate at short distances. He saw it as being much more humane. Within fifty yards, he was a deadly shot. He wondered about the "super" hunter he had met, John Hall. Did he really hunt? Or did he open up on his prey with a machine gun, like a lot of these so called hunters? His mind wandered as he drove with one hand on the steering wheel and the other stroking Brutus, who was asleep on the front seat. He had made this drive many times and enjoyed every mile in each instance. He looked at Brutus and laughed, thinking of Brutus chasing the chipmunk. "Brutus: deadly chipmunk hunter." He laughed again. He loved Brutus, as he felt dogs are far underappreciated. This tiny four pound canine would likely take on a bear and lay down his life to protect Ted. There is no loyalty like that of a dog to his master.

He made the turn on to a dirt road and was soon pulling up to his father's house. Though he had driven for hours on this day, it seemed much shorter, as it was such a pleasure. As he drove closer he could see his dad sitting on the porch of his home. It was a large house with a very small yard, considering the acreage his father owned. His father did not want to clear the acreage, and left it in its natural state. It appeared as if someone had dropped the house in a small clearing in the middle of this

DeathWalker

deep wilderness. His dad had it fully equipped and it lacked nothing. A satellite dish, a big screen television, whirlpool, and a hot tub, it had all the modern amenities. This was the ideal retirement home—or was, until his mother died.

There was no doubt in Ted's mind that his parents were in love. They did everything together. His father always appeared as the back bone of the family; he would order and roar, though gentle in nature, but always played the role of the "man" of the house. He grew up believing that his dad ran the show, with his mother in the background; secure, protected, and loved. It wasn't until she died that he learned exactly how much his father depended on his mother. It was the first time in his life that he saw his father cry. Not just weep, but fall completely apart. So much so, that Ted worried that his father might never recover. His father did eventually recover, but never regained the happiness he once knew.

He watched as his father walked toward the car. He noticed that his dad was walking a bit slower, and Ted suddenly felt a wave of guilt for not visiting sooner and more frequently.

His father called out to them. "Where's my Brutus?"

Ted opened the car door and Brutus ran to greet Ted's dad. The old man scooped him up and hugged the Yorkie, as Brutus licked his face. "How's my son?" he asked.

"Fine, Dad." Ted answered, hugging his dad.

"So, to what do I owe this pleasure?" he asked.

"I'm doing some research and was in the neighborhood," Ted assured him.

They slowly walked to the house. Upon entering, Ted noticed that his mother's favorite things were all still in place. He also noticed that her reading glasses and sewing basket were still exactly in the spot she left them. Even the picture that his mother loved—but his dad hated—still hung prominently in the living room. Ted knew it was his father's way of remembering mom.

"Are you doing okay, Dad?" Ted queried.

"One day at a time, Teddy, one day at a time."

"What are you doing with your time?" Ted asked.

"Christ! I have 300 channels to watch on satellite, and I do a lot of reading. Check this out!" He tossed Ted an electronic reader. "I can put hundreds of books on this thing! Any book I want, delivered to me within seconds! Who would have thought it? I still have my hobbies; still shoot some, but no hunting, only targets. I go to town from time to time besides church . . . it's as good as it can be, without your mother."

Ted glanced over at a pile of Minneapolis newspapers and noticed the dates to be old. "What? Not reading the paper anymore?"

"Teddy, I only subscribed so I could read your articles. Newspapers today are near worthless. All they do is reprint news we have already been bombarded with. They have all become like tabloids. I never imagined a celebrity's poor behavior would be front page news. To get serious uncensored news, I go online to other countries, like the BBC."

"That's why I left the business. News has become manipulated. It's become now that certain subjects are off limits. Newspapers always leaned to a political party, but today their blatant censorship includes religions, race, and even financial trends. Anyone who doesn't follow the agenda is quickly out of a job. A gay is harassed, and it's automatically front page news. However if a straight guy gets beaten up, it's back page. Anything Christian is automatically labeled conservative right-wing fanatical. A Catholic priest is accused of pedophilia, and it becomes front page. A Rabbi smuggling drugs is censored. As far as the economy, we can only write about optimism, rather than the fact we are up Shit Creek. There is no honest reporting anymore."

Ted proceeded to the kitchen and over to the refrigerator. In it was his Pepsi, as always. He popped open a can and flopped in the great room. Hanging on the wall, next to his father's gun cabinet, was Ted's crossbow. He studied his father. Once a huge, strong man, he appeared a little bit slower and a little bit weaker, as his huge frame sat on the couch. His brown hair was now thinner and no longer brown; it was white as snow. Ted realized that his dad was getting old. His father relaxed with Brutus on his lap. "Dad, why don't you get yourself a dog?" Ted asked.

"I'd take old Brutus here, if I thought the raccoons wouldn't eat him." They both laughed.

"That's the problem with this little guy. He would attack a bear if he thought he was protecting you. He has 200 pounds of courage in that four pound body. Speaking of bears, Dad, there have been some bizarre killings that have been attributed to bears recently, just south of here. I have been doing some research trying to find a story for another book, originally to be a novel. But now I tripped on this, and I'm wondering if there's a real story here. What do you think?"

DeathWalker

"I've never known bears to be aggressive, Teddy. Of course, you don't ever want to bother a mother with her cubs, and if you sleep outside, you don't want leave food around, but it's not their nature to attack people. A bear attack is actually very rare. How many are we talking about?"

"Three Dad, in our area, and I have a suspicion that there might be more attacks of the same nature up in Winnipeg."

"Winnipeg?" Ted's dad was surprised.

"Yeah, I stumbled across a similar situation on World News. In fact, I was thinking of going up there." Ted was looking for his dad's opinion.

"You go ahead and follow your instincts, son. There's a small prop plane that shuttles from Roseau to Winnipeg . . . only $75, one way. You could go up there and be back the same day. Your mother had relatives up there, you know?"

"No, actually, I didn't," Ted replied.

"Yeah, some of her clan was from Canada. Lots of Chippewa up there," he stated.

"Have you noticed anything up here that's changed?" Ted asked.

"Teddy, everything is different since your mother is gone. It's not quite the same. The sounds of the night seem different to me, but maybe it's because I'm alone and aware of it more now."

"Different? How do you mean?" Ted was curious.

"Now and then, the woods seem to get a bit too quiet. I mean, really silent, like you could hear a pin drop. I never noticed that ever before. Then again, I'm getting old, so maybe it's my hearing."

"Well, I'll be up here a few days and I know the sounds of the night. At this time of year it's almost a symphony out there. I've never heard it quiet, not at this time of the year."

Ted arose and removed his crossbow from the wall. "Come on Brutus, let's go outside." From the cabinet he grabbed a hand full of arrows and proceeded toward the door. "I'll see you in a little while, Dad."

He walked out to the back yard, where his straw target was still hanging on a tree, about 25 yards away. As he loaded his crossbow, he watched Brutus run about the yard frantically. His crossbow was a smaller model, only 18 inches long and 24 inches wide. It shot an arrow that was 18 inches long, with a shaft that was somewhat thicker than a normal arrow. It was a very powerful and deadly weapon at close range. He pulled the bow string back and cocked it; it was now ready to fire. Much the same as a gun, Ted took aim and slowly pulled the trigger. He buried the arrow in his target, dead center. Shot after shot hit the target in the center. *'It's like riding a bike . . .'* Ted thought. *'You never forget.'*

As Brutus chased chipmunks, a shadow moved across the yard. It was a large, hungry hawk. Ted looked up and watched as the hawk floated in the air overhead, watching his prey. Ted marveled at the sight of this magnificent bird, effortlessly defying gravity by floating in a wide circle, high up in the air. It took a second for Ted to realize that the hawk was likely watching little Brutus. *'Oh shit!'* he thought. "Brutus, let's go in, boy." Ted headed back to the house. Brutus was just the perfect size for the hawk's next meal. At this time of year, the hawk was likely feeding a family. He kept one eye on the hawk as he walked to the house, scooping up his loveable little companion.

The sun was starting to set as Ted made himself a giant sandwich. His dad was reading. There would be no formal dinners up here. His dad ate whenever he was hungry, with no specific set times. Ted wandered into the living room and sat down.

"I will go to Winnipeg tomorrow. Is that okay?" His father nodded an approval. "Will you watch out for Brutus?" His dad nodded again. "Pop, I don't want Brutus to become lunch for some hawk or fox." His father nodded once more. Ted didn't worry, for Brutus would stay at the old man's side. Ted smiled as his four pound watch dog curled up next to his father and fell completely asleep in seconds.

Ted ate his sandwich and watched as the sun went down in spectacular colors, as his father rested the book on his chest and was soon also sleeping soundly. Ted walked out to the porch and rested on the glider, slowly moving back and forth, listening to the sounds of the night. The crickets had started their calling, as thousands of them began singing in unison. Ted's writing mind took over as he thought of a way to describe the beautiful sound. "Sleigh bells" came to mind. Yes, thousands of tiny sleigh bells. Almost musical, was the sound. *'This is the good life,'* he thought, as he glided back and forth, listening to the symphony.

The sky was clear, but there was only a slice of the moon available to illuminate the earth. Without the full moon, it was dark in the woods—very dark. No car lights, street lights, or neon signs out here; just the moon and some bright stars. If the moon wasn't full, the deep woods became almost pure darkness, since the tall trees covered the faint light that was overhead. As he studied the night, the symphony of the crickets and frogs abruptly

DeathWalker

stopped. It became silent—so silent, that it was conspicuous. Ted took immediate notice.

From the sky, Ted's warm blooded body could be seen clearly by the female vampire, even in the dark of night. It was her presence that had switched off all sound. Suspended above Ted, she licked her lips thinking about the possible meal to be had. The only problem, was her mate, Christian. They had survived a century by leading a very guarded and disguised existence, and Christian would never tolerate risks that would expose the possibility that vampires were real. She hovered in the sky above him, enjoying the scent of warm human blood.

Ted thought about the silence. Usually, when a bear or wolf pack traveled through the woods, the section that they traveled went silent. You could almost track them by the trail of silence they created. But this was different, for it was total silence. Ted had grown up in these woods, but this was the first time he had ever experienced this. His writer's mind described it as a total, eerie quiet; a void of sound. His father was correct; you could almost hear a pin drop. The sounds of the night had been replaced by the irritating squeak of his glider. He wondered, *'What could cause such a wide spread silence?'*

He arose, walking to the edge of the yard, listening to the sounds of his own footsteps. He stood at the mouth of a path that led deep into the dark woods. As his eyes adjusted to the dark, he walked about ten yards down the path. It was so quiet that he could hear his own breathing. *'Unnatural'* was a thought that came to mind. His eyes scanned in all directions. Nothing could be seen moving, but he felt that there was definitely something out there. In fact, he had the distinct feeling that he was being watched.

Little did he know, he *was* being watched. The female vampire licked her lips as Ted neared the tree line. Should he enter, it would be an excuse for killing him and draining his blood. After all, if he was in the woods at this hour, he could be considered prey, and not a risk. She would not have to justify her kill to Christian. Christian frowned on any killing that might become questionable under public scrutiny. Their existence has been a secret for 100 years, and he wanted it kept that way. He enjoyed being regarded as a myth.

Unfortunately for her, Ted decided to go no further into the dark woods without his crossbow. He knew his curiosity would eventually get the best of him and he would have to explore these woods . . . but not tonight, for he had a plane to catch for Winnipeg, Canada, early in the morning. When he turned away and faced the house, she became discouraged, having been robbed of a meal, and quickly flew off. Had Ted looked upward a bit sooner, he might have seen her dark silhouette against the clear sky . . . but he didn't.

As he slowly walked back to house, the sound of crickets resumed as suddenly as it had stopped only a few minutes before. '*Curious*,' he thought. '*But, there is definitely a logical solution to this.*'

At least he could tell his dad to not worry. No, he wasn't going deaf!

In seventy-five of the rural communities, the position of Medical Examiner, {Coroner,} is a part-time function ... In fifty-five percent of these communities, no medical background or education is required to hold the position.

Department of Justice, report on crime, 2007.

Chapter Three

The steady hum of the plane engine changed to a low drone as the airplane circled, making its approach to the Winnipeg airport. It was less than a one hour flight from Roseau, Minnesota, and only about 125 miles away as the crow flies. Customs was fast and efficient, and Ted was soon in a taxi, on his way to the Winnipeg Police Headquarters.

The Canadian Police were far more formal than those in the United States, as Ted would soon find out. Once at headquarters, he asked for assistance in getting information on the tourist recently killed by a bear. He was told to wait and offered a seat in the lobby. He was impressed at the organized manner in which everyone functioned. There appeared to be none of the chaos common in the police stations that he was familiar with. Every officer was well groomed and impeccably dressed. Ted had the distinct impression that this was more of a military operation, given the visible structure.

Ted watched as officers moved in and out the station. He found it incredible that each person looked physically fit. No pot bellies here. He observed as criminals were brought into custody, with a few in handcuffs, and even they appeared much more clean and orderly than what Ted was used to seeing. A uniformed officer approached him. "Mr. Scott?" he asked. With his Canadian accent, it came off sounding like 'Mr. Skut.'

"Yes, sir," Ted answered.

"This way . . ." he motioned for Ted to follow.

Ted trailed along, observing everything as he walked the quiet halls. The walls were paneled in a fine dark wood. The floors were marble. Everything was immaculate, and a far cry from the States. He was led to an office that more resembled a successful attorney's, than that of a police officer.

"Have a seat, Mr. Scott." To Ted, it sounded like an order.

"I'm Lieutenant Caldwell. How can we help you today?" he asked.

DeathWalker

By the formality and cold greeting, Ted assumed that being an American, he was about to be dismissed. The Lieutenant, though Canadian, appeared English. Why? Ted didn't know. Maybe it was his tall, slender build, combined with his fair coloring and blue eyes. Maybe it was his hair, being slicked down in a style that reminded Ted of the roaring twenties.

"I'm a reporter and a free lance writer. I have interest in the tourist killing that was recently attributed to a bear. I'm not here in the capacity of a reporter, to put you at ease. I'm more interested in the aggressive tendencies of the bears recently. You see, we've had some bear problems on the other side of the border also, and I find it unusual, as I'm sure you do."

"Well, in fact, we have only had that one incident, Mr. Scott. It certainly was unusual, and we are sorry that it had to involve an American tourist. The poor fellow went nature walking in the evening. It appears he became lost, and wandered deep into the woods in confusion. Probably the poor fellow tripped over the bear, or antagonized him in some way. He was carrying a camera, you know. If he made the mistake of flashing a picture of the bear at close range, you know what that would do. The bear would have become angry and completely wild and enraged." The Lieutenant was tapping his fingers on the desk, as if counting down the time until this interview would be over.

"Did you check the film or memory card in the camera?" Ted asked.

"Why . . . I'm not sure." he scratched his head at the thought.

"Not sure?" Ted was dumbfounded that he actually admitted it.

The Lieutenant was now a bit nervous. "Well, ah, I guess because he was an American, we did not want to hold the family up here on an investigation for any longer than we were forced to. Uh . . . especially, due to the fact that the cause of death was quite obvious." He hoped his explanation would suffice.

Ted didn't pursue the obvious police blunder, and instead, pleaded for assistance. "I just have the need to explore if there are any other aggressive bear incidents, besides the confused tourist."

"If you really want to know the intimate specifics regarding bear behavior, it is likely the Indians would be a great help to you. Only an hour north is a large Chippeyan reservation. If the bears are behaving unusually, the Indians would surely take notice." This was an excellent suggestion.

"May I ask one just more question, Lieutenant?" Ted wondered.

"Sure, Mr. Scott." he answered.

"Was there any blood at the scene where the body was found?" Ted questioned.

"Blood? Of course, there had to be blood." The lieutenant scoffed.

"Why? Couldn't the bear have dragged the body a bit from where the tourist was actually attacked?" Ted expected to be stonewalled on this question. Instead, he was in for a surprise.

"Let me get the photographs of exactly what we found. I can't give them to you, but you can view them, if this helps you." Ted smiled as the Lieutenant left the room. Within a minute, he returned with a stack of photographs. He laid them on the desk and pushed them toward Ted. One by one, Ted sifted through them. Much like the pictures he had seen previously, the body was terribly mauled and there was no measurable amount of blood in view. He could see traces of blood on the clothes, but not in the amount one would expect when a body is torn to shreds.

The close ups were very clear. There was no blood on the ground or on the leaves of the surrounding foliage. Ted just sat, concentrating on this problem.

"Mr. Scott?" the Lieutenant asked.

"Yes," Ted answered, breaking his concentration.

"I don't suppose we would miss one of those photographs. I mean, if one was to be missing . . . we have our negatives and could make it over . . . if you understand?" Ted smiled, and quickly tucked one picture into his top pocket.

"Thanks, Lieutenant Caldwell." Ted stood up, and the Lieutenant walked him down the hallway and back to the lobby, wishing him a good day. Ted was pleased that his initial feeling that he would be merely dismissed, was wrong. The Canadians, as it turned out, were most helpful.

Ted walked to a corner where a number of taxis were parked. "How much would you charge to take me north to the Indian reservation?" Ted asked. All the drivers spoke at once.

"Twenty."

"Twenty-five."

"Twenty."

DeathWalker

Three instantaneous answers came in his direction. Ted became curious. He looked at the one driver and asked "Why are you charging me twenty-five?"

"Because I'm Chippewa and I can take you where ever you need to go. No problem."

Ted laughed, as he agreed that this was an advantage. Ted gave him the once over. He was wearing jeans, a plaid short-sleeve shirt, and stylish Nike running shoes. Recognizing he was getting the once over, the driver spoke.

"What do you expect? Buckskin and moccasins?" he asked.

Ted smiled. "Let's go, Mr. twenty-five." Ted jumped in the front seat.

"I'm Ted Scott, from the U.S., up here to research a story. I need to speak with a person that might know anything about bears and bear attacks."

"Shit, any Chippewa Indian can tell you about Makwa—I mean bear—Mr. Scott. By the way, I'm White Eagle, but most people call me Bob," he offered.

"Which do you prefer?" Ted asked.

"Bob," he answered.

"Well, Bob, what I'm really looking for is someone that might know if the habits or temperament of the bears up here has changed recently. I'm wondering if they've become more aggressive, or if there is something else that is attacking people, with it being blamed on the bears." Ted awaited Bob's thoughts.

"I think you may want to talk with Gray Wolf, he is the OgiMa, an elder of our Anishanabe tribe. An elder could be referred to as father or grandfather, out of respect, whether one is actually related by birth or not. An OgiMa is a term for one held in highest respect. He knows much history of the bear and has the ability to 'see' things. He will likely tell you everything you need to know."

Ted knew that the Indians we liked to call Chippewa, or Objibway, were the same that the Canadians called Chippeyan and the French called Ojibwe, or Ojibwan, were all Anishanabe and preferred that name. Pronounced "Anishaknobbee," Ted knew very little about true Indian culture, because his father had forbid it. From his mother he did learn a lot, but not anywhere near enough to be considered knowledgeable in Chippewa circles. He was not embarrassed of his Indian blood; only of the fact that he knew little of his heritage. He did know that the Anishanabe

29

were a proud race and he was aware of their preferred name. Although the Sioux were first to settle in Minnesota, and Minnesota itself was a Sioux word meaning "sky tinted water," it was the Anishanabe that held the largest population as the Sioux—or Lakota Indians, as they liked to be called—moved west with time. Unlike the Lakota or Sioux, the Anishanabe were not totally dependent on Buffalo. They were experts at living off the land, gathering wild rice, which grew with abundance in the marsh lands; fishing from the many lakes, and even drawing maple syrup from the abundant forests.

Raspberries, blueberries and chokecherries were made into jellies, or dried for winter. Though traditional "wigwams" were common, their actual shelters were made out of wooded frames, using a birch bark cover for siding, with many having pine floors made of large branches. With rounded roofs, they more resembled igloos.

The Chippewa (as we named them) were a proud race of people and though fearless warriors, were much more family oriented and peaceful in their preferred life. Given their natural expertise at thriving with nature, they became excellent hunting guides, as they could sense the slightest imbalance in their surroundings.

Bob was a wise choice on Ted's part. As they drove, Bob pointed out many of the historical sites while explaining their significance. An hour went by quickly, as they pulled into the entrance of the Indian reservation. It had the appearance of a tourist attraction, and was not what Ted had expected. Besides a number of traditional teepees, Ted could see some very attractive log cabins scattered about. The Indians walking around the village all appeared clean and very well groomed. They passed a cabin with a sign attached that stated "Moccasin Shop," with numerous cars parked out front. Next came another shop displaying "Crafts." It, too, had customer's cars parked out front. To Ted, it appeared that the Indians were very prosperous and very well integrated into the community. The vision of an Indian woman dressed in traditional fashion, weaving a decorative floor mat in the old method—using "rush," a thick, long grass—seemed like a glimpse of the distant past.

"Much experience with tourists?" Ted asked.

"Too much! I am always amazed that we don't have more accidents out here."

"Why?"

DeathWalker

"Well, the tourists act as if these woods are a giant theme park. They wander in the wild with no clue that there are rattle snakes, bears, and big cats out there. The rattle snake warns them, and what do they do? They move closer to get a picture or better look. They come upon a bear and instead of moving away or raising their arms to look as large as they can, they run away, screaming like little girls; or worse yet, try to pet it, like a dog. They view it all as entertainment."

Bob pulled his taxi up to very large cabin. This was the Tribal Lodge. Bob explained that this is where Gray Wolf spent most of his days.

Entering, Ted noticed small groups of older Indians scattered about the vast lodge. Some watching television, others playing cards. Bob guided Ted over to a chess game, where the opponents were deep in concentration. Bob softly asked, "Gray Wolf? May we bother you for a moment, OgiMa?" The old man nodded, offering a kind, warm smile. He was surely the OgiMa, or respected elder. Gray Wolf led them to a private table, where they all sat facing one another. He appeared ancient, with long gray hair. Wrinkled and weathered, his face was imprinted with deep tracks of wisdom.

Bob spoke softly. "Gray Wolf, I do not wish to interrupt you, but this is Ted. He has come a long way from the United States to speak with you."

"How can I help you?" the old man asked.

"I have been studying a number of attacks that have been blamed on bears," Ted began. "We have had some on the other side of the border in Minnesota, and recently there was one up here near Winnipeg. Is there a bear problem up here?"

What Ted didn't know, was that the Anishanabe held the bear in very high regard. If a bear was killed, a special ceremony was conducted for its spirit. They have a high respect for all animals, but the bear holds a special place in their culture.

The old Indian answered slowly. "There is no problem with our friend Makwa, Ted."

Ted pulled out his photograph. "What could do something like this?" he asked, as he showed the old Indian the picture given to him by Lieutenant Caldwell, of the tourist's mutilated body.

The Indian studied the picture in silence. Ted continued, repeating his question. "What other animal could do this type of thing to a man?"

The old man spoke. "This is not an animal attack. We call it Windigo. It is a creature of the night. He travels the woods at dark, taking life where he finds it. In English, it translates to 'Mover of Death' or 'DeathWalker'—NibookeBimozi."

"Windigo? What exactly is that?" To Ted, this sounded like an old Indian superstition that he had heard of many times before.

"A dark creature. He feeds off of life. When he visits, we do not travel alone in the woods at night. It is not our good brother, Makwa the bear, that causes such terrible death, Ted Scott."

"What is it? Do you believe it's an animal or a man?" Ted asked.

"He is not a man, no sir. He is a night creature. He is dead, but feeds off the living." The old man spoke as if this was a common fact, and not as incredible as it sounded to Ted.

"This sounds unbelievable. Has anyone ever seen this creature?" Ted questioned.

"Yes; he can appear as a man or as other creatures, if he wishes. He is smart. He might approach you as a friend would, but when your guard is down . . . he takes you."

Ted did not want to laugh and hurt the old man's feelings, but he was feeling as if his trip was totally wasted. The old Indian must have sensed this, for he offered reinforcement to his story.

"I will tell you a true story, Ted. It was once an Anishanabe tradition that if a member of this tribe violated certain tribal laws, he was expelled and banned from the reservation. This was many years ago. This was a punishment that was meant to be harsh, but not as harsh as putting the man to death. The person banned would make a place to live outside the reservation. His people could visit him, but he could not set foot on our soil. We stopped that punishment fifty years ago, when we found that it became a death sentence to those banished. Alone in the woods, Windigo would kill them. Today, banishment is now our new form of Nibooke." [Death] The old man watched Ted's reaction.

"If this is true, then why has no one ever heard of this problem?" Ted wondered. To the wise old Indian, this was a very naive question.

"Do you think that the white society cares if an Indian dies? Do you really think they would search for an Indian that we say has disappeared? No Ted, this is our problem. The white man, Chimookaman, does not care. But Windigo can be Chamookaman's problem, too, as you will find. No, it is not the Makwa [bear] that is the killer of man."

DeathWalker

Gray Wolf passed the picture back to Ted. "Your people, they will find a Makwa and kill him. They will then say that the problem is over. But it is not over. Windigo is smart. He will move to another territory for awhile, but he will be back . . . for he always comes back."

In order to placate the old man, Ted asked one more question. "How can you kill him?"

The old Indian arose. "You cannot kill what doesn't live. Only a giiwanadizi Chamookaman would ask such a stupid question." Gray Wolf turned, walking slowly back to his chess game while shaking his head. Ted thought *'Great, this really helped me. An Indian bogey man is the culprit.'*

"What the hell did he call me? It sounded like a mouthful!" Ted asked Bob.

Bob laughed. "It's similar to 'crazy white man'. Gii-wana-dizi is crazy, but traditionally, we never refer to you as white man, or pale faces like in the movies. To the Anishanabe, you are all 'long knives,' which translates to Chamookaman."

"So I'm a crazy long knife? Let's go, Bob. I've got a plane to catch." Ted arose and moved toward the door. He suddenly stopped and thought for a second, and then slowly walked over to the old Indian.

"Gray Wolf, you said that when Windigo is present, the Indians never go out wandering alone in the dark woods." The old Indian nodded an affirmative. Ted continued. "How do you know he is there? How do you know he has arrived?"

The old Indian swallowed and paused, as if deciding whether to divulge his Indian secret, and then he spoke cautiously. "Geyaabi. The woods will turn silent. Not just quiet, but dead silent. Geyaabi. So quiet that you can hear your own heartbeat. Windigo approaches from the night sky and sits high in the trees, for all the animals to see. They are geyaabi goshi; silent with fear. Then, you will know he is there. You will know. With Windigo comes nibooke, or 'death,' in your language."

"If you can't kill him, how does he leave?" Ted asked.

"We can only pray to KichiManitu, the great spirit, to take him away," the old man answered. "Do you believe in ManitoKa—spirits, Ted Scott?" Gray Wolf asked.

"Yes, yes I do," Ted replied.

"Good! Maybe you're not giiwanadizi after all. Remember Ted Scott . . . geyaabi. When the night is dead silent, he comes." Gray Wolf

33

turned and began walking away, but then stopped and focused his gaze on Ted's face. "You seem familiar to me, Ted Scott," he said softly.

"Maybe it is because some of your blood runs through my veins. My mother was Anishanabe and of the wolf clan. My father is a white man. I was brought up in the white world." Ted answered.

Gray Wolf moved toward Ted. "Give me your hands," he requested. As Ted extended his hands, the old man held them and closed his eyes. "I can feel that you are truly one of us, Ted Scott. You have a strong spirit. You will always be welcome here." Maybe it was Ted's imagination, but he felt a tinge of energy from the old man's touch. Gray Wolf reached into his pocket and pulled out a small leather pouch. "Keep this with you. It is strong medicine. Should you face death, it will help keep you strong." He then turned and walked away.

His words hit Ted with an impact. The first thing that the old Indian said that hit home was "dead silent." This was an appropriate way to describe the deafening quiet of the night. Ted fondled the pouch. "What did he mean, if I face death?"

Bob didn't answer. Instead, he walked over to where Gray Wolf sat and set a new pack of cigarettes on the table near the old man.

"What was that about?" Ted asked.

"When you visit the grandfather, you always leave a gift. It's tradition." Bob explained.

Ted took a last look at this way of life. It was so peaceful and orderly. Their way of life was guided by centuries of tradition. There were strong family ties, and all lived in close proximity. The respect for elders and authority was without question. In a way, he envied what these Native Americans held onto, regardless of their superstitious ways. He heard no cell phones ringing and saw no signs of stress. As they walked about, he saw the children playing physical games and running about without care or concern. The reason they resisted the white man's ways was all too obvious.

"Let's go, Bob." They were soon on their way, driving back to Winnipeg airport.

The flight back to Roseau seemed to be shorter than the flight to Winnipeg. This was only because Ted was deeply engrossed in sorting out the events of the morning. *Banishment from the reservation was equal to death*, was on Ted's mind. Of course it wasn't a mythical creature, Ted reasoned. Indians have a way of making everything sound mystical and

DeathWalker

mysterious. To the Native American, the sun itself rising was a major holy event and minor miracle. Native Americans had a way of interpreting everything in a wondrous way. "Shit happens" was not something that they believed in. To them, everything had a significant reason or purpose.

It was 5:00 p.m. as the plane landed, and Ted hadn't eaten anything all day. He was starving. He walked over to a restaurant near where he had parked his car, and wandered in. He sauntered over to the counter and sat down on a stool. Looking around, he recognized a familiar face. Sitting in a corner booth talking with two Indian companions, was John Hall, the hunter he had met the previous day. Ted ordered the half pound cheeseburger and a large Pepsi. As he ate, he watched as Hall and his companions seemed to be analyzing a map and taking notes. After devouring his food, he strolled over to their booth.

"Hello, Mr. Hall," Ted greeted him.

"Mr. Scott, if I remember correctly? Please, sit with us, if you like." John Hall seemed friendly enough, and Ted sat down.

"What brings you up here to Roseau, Mr. Scott? I thought you were from Minneapolis," Hall questioned.

"My dad. He lives up here so I'm here visiting. How did you drift this far northwest?" Ted queried.

"Well, I have a team tracking the territory south, so me and the boys thought we would anticipate this animal's next move, in case he's changing territories. Likely, he would head north into the deeper woods or the wildlife refuge." Hall's logic seemed sound enough to Ted.

Ted looked toward the Indians. "Windigo," he blurted out, and watched for a reaction. Only one Indian raised an eyebrow, but it was John Hall that answered.

"No, Mr. Scott, not likely." Hall grinned. He continued. "I'm sorry; I never introduced Joe and Pete, my Chippewa friends here. This is not Windigo; it is a bear. Windigo is a myth. It is a way for the Chippewa Indians to bring reason to inexplicable events. Someone dies a strange death and it's the dreaded Windigo. Someone runs away and disappears and it's the Windigo that took him. It's all old Indian folklore; it's just a bunch of Chippewa Indian crap." Hall watched Ted's reaction as he continued. "Do you know what the real English translation is?" Hall asked. Ted nodded negative, sheepishly.

"Vampire! Windigo is an Indian version of our Vampire. It's a being that can appear as a man, but can pick you up and carry you away, sucking

35

the life from you. They call him DeathWalker, but it's a vampire to us. It's a bogey man, for Christ sake!" Hall paused and took a drink of coffee before continuing.

"I've seen mean nasty bears in my life. Some are old, some lame, but whatever the reason, they get mean and dangerous. They become unpredictable. It no longer becomes a question of food, as they enjoy being aggressive. Maybe it's a bad tooth ache, I don't know, but it happens. They don't just pick on humans; they will tear up anything in their path. This is not a new problem. In fact, this is the third animal we've tracked this year." Hall smiled. "Do you hunt, Mr. Scott?"

"I used to," Ted answered.

"What with? If I may ask . . ." Hall queried.

"Crossbow, mainly, but I always carry a large handgun as a backup," Ted answered.

"Interesting. I use the crossbow also, especially at night. I don't like shooting a high powered bullet into the darkness. I might hit something I hadn't planned on," Hall stated.

"Well, Mr. Hall, I must go. If you'll please excuse me. I wish you luck. Catch him sooner, rather than later." Ted shook his hand and looked away, as he was embarrassed about suggesting that the problem might actually be a mythical Indian creature.

"We will catch him, Mr. Scott. We will!" Hall sounded certain and confident.

✳   ✳   ✳

As he entered the house, Brutus came running to greet him.

"Hey, my little man, come to papa." Ted picked him up and gave him a hug. "Did you take care of your Grandpa while I was gone?" Ted asked, as Brutus licked his face.

"Teddy! Come talk to me," His father called. "So, how did you do?" he asked.

Ted flopped on the couch and reviewed the day's events. His father listened intently. When he finished, he asked for an opinion. Ted's father laughed.

"Those Indians always have a tale to tell, Teddy. If there's too much rain, the Gods are angry. If there's no rain, the Gods are angry. They are a very superstitious people. If you ask me, I'd write that part off. This Hall fellow, he seems to know his stuff. But the whole bear thing seems like a crazy coincidence to me. Stick to your novels, son. You have a good mind and are a hell of a writer, so why waste your time on this bear thing? You can make up a better story than that." His father's comment was a valid one. He began to wonder whether he was wasting his time on this entire bear business.

"Maybe you're right, Dad. Maybe I'm trying a little too hard to make something out of nothing. I do have other ideas, you know," Ted stated.

"Teddy, you do what you have to do. You always had your own mind and it has served you well. I'm just giving you my opinion. I also have to give you the flip side. Your instincts have always been true to you. So if there's that fire in your gut that's telling you to stick with it, follow your gut hunch and the hell with what anyone thinks, including your old man."

"Dad, I was up at 4 A.M., I'm really bushed. Would you take Brutus out before you hit the sack? I'm going to bed."

As he drifted off to sleep, he knew that the feeling in his gut was telling him to stick with it. Ted had a strong feeling that something was behind these random deaths, and maybe it was something that couldn't be explained away.

Chapter Four

When Ted's father awoke and went to the kitchen to make coffee, he found a fresh pot ready and waiting. Sitting at the kitchen table was Ted, banging away on his laptop computer, typing furiously.

"What are you working on, son?" he asked inquisitively.

"I'm starting my new novel, '*No Trace of Blood.*' I have the beginning running through my head and I'm going with it." His fingers were flying as the keyboard was clicking furiously. "If I'm lucky, I'll get four or five thousand good words down today." Ted never lifted his head from the small computer screen.

"Teddy, I'm going to town today for some shopping. How long do you think you're staying? I'm just asking so that I buy enough food."

"Maybe a couple more days, if that's okay? I need to get back soon and do a few things in Minneapolis. I have to talk to the coroner and the detective, now that I have some more intelligent questions." Ted continued typing. Brutus was sitting on the table next to the computer screen. It appeared he was reading what Ted typed. Ted's dad laughed to himself as he went through his normal morning routine.

When Ted's dad returned from town it was late afternoon, and Ted was still in the kitchen typing. He noticed that Ted was typing a bit slower, having been at it for at least six hours.

"Teddy, take a break. You've been working all day!" his father yelled.

Ted must have agreed, for he shut off his computer and folded it up, packing it in the travel case.

"I really need some air, Dad. I'm going for a walk. Come on, Brutus, let's go!" Ted hollered as he headed for the door.

DeathWalker

Once outside, he decided not to walk the road. Instead, he would travel a path through the deep woods that led to a clearing. It was about two acres of meadow in the midst of deep, dense woods. How it came to be absent of tall pines was a mystery. This was his private place. As a boy, he would go there to practice with his bow and arrow. He often used it as a place of escape, where he could just go and daydream. There was a huge, flat-topped boulder in the clearing where Ted would sometimes lay tanning in the hot summer sun. Brutus stayed at Ted's side as they traveled the narrow path.

All the while, Ted studied everything about the path they traveled. Bothered by the silence of the previous night, he looked for signs of large game. Did the small shrubbery have leaves knocked to the ground? Were there any broken branches at walking level? Were there any tracks in the soft, black dirt, or in the carpet of moss along the tree line? It was late afternoon, but still bright and sunny, so his visibility was excellent, even in the thick shade of the huge trees. Beyond the path, he looked for shrubbery that was flattened, as if a big bear had slept there. He watched for claw marks on the trees, and found nothing. It was about a half mile to the clearing, and he examined every inch as he traveled.

He entered the clearing from the east, so the bright western sun hit him directly in the face, blinding him. As he stepped into the open field, Brutus let out a low warning growl, which then quickly turned into a higher, greeting bark. Ted shielded his eyes in order to see clearly. In his private meadow, on his personal boulder, was the figure of a woman lying down, enjoying the sun. Still blinded, he could barely make out her silhouette. It was almost a fantasy. Here, in his secret spot, was a woman sunning herself on '*his*' boulder, as the birds chirped and wildlife went about their normal routine. This was something he only imagined when he was fifteen. As he walked in her direction, she arose quickly and sat, facing his approach. Brutus was barking a combination "warning," and "hello." Ted was afraid he might scare her, as she was alone in these deserted woods, so he called out a greeting.

"Hello, please excuse Brutus' barking. I'm Ted Scott. I live a little east of here." He smiled, to put her at ease. With the sun in his eyes, he still hadn't seen her face. He could see her pull a T-shirt over the bikini top or bra, whichever she had been lying out in. Brutus had beaten him there and was climbing the smaller rocks toward the top, trying futilely to reach the boulders large, flat surface. She reached down, picking Brutus up, and he was licking her face as Ted walked upon them.

He was struck by her appearance, for she was simply beautiful. He watched as she cuddled Brutus, giggling at his affection.

"Brutus, cut it out," Ted ordered, embarrassed by his dog's behavior.

"It's okay, he's a real doll," she said, smiling. "I'm Kathy Baker. I live just west of here. I was out walking and followed a path that led here on the other side of this clearing."

"Just west of here is the O'Heath place. Related?" he asked. "I went to school with Bud," he offered.

"No, we bought the place about a year ago. At least, my mom and dad did. I'm just up here visiting from Minneapolis." She said.

"Minneapolis? That's . . . that's where I live. I'm visiting my dad; he lives here alone, now that Mom passed away."

Ted was a bit nervous. Something about her made him feel as if he had never spoken to a woman before. He felt like he was not in control and was blabbering. She had a very direct look, and he sensed confidence in her manner. He could tell they were near the same age. She had long brown hair and dark brown eyes, with a flawless smile. Perfectly proportioned, she was about 5" 4", as best he could tell. Her tan was golden brown and the sun had also given her hair blonde streaks that framed her pretty face. Most important, there was no wedding ring on her finger.

"What do you do in Minneapolis, Ted?" she asked.

Her words awoke him from a dream state. "I . . . I'm a writer. I was a reporter, but now I write books full time." He felt that his words were awkward and clumsy.

"I'm an attorney," she offered.

In a slice of wit, he put his head down and said, "Oh, I'm so, so sorry." Her laugh was music to his ears. "Remind me to tell you all of my attorney jokes," he continued. Ted felt his mental coordination coming back.

"I think I've heard them all, and then some. I'm just a staffer at HarCourt and Barnes. We do tax litigation primarily—boring stuff." Though she played her role down, Ted knew this woman was a ball of fire.

His courage now returned, and with not knowing if he would run into her again, he decided to be bold. "Kathy, can we have dinner some time? I know this may sound forward, but other than getting into tax trouble and

DeathWalker

having to call Harcourt and Barnes, I don't know if I'll ever see you again. Recently I've been on the move researching a story."

She handed Brutus to Ted. "Sure . . . call information. John Baker is my dad's name. Call tonight and I'll give you my number in the city and my cell, because I'm going back tomorrow." She smiled, turned, and walked to the west. There was a strange, overwhelming feeling that he had known her before. He knew they had never met, but a familiarity was there that he couldn't explain. He was drawn to her like a magnet. As he watched her rhythmic walk, he heralded Brutus. "You devil, you. You kissed her first. Gave her the tongue right away, didn't you, you devil you . . . I want that one, Brutus. I really want that woman."

His walk back to the house was a brisk one. All he could think about was how long to wait before calling her. Should he call immediately? Or, should he be cool and call later? "Piss on it, I'm calling her right away," he thought.

"Did you have a nice walk?" Ted's dad asked.

"Nicest walk I've ever had in my life!" Ted answered, with enthusiasm.

"I take it you ran into the Baker girl . . ." his dad said, wisely.

"You know her?" Ted asked.

"No, but I met her. Her parents bought the O'Heath place. Now Teddy, I saw that girl months ago and when I did, I thought of you. I swear it! She's a looker, isn't she? And smart, too!" His dad was grinning ear to ear.

"Dad, I swear to you . . . I have never met a woman and immediately felt like I feel. It's crazy. If she asked me to come over right now, I'd run there in my bare feet over hot coals. I even have this feeling like we've met before. It's crazy. This was the last thing on my mind." Ted was pacing while talking, almost to himself.

"Teddy, that's exactly how I felt when I met your mother. The minute I laid eyes on her, I never wanted to leave her side. Love at first sight, Teddy. Go with it," he urged. His dad sounded very pleased.

"It was strange, Dad. I walked to the clearing deep in the woods, and there she was. It was as though she was waiting for me, just lying on that boulder in the sun." Again, Ted was blabbering.

"Teddy, when it happens, it's sudden, believe me. When I met your Mom, it hit me like a ton of bricks. Once I met her, my eyes never wandered. We were married in less than a week. She was the sexiest woman

I ever knew. It's what's called chemistry, son." Ted's dad was reliving fond memories.

"Dad, please don't tell me any of the sexy parts, okay? I mean, she was my mom, for Christ's sake!" Ted scolded his father.

"Well, Teddy, I hate to tell you this, but your mom was a wild woman and I loved every damn minute of it!" he laughed.

"Dad, change the subject. Jesus Christ, give me a break." Ted covered his ears and began singing. "La-la-la-la-la! I can't hear you!"

"Okay, Teddy. Make your call!" his dad demanded.

Ted had to use the home phone, as most cell phones did not get reception in these rural areas. As Ted dialed, he tried to get his mind in order. He wanted to sound cool and aloof, and not nervous and anxious, as he really was.

"Is Kathy there?" he asked.

"Hello," she said politely.

"Kathy, this is Ted. I called to get your number?" he said tentatively, as though she possibly didn't remember the events of an hour ago. As soon as he said it, he recognized how stupid he sounded.

"Sure, Ted. 555-5555. That's my home. I live at Webster Place," she stated.

"Webster Place is almost across the street from me! I'm at The Oaks, on Tenth Street." This was an incredible coincidence. "Kathy, why don't we go out for dinner tonight?" He held his breath as he waited for the answer.

"Ted, I'm not dressed for anything and-"

Ted interrupted. "Don't bother, just go as you are. We'll just find a place in town to have a burger and just talk. Come on, you'll look fine." He knew that his cool and aloof attitude was lost, but at least he wasn't nervous.

"Sounds good to me. See you shortly." She hung up.

Ted quickly washed and brushed his teeth. He was still tucking in his clean shirt as he said goodbye to his dad. Dad and Brutus were curled up in front of the television. It was a country mile to her parent's house, and she was waiting at the driveway.

"Hi . . ." He opened the car door from the inside and swung it open.

"Where are we going?" she asked.

"A four star French restaurant, just a few miles from here," he replied, in his most serious tone.

DeathWalker

"What?" she panicked, glancing at her casual wear.

"Well, it's really not French; it's more like Frenchish Canadian. In fact, it's more like Polish. And they took the stars away a few years ago after a couple customers died of some disease. Moose burgers are their specialty now." Kathy was laughing at Ted, and it gave him a warm feeling. He loved the sound of her laughter.

"Are you crazy, Ted Scott?" she kidded.

"Sometimes," Ted answered. "I have an active imagination, which is why I enjoy writing."

"Are you successful?" she questioned.

"Not yet, but I will be. I have one book to be published soon, a novel. I didn't make that much on it, but it's a start. I'll get better at it. You see, I was used to writing articles. Some days, I could get by with writing 500 words. On a tough day, maybe I'd punch out 2000. It was easy. Writing a book is bit different. Instead of writing a few words with significant impact, you must challenge and engage the reader through 50,000 to 100,000 words. I don't think it is necessarily tougher; it's just different and I'm learning. But I'm committed . . . I won't give up." Ted was baring his soul.

"I like your attitude, Ted Scott. I feel the same passion for the law. I'm not exactly doing what I want right now, but eventually I'll get there. Right now I work behind the scenes, but some day, I'd like to be a trial attorney. I'd enjoy being the big gun, the one who faces the jury." Kathy was now the one baring her soul.

The ten mile drive was over as they pulled into a rustic looking pub. They entered and settled in a cozy booth. The pub resembled a hunting lodge, with animal heads hanging on every wall. The word "rustic" was a definite understatement. They automatically moved close to each other, sitting side by side. There were only a few people in the pub, but Ted couldn't believe his eyes. There, in the opposite corner, was the hunter John Hall and an Indian companion. Hall was occupied with conversation, never noticing that Ted entered. 'Small world,' Ted thought. He excused himself from Kathy and walked over to Hall's booth.

"I get the impression that you're hunting me!" Ted exclaimed.

"Ted Scott, we meet again. How are you?" Hall asked.

"Kind of far from where the action is, aren't you?" Ted queried.

"Well, I'm anticipating this animal's next move. I have a team south of us, but all the signs look like he's moving north. So, here we are." Hall explained.

"This bear would be moving rather fast, wouldn't he?" Ted asked.

"I once tracked a bear that traveled nearly seventy miles in one day! If one decides to move quickly, they move as the crow flies, with no terrain to stop them." Hall spoke with authority.

"Any signs of him?"

"Yeah, I believe so. One of the things we're seeing is a lack of large animal activity up here. It's as though something scared them off. He's either up here, or heading this way, all right." Hall sounded confident.

"You say there's a shortage of big game out here?" Ted questioned.

"I take it you haven't been hunting, Mr. Scott," Hall answered.

"Please, call me Ted. We've seen each other so much over the last few days that I feel as though we're old friends. But to answer your question, no, I haven't been hunting at all." Ted responded.

"Well, you should take your crossbow and give it a try. Good luck finding anything large, though," Hall replied. "Big game seems to have left this territory, for some strange reason."

"Well, I left my date sitting over there and I must get back. Good luck to you, John."

Ted returned to his booth and his comfortable position alongside Kathy.

"A friend?" she asked.

"Not really. He's a hunter with the Department of Forestry. He says there's a renegade bear that is possibly moving through this area. It's a story I'm following." Ted had an instant vision of Kathy sunning herself, alone, on that boulder in the middle of the woods.

"I know you're going back tomorrow, but should you return here soon, I wouldn't go deep into the woods alone for a while until they catch this renegade bear. They think he's killed a few people." Ted said.

"So that's your next story?" she questioned.

"I . . . I'm not sure yet," Ted responded.

"Is it the writer, or reporter, that's chasing this bear?" Kathy wondered aloud.

"Great question. Honestly, I don't really know. I think it's the reporter that's doing the investigating . . . but the writer is looking for a new creative

DeathWalker

angle. I know these are supposed to be bear killings, cut and dried. Maybe it's my imagination, but I feel that there's a little more to it. There are too many things that don't add up, and they make no sense. So, I follow my gut instinct." Ted made it sound similar to a game.

"I like you, Ted Scott. I think you'll be a great writer some day," Kathy said.

"Someday . . . yeah, someday," Ted answered.

"Yes, you'll be successful!" Kathy sounded assured.

"Why are you up here, besides visiting your parents?" Ted asked.

"Honestly? I love the solitude. My life is made up of urgent research, writing various legal opinions, cell phones, texting, meetings, and chaos, in a business sense. Sometimes, I just want to chuck it all and just get away. When my parents bought this house, I found my quiet place."

They quickly looked at the menu and ordered cheeseburgers and cokes. It was as if eating became secondary. They talked about their families, school, and growing up. Ted liked watching her eat. She took such small bites and always licked her lips afterward. '*Cute*,' he thought. There seemed to be no inhibitions between them, as though they had done this many times before. Ted felt no pressure to impress her, nor any urgency to put any moves on her. He knew in his heart that they would be seeing each other again soon. Driving back, he was already thinking of calling her, once he was back in Minneapolis. As he pulled up to her house, she suddenly leaned over and kissed him on the cheek.

"Thanks, Teddy. Call me when you get back. We'll get together," she offered, as she smiled and was soon gone. He was left watching her rhythmic walk move towards the house.

He drove home wishing that he would have taken his walk earlier in the day. Maybe they could have spent the afternoon sunning together, and talking privately on that big boulder deep in the woods. Parking the car and walking to the house, he noticed the total silence. '*Maybe I should put in a call for John Hall and have him come up this way*,' he thought.

Once again, he walked to the edge of the forest and listened, only to hear his own heartbeat, just as Gray Wolf had described. Ted was tempted to explore further, but felt the little hairs stand up on the back of neck, and a slight chill went down his spine. In his head, he heard the old Indian's word, "Nibooke," death . . . death . . . death. He caught himself looking about, as if to see someone watching him. He turned slowly and made his

45

way to house, looking back, as though expecting something to follow him from the dark woods.

"Hey, Pop!" he yelled as he entered the house. Brutus came running for him immediately and Ted scooped him up. "Did you guard your grandpa while I was gone?" Ted asked as Brutus licked his face.

Ted's dad was watching the local news and announced, "They found a body floating in the river near Pine Creek today. They say it was an Indian. They're calling it suicide. First one I have ever heard of around here." His gaze was fixed on the television.

"When did they find him?" Ted asked.

"They said late in the afternoon. A fisherman spotted the body and the officials said it looked like it had been in the water quite a while. It bothers me though, because Indians don't commit suicide. Nope! Don't sound right," he mumbled, as he was familiar with some of the local Indian ways.

"You know, you're right. It's against their whole philosophy. I never have heard of an Indian committing suicide, now that you mentioned it. Pop, where will this body end up?" Ted asked.

"Likely Rosawan, Teddy. That's where the local Coroner is."

"Then that's where I'm going tomorrow, Dad. I'm hitting the sack. Good night."

Suspended in the night sky, she watched the silhouette that was becoming familiar. She had watched Ted pull up to the house and followed his warm blooded glow to the edge of the woods. Again, she was hoping he would venture into the woods, but instead, he turned away. When he entered the house, she flew to her favorite boulder to enjoy the feeling of the night.

At nine in the morning, Ted was in Rosawan. The coroner's office was in the basement of a small county building. As Ted walked the stairs, he could smell an odor that told him that he was in the right place. He knocked politely.

"Come in!" A male voice beckoned.

"Hello, I'm Ted Scott. I am inquiring about the Native American that was found in the river near Pine Creek."

DeathWalker

"Are you a relative?" The man asked. He looked at Ted curiously, as if wondering why anyone would be interested in this case.

"No, a reporter." Ted held out his press card.

"I'm Dan Wilson . . . town doctor and part-time coroner. How can I help you, young man?" Ted took note of the fact that Wilson did look more like a country doctor than a coroner. He was a smiling old man, short and bald. Ted felt that Wilson didn't have the intensity that traditionally went with the coroner's position.

"Part-time?" Ted questioned.

"Sure. Not much need for a full time coroner up here. Fortunately, most people in these parts die a natural death of some sort. This suicide is unusual." Wilson stated.

"Why do you think suicide?" Ted questioned.

"Pretty simple, really. The body was found in the lake. He was fully dressed and had his wallet in his pocket. This makes it pretty clear that he wasn't swimming, so not likely a drowning accident. The wallet had a few hundred dollars in it, which rules out a robbery or obvious foul play. The extensive damage to the body appeared to be made by the fish and turtles after he died. It was pretty evident that there are no wounds on the body that could be determined as the cause of death." Wilson sounded confident. "What else would it be, if a fully clothed man dives head first into some rocks in shallow water? I mean, this guy was fit. This was no accidental fall."

"Water in the lungs?" Ted asked.

"Well, he was pretty torn up by the fishes, but yes. There was very little in the lungs, but not enough to fully diagnose a drowning," he answered.

"Then, why is the assumption suicide?"

"Well, what am I to say? He is too young for natural causes. I see no evidence to call it a homicide, so I assume he dove in and likely hit his head. The head trauma is enough to be the cause of death. I examined no evidence that he put his hands forward to even break his fall. I start screaming homicide, and I must call in the state and possibly the FBI, for what? I will make the whole community paranoid."

To Ted, he didn't sound that confident. "Can I ask if there was blood?"

"Blood? What exactly do you mean?"

"Was there blood in the body?" Ted blurted, repeating his question.

"No, not a lot. It appeared as standard hypovolemia. The head trauma alone would be a source of massive blood loss. I said he was torn up pretty bad, and spent days in the lake. Why would you ask that question?" Wilson inquired.

"Curiosity. Just curiosity," Ted responded.

"Want to see the body?" Wilson asked, raising an eyebrow.

"Sure," Ted answered.

The coroner led Ted through a heavy metal door. Behind it was a refrigerated room. On a cold, stainless steel table, laid the body, covered by a black rubber sheet. Wilson threw the sheet back and Ted flinched at the macabre sight. The body was bluish white and severely mutilated, covered completely with variously sized gaping wounds. It was evident that it was completely drained of blood. There were huge wounds across the trunk of the body, including a large cavity in the chest. Chunks of flesh were missing from head to toe.

Ted swallowed hard. "You think fish did this?"

"Have you ever seen what a Northern Pike or a Muskie can do to a piece of meat when they're hungry? Not to mention a big-old snapping turtle," the coroner stated.

Ted covered his mouth and nose as he moved closer to the body, examining the wounds. He could clearly see that some of them fit the description of being fish bites. But two huge openings in the chest and abdominal area looked suspicious.

To Ted, it was obvious that this was not an open and shut case of suicide. The damage to this body was too extensive. The fish story made some sense, but not to the extent that this body was mutilated. Ted knew that Muskie, a huge fish that grew over four feet long, rarely attacked anything that wasn't alive, and almost never anything that was larger than it could swallow whole. It just didn't make sense.

"Did he have family?" Ted asked.

"No family that we can find. He lived alone in a cabin. He probably just decided to end his loneliness." Wilson had it all figured out, and his determination, justified. "Believe me, the local police found nothing suspicious. I will likely find a good amount of alcohol in his system, or another remote possibility is sudden death, and his heart just stopped."

The coroner's job in most small towns is a part-time position. In fact, it isn't even a requirement in many towns that the coroner have medical experience. So this old country doctor was used to people dying of a ripe old age, a fact not so uncommon in Minnesota. The people of Minnesota have the highest life expectancy of the mainland United States; the only Americans to live longer are the Hawaiians, on average. So, the good doctor had made his simple diagnosis—suicide. And Ted didn't believe it. He thanked the doctor for his time and was soon on his way, driving home.

What could he make of all this? This fit the description that old Gray Wolf had talked about. This was a clear case of an Indian living alone being condemned to death and killed by the "Windigo." The coroner says it's drowning. John Hall would likely say that it's a bear attack. Ted couldn't help this feeling in his gut that said it was neither. He had to find out what exactly was going on. Ted knew he was doomed to follow this story through to the very end.

He couldn't help but believe that it was possible for something to be falling between the cracks, as far as facts were concerned in these cases. He was fully aware of the tendency in our culture to provide quick and easy explanations for everything, both by the authorities and by the media. Maybe, just maybe, there was something strange and sinister behind these killings, something that wasn't so easily explained. It was something that possibly no one wanted to think about, much less hear about. Ted was on the verge of a discovery, of the very ingredient that nightmares are made of. He would soon find the source of what would send chills down his spine.

Chapter Five

Ted was literally scratching his head in confusion. "It was bullshit, Dad," he explained. "This Indian's body had some major wounds on it. The coroner attributed them to the fish tearing at it. I think the whole thing stinks. I'm not sure what it was, but I'd bet the farm it wasn't a suicide. The chest wounds alone were too deep for any fish. They resembled the other deaths."

"Like I said, Teddy, Indians rarely commit suicide. Never have I heard of a valid case. They believe that a suicide destroys the spirit forever. So you're probably correct on your hunch. The real question is; what to do about it?" his father asked.

"I'm not sure, Dad. But I'm learning how incompetent our system is in determining a cause of death. It's almost a rubber stamp." Ted replied quickly, with a hint of disgust in his voice.

"Son, if you think that's ridiculous, read this book. A fellow named Henry Marshall was found in Texas with five slugs in his chest from a bolt action rifle. They called that suicide, too. It's a real education." Ted looked at the title. '*Unsolved Texas Mysteries, a non-fiction work.*'

"Well, I'm not out to fight the system. I only want to get a story. I think I have one, but I'm not sure what it is. I have certainly met some great characters. The problem is that if I use this stuff in my novel, it's almost unbelievable. Reality can be much more frightening than fiction!" Ted exclaimed.

He opened his laptop computer and started typing his notes. His words painted graphic descriptions of everything that had transpired to date. As he typed, the hours flew by. The sun was beginning to set when he stopped to make himself a sandwich. He made up his mind that he would leave for Minneapolis in the morning. Ted needed to speak with his detective friend, Mike Evans, not to mention wanting to see Kathy again. He held on to the vision of Kathy lying on that boulder in the sun

DeathWalker

vividly, in his mind. He shared bits of his meal with Brutus, who was always hungry.

"We're heading back home tomorrow, boy. Is that okay with you?" Brutus cocked his head, as if understanding every word. Together, they walked to the porch and watched as the sky turned dark. Ted listened as the silence of evening was replaced by the standard sounds of the night. He studied the noises intently, as he tried to separate the various sounds. Thousands of crickets and an occasional hoot of an owl or screech of a hawk could be heard at random times. Layer after layer of night sounds, becoming louder and louder the darker it became. He sat back, petting Brutus and enjoying the pure sound of nature.

Suddenly the woods became silent. It was as if someone had turned off the volume on a radio. The only sound Ted could hear was the sound of his own breathing. He listened, trying to hear some sign of life, but there was none. Even Brutus was aware of the change, as he began pacing the porch in a state of vigilance.

"Come on, boy. You go inside. I'm going to investigate."

Overhead, she hovered, observing her familiar prey and his little warm blooded pet. At her presence, all the creatures of the night became silent, as if in fear that their sounds might attract her. She watched Ted rock back and forth before entering the house. At that point, she thought she had lost him again and proceeded to her favorite resting spot, the large boulder in the clearing. Little did she know that instead of staying in the house, Ted was about to venture out and was on a collision course to meeting the "Windigo."

Ted grabbed his crossbow from the hook on the wall. He tucked a few arrows in his back pocket.

"Dad, I'm going for a stroll." His father nodded and continued watching television, paying little attention.

Walking outside, Ted would follow his path deep into the woods toward his private clearing. The moon was only a quarter, but the sky was clear and created an eerie glow; however, the glow would all but disappear once in the midst of the tall pines. As his eyes adjusted to the darkness, he proceeded down the path. As he continued, he loaded an arrow into his crossbow. He carried it, holding it with both hands across his chest, ready to fire. It was so quiet; he could almost hear the sound of his own footsteps echoing.

51

Ted found it amazing that there was no sound at all, not even in the distance. As he walked slowly, his eyes scanned in all directions. Even the noise of a large thrashing bear would have been a comfort, if only for the sound. He walked very cautiously, because with the limited light from the sliver of the moon, he could barely see a short distance up the narrow path. It occurred to Ted that somewhere in these woods, John Hall, the master hunter, was likely doing the exact same thing that he was. *'Wouldn't it be funny if it was me that took this renegade bear down?'* Ted thought.

Ahead he could see the path, ending with the bright glow of the moon and stars in the open field. He continued his slow pace, anticipating seeing something in the clearing, even if only a deer. He quietly stuck his head out of the woods, surveying the landscape. There was nothing to be seen that was moving. He walked into the clearing, thinking that he would climb the boulder to get a better view of the surroundings. As he looked toward the boulder, he froze at the sight of a dark silhouette. It was a woman, lying on the boulder, looking up while staring at the sliver of the moon.

Just as Kathy had been lying in the sun, this woman seemed to be enjoying the night glow coming down from above. Ted rubbed his eyes, making sure he wasn't seeing things. Having envisioned Kathy lying on that rock, he wondered if his imagination was working overtime. As he approached, he wondered what a woman would be doing in these deep woods, alone at night? Then it struck him. Maybe she wasn't alone. He scanned about, looking for her companion, and could see no one else on the boulder or in the clearing. Then it also occurred to him that if she really was alone in these woods, maybe she was armed . . . so he cautioned that he had better be very careful. He decided to show her a sign that he was no threat. He raised his right arm, as in a gesture of peace, as he walked slowly forward. As he walked, he felt a chill run through his entire body.

She was gazing up at the night sky when his strong, warm blooded scent filled her nostrils. She turned, and could immediately see his warm blooded glow approaching. As she sniffed the air, she realized it was a familiar scent, and one she longed for on a number of occasions. She watched him, and knew he was hers to feed on. Alone in the deep woods, she was taking no risks, and therefore, was free to enjoy what was there for the taking. She began to salivate at the very thought. He was all hers, and Christian could have no objections.

DeathWalker

As he moved closer, he could see her rise from her prone position. In the blink of an eye, she was on her feet. Her movement was so quick, it caused Ted to stop dead in his tracks. He stood, staring at her silhouette against the crescent moon. Something about this just wasn't right. Instead of climbing down to the ground, using the smaller rocks that were surrounding the boulder, she bounded in the dark from the top of the huge rock, fifteen feet to the ground below. Almost catlike, she landed light as a feather. *'She is either some kind of incredible athlete, or something is terribly wrong,'* Ted thought, as a cold chill ran down his spine.

She walked directly toward him at a fast, confident pace. As she approached, and as the silhouette took a clearer form, he could see her white porcelain skin almost glowing in the dim moonlight. He felt the chill turn to a shiver, for her skin was far too white, almost like that of a mime. Then, he glimpsed at her eyes, and knew that he was in big trouble, for they were glowing a bright amber, and they were focused directly on him as she made her approach.

He was about to introduce himself at a distance, so as to not frighten her, but changed his mind very quickly, as all his instincts screamed at him to run. *'Screw this!'* he thought. *'I'm out of here!'* He had no idea what she was, but he listened to his instincts as they told him to run and run fast. As he turned to flee, he heard what could only be a deep snarl and a loud hissing sound. Full fear set in as his legs took off running. He couldn't feel his legs move, but he knew he was moving as fast as he possibly could. Everything seemed in slow motion as he tried to reach the path into the woods at the mouth of the clearing.

She smiled as he turned to run, for she knew it was such a futile human effort. She almost wished he was a bit further away, as she enjoyed the thrill of the hunt and the anticipation of the kill. She would tease him a bit before feeding and killing him, like a cat toying with a mouse. She knew the very sight of her would cause such fear that the air would be thick with the scent—and she loved the smell of fear. She also relished the thought of his heart pumping the blood faster.

As Ted ran and the path became closer, he felt sharp claws run the full length of his back, and could hear his shirt and flesh tearing away. The pain was not as frightening as the fact that he knew she was upon him. He also knew that at this point, outrunning her was impossible. Still clutching his crossbow with both hands, he turned quickly to face his nightmare. He wasn't prepared for what he would see. The fangs protruding from her mouth were sharp and glistening, and he could see saliva dripping freely down her chin. The once bright amber eyes, now were blazing a bright red. Her body was that of a woman, but her face was that of a tortured animal. He screamed, "No! Get back!" but before the words completely left his mouth, he was pushed backwards to the ground with great force. He had only a moment to look up at her as he lay on his back, in pain. As she fell upon him snarling and clawing like a wild animal, he raised his crossbow as a protective reflex, and she fell directly on it. Only the short distance of the crossbow separated their bodies. As he stared into her demonic red eyes, his trembling finger pulled the trigger, releasing the wooden arrow at full force, deep into the center of her chest and into her heart.

She screamed an ear piercing shriek as she arose, standing directly over him. Both hands were clutching and tugging at the small stub of an arrow buried deep in her heart. He gagged from the foul odor that surrounded him. Ted stayed on the ground and watched in horror as she screamed and moaned, clawing at her own chest. He could see the steam rise from the blood pouring out of her wound, and stared in a frozen state as she tore at her own flesh. Then, suddenly it stopped, as she fell to the earth. Then, there was total silence. Her body rested on the ground, completely motionless. Ted knew he was in shock as he sat shaking, watching the blood slowly ooze from her chest. He realized that he had delivered a perfect shot, directly to her heart, in a stroke of pure luck.

He too, could feel the sensation of warm blood running down his back and chest. His shirt was torn to ribbons and he was beginning to feel pain, despite the state of shock he was in. He arose, still shaking uncontrollably as he took one final look at his attacker. Her face seemed to shrivel and wrinkle, but that was not as alarming as the expression. It was pure evil. Still shivering, he turned and ran down the path toward home. He was still filled with fear and flinched at each shadow he encountered as he walked. The pain was excruciating, and it was only the pain that kept him from believing this whole event was nothing more than a hallucination of some sort. As a second thought, he reloaded his crossbow, although trembling, and kept his finger on the trigger. He increased his speed as much as possible, until he saw the comforting lights from the house in the distance.

He couldn't get into the house fast enough. Brutus was barking and his dad arose from the couch. He took one look at Ted and gasped. "What the hell happened? Teddy, you're hurt!"

DeathWalker

"Dad, I killed something out there," Ted blurted.

"Killed what?" his dad asked, rushing to the bathroom to grab a medical kit.

"I . . . I'm not exactly sure. It looked like a woman, but it wasn't. Her claws almost cut me to shreds." Ted looked down at his wounds as his father stood, dumbfounded.

"A woman? A woman? Teddy, take your shirt off!" his father insisted.

Ted removed his shirt and his father put his hands to his head, as if not believing what he was seeing. He examined his son's wounds as Ted sat, staring in a trance-like state and shivering as if he were freezing to death.

"Jesus Christ, Teddy, you need to go to a hospital. You're going to need stitches. Some kind of animal did this, for Christ sake. Come on, let's go!"

"Dad, grab your gun," Ted ordered.

"What?" his father asked, in disbelief.

"Dad, I said take your gun, or I will. You have no idea what else could be out there!" Ted ordered.

His father went to the gun cabinet, taking out a large handgun. He took time to load it with six shells. "I'm doing this for you, Teddy."

Ted's dad saw five perfect lines down Ted's back; so perfect and deep that they could have been done by a surgeon. On Ted's chest were ten more. He retrieved his terry robe for Ted. Wrapping him in it, he led him to the car. They were soon speeding on their way to the Roseau Clinic.

"Dad, once we get there, there's no way I can tell people what I really saw out there. If I do, they'll lock me in a padded cell. I'm going to say it was a bear, but it was dark out there so I'll be vague on this, okay? They'll think I'm nuts if I tell them the truth. They'll think I'm completely crazy!" he raved.

"Teddy, say whatever you like. I don't know what you saw, but I think you may be in a great deal of shock. With the wounds you have, no one will think you're crazy, believe me. We can talk about it later," he responded.

They entered the emergency room and were tended to immediately, as there was no one else there. Ted told the doctor that he had been clawed by a bear. They quickly went about cleaning and stitching his wounds. The Clinic also placed a call to the Department of Forestry and to the local police, notifying them of the attack. Noticing that Ted was not bitten, rabies was not a concern.

The doctor explained to Ted that each claw mark graduated from a shallow scratch, to a deep cut. He would stitch the deep wounds. Fifteen places in all, each getting three-to-eight stitches. It was an hour and eighty-three stitches later before Ted was finally ready to go home. His father had given the police a report, which satisfied them for the moment. The doctor had given Ted a morphine injection for the pain, which left him drowsy. Within a minute of getting into the car, Ted was fast asleep.

His father was confused. He had never known Ted to imagine things or exaggerate to this extent. His son always kept a clear head. As Ted slept, his father sat up worrying that whatever it was, it had scared Ted to death and then some. He only hoped the morning would bring with it an explanation.

While they were at the hospital, a great cry of anguish was heard echoing in the wilderness. It was Christian, her mate. He landed on the great boulder and knew something was wrong, as Anne was always there waiting for him. He could smell her in the distance, and also picked up another warm blooded scent. "Anne?" his voice boomed across the clearing.

It took but a second to find her limp body, and in less than a second, he sent an inhuman cry heard for miles. The arrow had destroyed her heart, and he knew she would never "live" again. Christian cried in sorrow as he tenderly carried her body to one of the many resting places they had used to escape the sunlight. There he would leave her and seal it, so he could never use it again, for it would become Anne's resting place for eternity. When finished, he returned to the site where he had found her body. There, he picked up a clear scent of her killer, as his blood was everywhere. He rubbed his long, thin finger into the drops of blood that littered the surrounding foliage, and tasted it. He decided his eternity would be spent searching for the man whose blood he tasted. When he found him, he would tear his heart from his body and drink until his thirst for revenge was satisfied. Christian, whose existence was one of living outside the population in wilderness, was now prepared to pursue Anne's killer to wherever he could reap his justice. Christian who had enjoyed their solitary existence wanted only to kill. He wanted Anne's murderer and would kill anyone who might become an obstacle. He wanted blood!

DeathWalker

*   *   *

The next morning, Ted awoke hoping it was all a bad dream. The pain (and the bandages) told him differently. Ted could not get the image of her face from his mind. It was the most horrible face one could imagine. He put on a robe and went down the stairs to the kitchen. There sat his father, sipping coffee and talking with John Hall. Ted was not unhappy to see Hall, but was upset at not being able to discuss in private what actually happened with his father.

"Ted, how are you?" John asked.

"I'll live . . . I think?" Ted answered.

"Our paths cross again. The Department sent me here to capture the details and pick up the trail from your attack. Can we talk about it?" John asked.

Ted looked to his father, giving him a look, as if to ask whether anything had been said. His father nodded negative.

"I'd rather take you there, so you can see for yourself," Ted replied.

"Hey, if you are up to it, I'm game," John responded.

"Give me a few minutes to get dressed . . ." Ted turned and walked back up the stairs.

"Jesus Christ, he's wrapped like the mummy!" Hall gasped.

"Eighty-three stitches, Mr. Hall. Whatever he encountered was out to cause some serious damage," Ted's dad mumbled.

"Did he at least get a good shot off?" Hall asked.

"To be honest, I don't know. He was in shock when he got here and bordering on hysteria. When the doctor finished with him he was really drugged up, so we never had a complete conversation. All he did was mumble a lot," Ted's father responded.

Ted returned, walking to the gun cabinet. He removed a pump shotgun and loaded it with five shells while they watched. "Let's go, John," he called as he walked out the door. Although in some pain, Ted was anxious to see exactly what had attacked him while they were now in broad daylight. He would say nothing to Hall until they saw the body, and then John Hall could make his own determination.

As they walked the path, paranoia set in, and Ted's eyes darted in all directions. He held the shotgun tightly.

"Did you get a shot off?" Hall asked.

"Oh yeah, a good one. I buried an arrow in its chest. Believe me, it was point blank," Ted replied.

"Then we should be seeing a carcass up here," Hall stated.

"I think so." Ted responded. He would say no more, and he would let the body speak for itself.

As they approached the clearing Ted held his breath, expecting to view this unearthly corpse. He knew the sight of it would astound John Hall. As they entered the clearing, Ted pointed just ahead. Reaching the exact location, there was no body. Ted looked around in amazement. Since Hall had never been told that Ted actually killed anything, he went about his business checking out the area. They were standing at the exact point of the struggle. It was evident that a fight had taken place on this spot. The weeds and grass were flattened and there were deep claw marks and blood in the ground . . . but no body.

"How exactly did you get away?" Hall asked.

"I told you, I buried an arrow in its chest . . ." Ted answered.

Hall carefully studied the ground. "I don't see any trace of blood, other than that going back down the path, which is obviously yours." He was scratching his head in confusion.

Ted looked at the exact spot where he had watched her blood oozing on the ground freely . . . but there was not even a trace. He was beginning to doubt his own sanity and state of mind.

"Ted, I see deep claw marks on the ground, but there are no bear tracks? I don't see a bear track anywhere." Hall was now very confused.

Ted took a deep breath. "It may have not been a bear."

"Not a bear? Then what the hell was it?" Hall questioned.

"I'm not sure. I first thought it was woman, until I got close to it . . ." Ted answered softly.

"A woman? It looked like a woman? Are you serious?" Hall was looking at him as if he were nuts.

"Okay, okay, don't look for bear tracks. Look for footprints coming in this direction from that boulder." Ted pointed straight ahead.

Hall examined the ground as he walked to the boulder. "Yeah, I see what could be a woman's footprint. She was wearing moccasins. So it was a woman that attacked you?" Hall was confused.

Ted carefully opened his shirt, and then gritted his teeth as he removed the bandages from his chest area that were covering the wounds and his stitches. Turning to Hall, he displayed his mangled chest.

DeathWalker

"You can laugh if you want to, but this was the result of her work." Ted watched as Hall winced at the sight of the huge claw marks and the dozens of stitch marks. "All I know is she looked like a woman from a distance, but had the face of an animal. She attacked me and I buried an arrow in her chest. She fell right here and I made my way home. And no, I wasn't drinking or doing any drugs. I know I killed it. Someone or something must have taken the damn body. I don't know . . . I just don't know. I'm going home." Ted buttoned his shirt, picked up the shotgun and walked toward the path.

Hall picked up a shred of Ted's bloody shirt lying on the ground. "I'm going to stick around here a while. I'll stop by, before I leave." Hall walked in the opposite direction still scratching his head.

As Ted slowly walked back, his mind started to replay what he had seen the previous night. Pasty white skin and huge fangs, with eyes that went from amber to red, plus the agility of a feline, all rolled into a single human body. Windigo, Deathwalker, or vampire, he had come face to face with it. His little wooden arrow fired from the crossbow was the perfect weapon. If it was truly a vampire, it provided the perfect stake through the heart. But what of the body? Was it like in the movies, where it evaporated in the sunlight? If it did evaporate, where was his arrow? No, someone moved the body . . . but whom? He shuttered as he realized that likely there was another vampire to deal with.

As crazy as it seemed, the thought of a vampire answered a lot of questions about the killings that Ted had investigated. One look at his own chest and he knew how easy a body could be torn to shreds. This certainly would explain the lack of blood at the scene of all the bodies found. The thought of a vampire certainly made sense. The problem was that at this point, it would only make sense to Ted and possibly old Gray Wolf, the wise old Anishanabe Indian.

Ted was thinking that the whole episode was finished with only a mystery to be analyzed and solved. He thought that by the time his wounds healed, that he could also heal his emotions by writing of it and releasing his fear. Instead, this was only the beginning . . . but Ted didn't know it!

Chapter Six

ohn Hall stayed at the site of the attack, carefully studying every inch of ground and blade of grass. He could see where Ted had fallen and had moved about when attacked. At the location were shreds of Ted's shirt and sprinkles of blood, still clinging to the weeds. He followed the scene backwards. Ted's tracks were clear. They were deep, as if running, and they were pointed in the direction of the path. He could also see Ted's original tracks walking toward the boulder, and he followed them.

He could spot where Ted stopped dead in his tracks. Now, the only tracks were those of what appeared to be a woman in moccasins, pointed in Ted's direction. He followed those prints to where they originated at the base of the boulder. He could clearly observe that her prints originated at the base, and he scratched his head as he looked over fifteen feet straight up, from where she must have jumped. He found no other fresh tracks. Hall climbed the rocks to the top of the boulder, surveying the clearing. *'If she was on top of this rock, how the hell did she get down from here?'* Hall was now very confused, as none of the moss covering the lower rocks had been recently disturbed.

Hall recalled the old Chippewa tale of how the Windigo would lift his victims to the air. The Chippewa, searching for the victim, would see footprints that gradually became further and further apart . . . until they disappeared. *'No damned way . . .'* he thought, shaking his head.

Hall decided to call in one of his Chippewa companions and make camp on the top of this boulder. If there was something here, he was going to find it. There was no way Hall could reason that an ancient Native American myth could possibly be real. Whatever it was just might return, and if it did, he would kill it. He had never encountered anything that he could not handle, so there was no feeling but total confidence.

DeathWalker

*   *   *

"Dad, there was no body back there. No blood—not a trace! I think Hall believes I've lost my damn mind. I'm not sure what exactly happened now. I swear that I buried an arrow in its chest, and saw it die at my feet. I will never forget it." Ted was visibly upset and pacing the room.

"Teddy, you need some rest. I know there's an explanation for all this, and we'll find it. Rest is what you need right now," his father responded. "Please sit, or you'll bust those damn stitches."

"Oh, I know what it was all right. But if I tell you, you'll think I'm completely nuts. Dad, I think I was attacked by a vampire of some sort. Don't say anything, just listen to me. It did appear to be human from a distance. I saw her jump off the boulder from over fifteen feet high, and land, light as a feather! Dad, I had a thirty yard head start, yet she caught up to me in two seconds. I mean, two seconds, flat! The eyes, the fangs . . . I know it was a damned vampire! That's how I killed her, with an arrow through the heart. Think about it—a stake through the heart, just like in the movies!" Ted rested his case.

"Teddy, if you killed it, then where's the body?" his father patiently asked.

"I . . . I don't know. There wasn't a trace. I saw blood gushing out in gallons, but there wasn't a damn drop to be seen. No arrow . . . nothing. I don't know." Ted covered his face with his hands in utter frustration. "Pop, I feel like I'm losing my mind!"

"Teddy, I don't know what you saw out there, but vampires don't exist. Maybe a crazy person dressed up like one could be the answer, but vampires are a myth, sort of like the bogey man. Son, I don't have all the answers, never did, but this sounds like you were attacked and now you have become a bit hysterical. The mind can play games at a time like that. I know what you think you saw, but let's face it, there is no body. Maybe this whole thing is connected to that story you been chasing, subconsciously. I'd get some rest."

"Dad, I know how this sounds and I will ask only one thing of you. You must make me a promise. I want you to promise me that when I go back to Minneapolis, you will do one thing for me," Ted pleaded.

"What, son?"

"If the woods become quiet, so quiet that it becomes dead silent, promise me that you will never go out. Not on to the porch, not out to the car, not anywhere. Promise me, Dad. Promise me," Ted begged.

"I promise, Teddy. If it will make you feel better, I promise you."

"Dad, you must understand. If the body of that thing, whatever the hell it was, is missing, then someone moved it. It is only logical that this someone is a damned monster like she was. Therefore, he or she is still out there. Dad, I need to know that you won't go out there at night."

"Teddy, I'm an old man. I don't have a reason to go out at night, much less in the woods. If anything looks or sounds unusual, I go for the shotgun, anyway. So . . . I promise!"

"I need to get to back to Minneapolis. I know there must be someone in town that knows about these things," Ted stated.

"Well, for now, Teddy, you rest. Go sack out on the couch. Take one of those pain pills," his father suggested.

Ted took two pills and sat back on the couch. He clicked on the television. Within minutes, he was out like a light, snoring loudly. His father was worried. He knew Ted never had the tendency to exaggerate or lie. Ted was always conservative in the reporting of facts. This is what most likely made him a good news reporter. So, what really happened to his son out in those woods? As he sat on the porch pondering that very question, John Hall came out of the woods from the path.

"Is Ted around, Mr. Scott?" he asked.

"Yeah, but he's sleeping. He took a couple of pain pills and will probably be knocked out for hours. Do me a favor, call me Ray," he replied.

"Well, Ray, one of my companions is headed this way. He and I are going to camp out in that clearing for the next few days. It's weird, very weird. Nothing makes any sense. Incredible as it sounds, there is evidence that a woman was out there last night. The prints are very clear, even though they don't make much sense. But, I'll find the answer. There's always an answer," Hall stated.

"What doesn't make sense?" Ray asked.

"Well, the fresh prints just sort of appear at the boulder in the middle of the clearing. Then, they point away from that point. There are no similar tracks leading to the boulder. None! That is, unless she flew in on a helicopter." Hall laughed.

"Yeah, that's one answer," Ray responded.

DeathWalker

"Ray, I don't know what happened out there. I do know that there are a woman's prints, and I do know that Ted looks like a bear sharpened his claws all over him. Whether there was a woman and a bear, or how this thing developed, is all very confusing. It was very dark out there, and maybe Ted was confused. The only thing that really puzzles me is the fact that there is not one bear track in that clearing. Not one!"

"Well, if you need anything, just ask. I'm glad to help you. I certainly would like an answer to all this," Ray replied. "I have never seen Teddy in such a state. Considering his wounds, there is no doubt that he faced off with something powerful, and he was lucky to escape with his life."

"Whatever it is, I sure would like a crack at it." Hall shifted his weight. "Well, we won't bother you. Just remember we're out there and please don't do any shooting in our direction," Hall requested.

Ted slept the day away, rising only to swallow a few more pills; it would be the next day at five in the morning before he would be ready to begin living again.

"Dad, I'm going to back to Minneapolis," were his first words to his father.

"What about your stitches?"

"I'll get them taken out at the Medical Center, around the corner and up the street from me. I'll be back in a week," Ted answered.

His father hugged him gently. "Teddy, you take care. Please make sure you get those stitches taken out and looked at."

*　　*　　*

Ted spent the first day home, opening mail and conducting business. He called Kathy and invited her to dinner at his apartment, which she accepted. He feverishly started making calls trying to find material on vampires. He quickly found that the problem was that everyone had fictional material, but no one had anything that was based on facts, whether theoretical or not.

Eventually, by searching the web, he acquired the name of Professor Steiner, who was located at the main campus of University of Minnesota. He made an appointment for the same afternoon. Just walking across the campus brought Ted memories that seemed like yesterday. Ted could have attended almost any one of the twenty-seven colleges in Minnesota,

63

but he had chosen this one. He loved the location and the Ivy League atmosphere.

He remembered walking to class, imagining himself as the next F. Scott Fitzgerald. Or on his better days, the next Sinclair Lewis—the first American to ever win the Nobel Prize for literature! Every time he traveled over the old stone bridge, his aspirations seemed to grow.

His daydreams burst at the entrance to the Professor's office. Once there, he found the Professor reading. The Professor resembled Santa Claus, but shorter. White hair and beard, round and stout, with a pair of gold wire rimmed glasses, balanced delicately on the tip of his pink nose. He looked up, as if sensing he was being watched, and smiled a warm, friendly smile.

"Professor Steiner? I'm Ted Scott."

"Yes . . . yes, Mr. Scott. How can I help you?" he questioned.

"Vampires. I need to know about vampires," Ted stated bluntly.

"So you need to know about vampires, young man? Why, may I ask?" The old man continued smiling.

"I'm doing research on the subject. I'm a writer," Ted answered.

"Well, come in and get comfortable. I enjoy talking, you know, and I love discussing vampires. They've been an interest of mine for a very long time." He sat back, preparing for a long chat.

"Well, where do we start?" Ted asked.

"Let's start with the concept. Vampires were once real, and may very well still exist. So you will have to excuse me if I switch from past to present tense at times." The Professor stated, watching Ted's face. He was looking for skepticism, but was finding none. "May I say that if you're looking for the creature that likes to have coffee with humans, or sparkles while it walks about in the sunlight, that this is not what a real vampire is about. They are dark, solitary, nocturnal, and simply view us as food."

"I know . . ." Ted replied in confidence and complete attention.

The Professor was puzzled by the immediate acceptance. "The vampire is a very incredible creature, Mr. Scott. Yes, he did feed off of blood, but not as it's portrayed in the movies. The vampire preferred human blood, but could survive easily on any large mammal. They were once very common in Europe, and a few migrated here in the early 1800's. It was not easy for them to get to this country. Isolated aboard a ship, they could be discovered easily should they travel as a passenger, so most transported themselves in crates. Stored deep in the holds of the ships, they lived

DeathWalker

off rats for months. But America was not what the vampire expected. Because of our sparse population at that time, they became obvious and were hunted down and destroyed rather easily. Europe was a much more comfortable environment for the vampire," The Professor explained.

"But, don't they multiply quickly?" Ted questioned.

"No, no. The vampire is a solitary creature. They are sometimes known for taking on a mate of the opposite sex, but to multiply? Two males could never get along. No, no, no . . . they have a strong sense of personal territory and domain. Put two males together and they will fight to the death. Sharing is out of the question. Vampires are not stupid creatures, Mr. Scott. If they multiplied, it would create a food shortage, and the carnage would be visible and obvious, thus creating a situation where their presence would become widely known. They would be hunted down and exterminated, just as in the 1800's. It is one of the areas that have always confused me. Why does a vampire ever create another vampire? I believe that in many cases, it is accidental. I don't think it is an intentional decision. Other than creating a mate, there is no reason for them to multiply. Procreation is not an instinct necessary for a 'dead' species. But should they drain someone to *just before* the actual point of death, and should that person survive being taken over the threshold, theoretically, they then become a vampire, themselves. I believe that is why they mutilate their victims, in most cases. This is to assure that they will not survive and compete with them for food. Imagine if every vampire created more vampires, and those created more, etc. If you simply do the math, more than half our population would be vampires within a few months."

"How many do you think really exist on this continent?" Ted asked.

"Oh, I could only guess, but I would say maybe a hundred at most," The Professor answered.

"There could be a hundred? Why wouldn't we be aware of them?" Ted asked.

"Well, the FBI reports that seven hundred thousand people disappear in this country a year. The FBI admits that maybe half of those people intend to disappear for some personal reason. That leaves over three hundred thousand actually missing. If my knowledge is anywhere near correct, a vampire would only need between a hundred and two hundred kills to easily exist—let's say comfortably—for a year. I expect that their territories are vast, so if a mere few thousand people become their sustenance, who would take notice?" he explained.

Ted was completely amazed that the old Professor was speaking of vampires as real and common, as if they were any other animal. "Professor, you make this sound as if we are speaking of a common animal," Ted stated.

"Oh, Mr. Scott, many people think I'm as crazy as a loon. But I can assure you that I'm as sane as the next person. People don't want to believe in something that they have no control over. Anthropology is my specialty, but vampires and their history have always been a personal passion. As a child, my grandfather once told me a vampire story that he claimed was true to the day he died. This became the basis of my curiosity."

"How can one kill them?" Ted inquired, looking helpless.

"Only three ways, that I know of, will dispatch them. Direct sunlight is their enemy. It will destroy them in minutes. The ultraviolet rays of the sun react to a vampire as a microwave cooks an egg. A stake through the heart is next. It doesn't have to be a traditional stake. It could be a wooden branch or an arrow, but it must cause a massive puncture and destruction of the aorta. Last, is the removal of the head. If a vampire is beheaded, he dies." The Professor sounded confident. "Guns, bullets, metal knives, all a waste of time," he scoffed. "Fire, however, is debatable."

"Tell me more about how you might recognize one."

"They are said to have a foul or musty odor when you are close and upon them. They can disguise the odor with perfumes, but eventually it seeps through. Recognizable, it is the smell of a dead body—like rotting flesh. If they have been in a room, you will be able to smell their presence, even hours later. In the wild, the other living creatures will sense their proximity and become silent. It is like all wild creatures sense their deathly presence. This is another area that puzzles me. To my knowledge, the same is not true of domestic animals. Domestic animals are said to react with fear and hostility. It is true that they have no reflection. Also, you cannot take their photographic image, as it does not produce on film, and it will not reflect to record digitally. Here, let me show you something."

He reached into his top desk drawer and produced a large photograph. As soon as Ted laid eyes on it, he could recognize that it was very old by the color and condition.

DeathWalker

"This picture was taken at a political rally in Chicago, sometime around 1890. Take a close look at the crowd, Mr. Scott," the Professor urged.

Ted looked at the photo. It was taken at what appeared to be at a hotel ballroom in Chicago. A banner in the background read, "Welcome to Chicago, Candidate Bennett!" It was an image of the political candidate standing on a platform giving a speech, surrounded by a dense crowd of supporters. He saw nothing of real interest, and looked to the Professor with a perplexed expression.

"No, no; look closer, Mr. Scott," the Professor, once again, urged.

Ted scrutinized every inch, looking for anything unusual. Then, he saw it. It was clear as day. In the midst of this crowd of hundreds of people, stood a suit and a hat . . . without a body!

"Holy shit!" Ted exclaimed, as his eyes were glued to the picture. "Holy shit!" he said again.

"I assure you that this is not trick photography," the Professor stated. "This is a great example of as close as one will ever get to record a vampire on film."

"Tell me more, Professor," Ted probed.

"They despise garlic and will shun it, as though repelled by the odor. People would wear necklaces of garlic as protection, many years ago. Unlike in the Hollywood movies, I believe a crucifix has no affect what so ever. I do not believe they are afraid of the cross. It is my theory that this was a myth started by the religious community centuries ago, and is likely untrue. I always wonder how many people may have died, if it is truly a myth. But, quite honestly, I can say wearing a cross would be the prudent thing to do, because my opinion on that is only a theory. I believe it is similar to the myth the church started that an exorcism can remove ghosts. Ask your local priest to exorcise a ghost and see what happens, Mr. Scott." The old Professor laughed. "Demons can be dealt with, but never a ghost."

"No, they don't need special soil to sleep on, and no, they don't need a coffin to sleep in. They can rest anywhere, as long as they are protected from the sun. They can travel and rest in a cave, a sewer, even an apartment." He snickered again.

"You seem to really know this subject well, Professor," Ted said. "Have you actually ever seen or confronted one?" Ted inquired.

67

"No, I'm sorry to say that I haven't. It is my dream, someday before I die, to observe a vampire in the flesh." The Professor paused, as if enjoying the very idea. Then, he continued. "You seem to have a very serious interest, Mr. Scott. Somehow, I feel this goes beyond common research. Am I correct?" he quizzed.

"Yes, you are correct. I . . . I may have a problem with a vampire, Professor."

"Go on, Mr. Scott," the Professor urged, anxiously. The Professor's heart was pounding at the prospect of a real vampire sighting.

"Professor, I mean no disrespect, but I need to verify that you truly know of what you are speaking. This may sound insane, but I might be in a position of confronting a real vampire. What if I cut off his head and he laughs at me, Professor? I need to know all the means of killing one, and be totally sure that it will work," Ted explained.

The old man turned slowly and walked to a credenza. On top, was a very expensive looking carved wooden box. On the box was a gold padlock. Taking a key ring from his pocket, the Professor unlocked the padlock and walked toward Ted, holding the box.

"Mr. Scott, I'm very old, but I'm not senile or stupid. I sensed the minute I saw you that you are bothered. Whether it is by a real vampire or not, I'm not sure. Here, look for yourself. I found this, buried in England. After studying records of vampires, I followed the records of one that was hunted down and beheaded. I brought this back." He opened the box, handing it to Ted. "Believe me, Mr. Scott, if you cut off his head, he won't be laughing at you." The Professor watched Ted's face as he gazed into the carved wooden box.

Ted's face drained of color as he viewed a familiar sight. In the box was a skull. It could have been a human skull, except for the teeth. The upper teeth had two protruding fangs, over three inches long. The remaining teeth had a similar configuration to ours, except they were all very pointed and sharp. He stared in awe.

"This could be the missing link, except that this skull was tested and found to be only two hundred years old. What do you think it is, Mr. Scott?" The Professor smiled.

As the Professor took back the box, locking it, Ted asked a question that was bothering him.

"Professor, if a vampire was killed by shooting a wooden arrow deep into its heart, and left in the woods at night . . . and the next morning the

DeathWalker

body was gone, what could have possibly occurred?" Ted waited anxiously for the response.

"Well, Mr. Scott, no animal in the wild would touch it. When the sun rose, it would be reduced to skeletal remains. But, if it were gone altogether, it was likely taken and hidden, or buried, by its mate." The Professor could tell by Ted's expression that this answer was most troubling.

"Oh, God. This means there has to be another one," Ted mumbled.

"What?" questioned the Professor.

"Can they really fly?" Ted asked, quickly changing the subject.

"Yes, yes, they can. And very fast, too. A single vampire's territory could cover hundreds of miles. They may have as many as a dozen safe sleeping places in their territory," the old man stated.

"Professor, is there anything else I should know?" Ted asked.

The old man thought for a second. "Yes. They do not necessarily bite you neatly on the neck, as in the romantic Hollywood movies. They are violent and messy. There is no self control if they are truly hungry. It becomes a feeding frenzy. They just might tear your heart out and drink directly from your chest."

Ted produced the Canadian snapshot from his pocket and handed it to the Professor. "Could this be an example?" Ted asked.

The old man carefully studied it, and then answered slowly. "Yes, it could possibly be. Where did this happen, Mr. Scott?"

"Canada . . . Winnipeg, Canada," Ted answered.

"What did they attribute this death to?" the Professor asked.

"A bear. They said it was a bear. The problem, is that I have knowledge of at least four similar deaths here in the upper part of the state," Ted offered.

"A vampire? Here in Minnesota? Interesting . . . you know, if it were true, this is a perfect environment. Large mammals, caves, secluded wilderness, storm drains, and humans. All of which would provide a virtual paradise for an isolated vampire. God knows with our current society, that he could walk around the city with great ease and no fear of standing out. With all the kids walking around with pierced faces and dyed hair, a vampire might appear rather tame and harmless—if not vulnerable—walking around at night."

The old man looked bothered, but enthusiastic that this may lead him to finally confront his lifelong passion. He went to his bookcase and produced a thick note book, handing it to Ted. "Here, read this. It may help you. It is my work, but it has never been published. It is nonfiction and the publishers wanted me to publish it under fiction, as if it were a fairy tale. I refused. So I sent it to the Copyright office and had a few copies printed. In it is everything I know on this subject, along with the topics in which I am still doing research. Read it, Mr. Scott."

Ted looked at the title page. "*The History of Vampires.*" He smiled, for he knew all too well why the publishers wouldn't touch it as a nonfictional work.

"Here, Mr. Scott, my home number, should you need it. If you should need assistance, I'll help you anyway that I can. If there is a chance that you are truly on the trail of a vampire, I would consider it an opportunity of my lifetime to be involved. My whole life I have searched to find a complete example. Just the thought of confronting one is like a wish come true." They warmly shook hands.

"We'll talk again. Thanks, Professor." Ted left, knowing that the good Professor had no idea what he was asking for. Facing a vampire is not something one wants to do. It is a nightmare that stays with you for life. He found the professor a bit naïve, thinking that this may be a creature he could 'study.' The horrible image of those fangs, and the look of a beast intent on tearing one apart, is nothing any sane person would look forward to.

Ted walked away feeling validated that his fears and experiences were real, but frightened at his dilemma. He had to get home, for he had reading to do. If he actually did kill a vampire and her body was taken away by her mate, then it might still be out there, camping out near his father's house. Once home, he buried himself in the Professor's book. He found some comfort in the fact that a vampire cannot enter a private residence without being invited, if the Professor's theory was correct. He knew his father wouldn't invite a stranger in for a visit. But he would call to remind his dad of the promise he had made—not to go out into the silence of the night. Ted knew that he had actually killed a vampire, and thought that if one did exist, then it was possible that others were out there.

There actually was one more vampire out there, but he presented no danger to Ted's father. What Ted didn't know, was that the vampire was now searching for him!

Chapter Seven

John Hall and his Indian companion had spent two nights sleeping on the boulder in the clearing. They had spent their days combing the woods for any signs of large predators and had found nothing. This would be their last night in the area before giving up and heading further north. Hall was certain Ted had been attacked, but was skeptical of Ted being sober on that night. John and Joe sat by the fire they had made at the top of the boulder, talking about other hunting experiences they had enjoyed. They always enjoyed kidding each other about their heritage.

"Why is it that you Indian people like music so much, but only use rattles and drums to make noise?" Hall asked Joe.

"Little you know, Chamookaman. We use flutes in our wedding ceremonies," Indian Joe snapped back."If you want to know about the Anishanabe, let me tell you of the fifty year war that the Anishanabe waged on the Lakota," Indian Joe suggested.

"Not again? I've heard that story a hundred times. Every damn Anishanabe wants to tell the story of the fifty year war. Oh, the fifty year war. Ever hear about World War II?" Hall barked.

"Yes, maybe I can tell you how our Navajo became the 'wind talkers.' The government found out that the enemy could not understand nor break down the Navajo language, and thus, used it as a way to send messages that could not be deciphered. Native Americans helped win that war. Not that we would ever get any credit . . . all you white men do is picture us as sitting around a teepee, smoking peace pipes all day! But about the Lakota fifty year war . . ."

"Give me a break. I've heard that story a hundred times!"

"I like telling that story," Joe replied.

"Yeah, it's a good one, but I've heard it far too many times. I could probably tell it better than you!" John responded.

"Maybe you would rather hear about what the Lakota did to Custer?" Joe suggested, with a laugh.

"Custer was a moron!" John Hall laughed.

"I'll say! If he would have had Anishanabe scouts instead of 'Chamooka's,' he never would have had such a bad hair day!" Joe smiled. "Yeah, you white men took an ass whipping that day!"

"Yeah, blame it on the stupid white scouts. If all of us 'Chamooka's' are so damn dumb, how come we're not the ones on the reservations?"

"Shit, I should be safe at home with my wife and family instead of acting like a great 'Giiwosewinini Wag,' [hunter] leading a Chamookaman around . . ." Joe mumbled, shaking his head.

They verbally bantered back and forth, as that was their way of kidding each other and lightening the atmosphere. Joe respected John Hall's expertise as a hunter, but knew he could never match skills with an Anishanabe. It had been dark for some time when John started to feel as though they were being watched. They both sensed it and said nothing. They just sat, silently aware of every movement and sound around them.

Directly above them floated Christian, watching their moves intently. This was the first time he returned to this rock since his Anne had died. He could smell the scent of the two warm blooded beings, and also a scent that he had tasted in anguish. He knew one of them was Indian and the other a white man, who was carrying the scent that was the target of his revenge. Christian realized that the white man could likely direct him to the target of his revenge. He decided to land and let fate run its course.

"Joe, do you feel it?" John Hall asked.

"Yeah, I do . . ." The Indian sniffed at the air. "Geyaabi! It is too quiet and I smell something in the air. It's not a good odor. It's bad, very bad . . . getting stronger . . ." Joe responded.

"Put the fire out," Hall ordered.

As the Indian poured water on the fire, extinguishing it, John Hall looked about for anything moving. Hearing a strange hissing sound, it was Joe, the Indian, who turned completely around to see what appeared to be a man standing at the edge of the boulder, directly behind them.

"John? We have a visitor . . ." Joe said softly, stepping back.

Hall turned quickly, surprised; he immediately put his hand on his hunting knife, which was strapped to his thigh. They stood ten feet apart, facing each other, in the faint light of the moon.

John heard Joe whisper, "Windigo."

DeathWalker

"We never heard you arrive," Hall stated.

The figure stood silently, as if deciding whether to speak or not, and then it spoke. "I know," came the abrupt answer, in a deep, chilling voice, slicing through the silent, cool night air.

"Who are you?" Hall asked, feeling a chill in his spine.

"Does it matter to you?" the indignant stranger replied.

"Well, excuse my rudeness, but I'm John Hall and this is Joe. Now, who the hell are you?" Hall was not afraid, for he knew he could bury his hunting knife in this target in two seconds flat, should the need arise. To John, this seemed a strange, dangerous game this fellow was playing.

"I am called Christian," the dark figure responded, offering nothing more.

Hall studied the figure standing in the dark, only visible for the moonlight. He was about 6' 3" tall, and looked lean and fit, with a deep, confident voice. Hall could see that his hair was long, dark, and shoulder length.

"How did you get up here?" Hall asked.

"That is not very important, Mr. Hall. Your problem is that I am here," Christian responded, as if he resented the very question.

"Then what the hell do you want?" Hall snapped, agitated.

Christian took a number of steps forward. So quick, that it caused John Hall to grip his knife tightly, pulling it from its sheath. Hall could now see a pale white face and two large black holes, where eyes should normally be. Indian Joe started to tremble, as he sensed this was no normal visitor, but faced him bravely, nonetheless.

"Revenge, John Hall. I want reeevennnnggge!" he screamed.

The words cut through Hall like the knife he gripped, and he shuddered at the sound. The word 'revenge' came deep from this man's soul.

"For what? Revenge for what? We've done nothing to you?" Hall responded, trying not to make his fear known.

"But you know who did, Mr. Hall. You know who did. I smell the scent of his blood on your very person. There, in your pocket." Christian pointed toward John Hall's breast pocket.

Hall noticed his unusually long finger and the claw-like finger nail. He now had the distinct impression that he and Joe were in mighty big trouble.

Reaching into his pocket, confused, Hall pulled out the only thing there . . . it was the tiny tattered piece of Ted's bloody, shredded shirt, that he had picked up days ago.

"Where is he?" Christian demanded.

"He is not here. He is in Minneapolis somewhere," Hall answered. "Why do you seek revenge? For what? What did he do to you?"

Christian ignored the question, as if never asked. "What is his name?" Christian demanded to know.

"I don't know . . ." Hall answered.

"WHAT IS HIS NAME?" Christian screamed, in a tone that was both threatening and frightening.

"I don't know. I just don't know," Hall answered, glancing at Joe.

In a blur, Christian moved, grabbing Joe by the throat. The Indian's eyes grew to the size of silver dollars, and he was shaking uncontrollably.

Hall became furious. "You hurt him and I'll cut your fucking heart out!" He held his knife up to Christian's face.

Christian smiled, as though he was enjoying the very prospect of a bloodletting. "Have you no idea what you are dealing with, or who I am?" Christian asked, in a mocking tone.

"Watch closely, John Hall . . ." Christian smiled and his eyes became visible, glowing a bright red. As Hall froze in fear, Christian lunged at Joe's throat, tearing away a six inch portion and spitting it to the ground. Hall was paralyzed at the sound of tearing flesh. Indian Joe never had a chance to draw his last breath—much less scream—as his body simply went limp, almost instantly. Christian buried his mouth in the stream of red blood flowing, and drank freely from Joe's throat. Hall stepped back in horror as he heard the gurgling and gorging sounds coming from Christian. Trapped on top of the boulder, there was nowhere to run and nowhere to hide.

Christian lifted his head, tossing Joe's body off the top of the boulder, as if it were a mere piece of garbage. Hall could see blood dripping down his chin, and his huge white fangs shining in the moonlight. Christian stepped forward, fixing his gaze on Hall.

"Now, do not affront me with another untruth. I will ask you one more time. What is his name, Mr. Hall?" Christian asked again.

Hall could think only of survival. "Ted . . . Ted Scott," Hall uttered.

Christian smiled, enjoying his victory.

DeathWalker

"Put your knife away, it is useless." Hall's trembling hand slowly slid the knife into its sheath.

"I will let you live, Mr. Hall. But I pray you to deliver a message for me, to Mister Ted Scott. He killed my mate. She was my mate for one hundred years, and I loved her dearly. I will be coming for him—you tell him that." Christian paused, licking his lips, as if contemplating the sweet taste of revenge. Slowly, his fangs retracted and his eyes ceased to glow. "I want Ted Scott's blood. You tell him that there can be no doubt that I will I find him, and I have all eternity to do so. I know his scent and have tasted his blood, so there is no way for him to escape me. She was the only thing I ever loved, Mr. Hall. I will kill Ted Scott for what he did. I will kill him slowly and painfully. I will taste his fear and his blood." The vampire was pacing back and forth.

Hall watched as Christian's face transformed from a monster to near human. Hall could tell that Christian was once a normal man, and could appear as one at will. In his shock, he wondered how this beast came to be? He could see the raw emotion in the vampire's face as he spoke again.

"I will drain his life's blood as he did my Anne's. He killed my Anne. She was the only thing of beauty in my existence. Do you possibly have any understanding of losing a mate that you were destined to spend eternity with?" Hall was silent, as Christian laughed.

"Ha, ha, ha! How could you?" He said with distain. "You have no concept of what eternity is. Ted Scott robbed me of eternity and he will pay. Yes, he will pay dearly. This I will greatly enjoy." Christian was now near human in form as he paced, with his eyes fixed on Hall. "You feel frightened, don't you, Mr. Hall?" Hall nodded affirmative. "You feel alone and vulnerable, don't you?" Again, Hall nodded affirmative. "You will never know the definition of the word 'alone' as I do, Mr. Hall. You can never *possibly* imagine what it is to be 'alone' as I live it. My Anne kept me from being alone, and now she is gone." There was great anguish in his voice.

"I do apologize for your native friend, but natives have no problem understanding the cycle of life and death. Don't worry about explaining his death. When they find the body, they will swear the wolves had at him." He studied Hall trembling in fear. "Understand this was necessary, as somehow, I felt that you would not easily accept the role of a messenger when I first came upon you, unless I truly convinced you of what I am." Christian looked to Hall, almost embarrassed at his display of emotion,

75

but his expression changed in a heartbeat. "I trust you will deliver this message for me?" Hall nodded, for there was no way he could speak. "You are a hunter, Mr. Hall?" Hall nodded yes, quickly.

"Deliver this message, or you, too, will become hunted, Mr. Hall. I, like you, relish hunting. The thrill of the hunt is almost more enjoyable than the kill itself." Christian smiled, as if delighted by the very thought. "Now it's time that I quit engaging in conversation. Tell him to prepare to meet me, Mr. Hall. You tell him that Christian is coming for him. He will feel my wrath! Christian is coming for him!" In a flash, Christian leaped from the boulder into the darkness. John Hall stood frozen as he heard Christian shout his final demand. "**You tell him, Mr. Hall. You tell him I'm coming for him. Tell him that Christian is coming!**" he screamed, as he arose into the air and disappeared into the night.

John Hall would spend the night sitting in the darkness, afraid to move a muscle, and praying for daylight. Hall had never felt fear as he did this night. He had never felt as helpless as he felt the moment that this monster killed his companion, Joe. He also felt guilt, for to spare his own life, he had betrayed Ted. In his moment of pure fright, he did something he never thought he would do, and he was sorry, in retrospect. He had to get to Ted and help Ted defend himself. He sat in a near trance. He had actually met a vampire. A creature that he thought only existed in the minds of the writers of horror stories. He sat cross legged, rocking back and forth in the darkness, unable to get the sound of Indian Joe's blood gurgling from echoing in his mind. There, he would sit until the light of day.

In eleven percent of all homicides, there is a noticeable absence of blood.

This is assumed normal, due to the fact that the person has been killed elsewhere and the body relocated.

FBI Report on Violent Crime 2006.

Chapter Eight

It was 1885, and a thirty year old Christian left his family and friends in Boston, to seek his fortune in the West. Educated at the finest schools the East had to offer, Christian was convinced that he could capitalize on the many opportunities offered by the developing western states. A handsome young man, Christian stood 6' 3", which was tall for a man of this time period. Long brown hair, blue eyes and square chin, he did not appear as the classic eastern intellectual, and given more casual wear, he might even appear rugged.

The son of a banker, he projected the image of a man of great means in his tailored suit, with fine leather shoes and a gold chain attached to his vest. At the end of his chain hung a fine gold watch, which was a gift from his father. Traveling by train to the west, he had no itinerary. He would exit the train at will, spending time in various cities, surveying the real estate and other opportunities. Once in town, he would acquire a horse, and was comfortable riding the countryside, exploring his interests. His only goal was to eventually settle west of Chicago and east of Los Angeles.

He had exited the train at Germantown, a small town just north of Peoria, Illinois. He found the town interesting, for it was along the railway, and also close to the Illinois River. After spending a few days there, Christian decided to travel by carriage, south to Peoria, and after sightseeing, he would catch the train to his next stop at Springfield, Illinois.

It was early evening when he checked out of the rooming house at Germantown. Trading his horse for a carriage, he figured he could reach Peoria in four short hours, at most. He enjoyed traveling alone, and for the first time in life, felt truly independent. He had lived in the shadow of his father's success, and was glad to finally be in control of his own destiny. His father had guided him through college and graduate school. After graduation, he was automatically seated in an executive position

DeathWalker

at his father's prosperous bank. Life was very good, but far too easy and predicable for a young and curious Christian. He wanted more.

As he drove the carriage south to Peoria, he inhaled the fragrance of fresh evening air, savoring his new found freedom. Christian had a vision that many of the already established cities west of Chicago would be growing by leaps and bounds. He figured to find a place where he wanted to settle, and buy up surrounding real estate. Once established, he would invest in the construction of housing to accommodate the migration of the population moving to the west. Christian had big dreams, which included owning his own bank someday. As the summer sun was setting, he took one final glance at his watch. As best as he could determine, Christian would arrive in Peoria in another three hours.

Christian listened as the crickets started singing in the cool cover of night. He could see the landscape dotted with lights from the farmhouses, spread sparsely across the hills. Almost hypnotized by the rhythm of the horse's pace, he could easily see the wide road ahead in the light of the full moon. He awoke from his trance when the horse stopped suddenly. It was when the trotting of the horse had come to a stop that Christian took notice that so did the singing of the crickets. This left him engulfed by silence. He snapped the reins, ordering the horse, "Let us move forth, gelding!"

The horse remained perfectly still, resisting Christian's command. "What is the cause of this complexion, boy? Is there something in the road?" he asked; but as he stood up to view the road ahead, he was knocked over. He felt pain as he fell backward over the seat to the rear of the carriage, and was quite confused. Regaining his senses but still puzzled, he attempted to rise up from his prone position. He looked up, and was shocked by the horrible glimpse of the monster that nightmares are made of. Greeted by the vision of red eyes and huge fangs, he reacted by screaming, "No! No!" His attempt at protecting himself became feeble, considering the overwhelming power and strength of his foe.

Christian felt the bite on his neck, and heard the sickening sound of the tearing of his own flesh from his body. Powerless, he blacked out completely and was certain he was on his way to an inevitable death. The pain ceased, and he fell into an abyss of darkness. His horse bolted and took off running down the road in a full, uncontrollable gallop. The vampire rode along, drinking his fill from Christian, before taking flight and disappearing into the night sky, sure that his victim was dead—or soon would be.

It was mere fate that drove Christian's carriage to a near collision with another carriage, which was going in the opposite direction on this dark night. Both carriages stopped. The carriage going north was driven by a nurse on her way to Germantown to help with the delivery of a baby. Her name was Anne Witherspoon. Lighting a lantern, she could see a body lying in the rear of the carriage. Climbing aboard, she realized he needed treatment urgently. The gash in his throat was huge, and although not much blood was present, she could see by his coloring that he had lost much of his life's fluid. She quickly retrieved her nurse's case and went to work by the dim light of the flickering lantern.

Working feverishly, she repaired and stitched Christian's wound as best as she could, thus saving what little blood he had left. In doing so, she allowed Christian to survive his journey to the brink of death, and not cross completely over. This was the very formula necessary to pass on the curse of becoming a creature of the night. Vampires usually take great care to insure that their victims die, but the vampire that had attacked Christian had no idea that fate would allow Christian the chance to survive and transform into a whole new world. Anne was the daughter of Doctor Henry Witherspoon, a prominent Midwest healer. Trained at medicine since adolescence, she could have easily been a doctor herself, had women been considered for the occupation. Unfortunately, this left her with the next best thing—becoming a nurse.

Anne worked hours on the stranger before finishing as much as could be done, with what little she had at hand. She transferred her belongings to Christian's carriage, as he was far too big to move. At 5' 2" and scarcely one hundred pounds, this was her only alternative. As fast as she could, she drove the horse toward her destination, racing through the dark night with her long, raven hair flowing in the wind. Once there, Olaf Johnson helped her unload Christian into the comfort of a bed. Olaf's wife, Helga, was pregnant and expecting any day. Anne was to stay with them acting as a nurse and midwife until the baby arrived. Olaf, a farmer who worked in the fields eighteen hours a day, would leave Anne to care for his wife and Christian, and would wait to help with his new arrival.

For three days, Christian slept with only brief moments of consciousness. In his dreams, it was dark and frightening, with visions of demons chasing him relentlessly. He felt fangs ripping him to shreds,

DeathWalker

with the feeling that his whole being was on fire. He was running with the sensation of fear and despair as he had never known. He dreamed he was falling endlessly into a bottomless cavern. The only comfort he saw was an occasional fantasy of an angel standing at his side, protecting him, which would flash before his mind from time to time. These nightmares were just dreams, but his angel was for real. The warm brown eyes he imagined belonged to Anne, as she was there at his side for three days, tending to his fever and wiping his brow. She had delivered a healthy baby boy for the Johnsons', and now waited for Christian to be healthy enough to travel to a hospital.

It was sunset on the third day that Christian awoke from his sleep. When he opened his eyes, his "angel" was there at his side. As if programmed by instinct, Christian's first words were, "We must go."

From the moment he awoke, he knew he had changed. It was as if he was born again, with a heightened awareness. His human concerns were gone completely. He could smell and identify every scent in the air without an effort. The scents were so separated, so specific, that Christian's new brain computed everything in the air and read him the instant analysis. His vision was sharp and enhanced, and even in a darkened room, he could easily see an insect flying in the blackness, as if it were broad daylight. His hearing was magnified; easily identifying the farm animals moving about outside the house. But there was also a new uncontrollable hunger rising up from the depths of his soul.

"We must go," Christian said once more.

"I pray where to?" Anne questioned, confused.

"We must rush away from here immediately," Christian replied. "Come with me," he beckoned.

As if mesmerized by his spell, Anne quickly started gathering her things. As they walked from the darkened room, only Olaf was awake, but was preparing for bed. It was the first time he had actually seen Christian since the night he had helped carry him into the house. Olaf knew immediately that something was not right, but a tinge of fear kept him from reacting in any way other than "normal." With his eyes fixed on Christian, he asked Anne, "Where are you going at this time of the night? I do not wish to pry, but things seem confusing."

"I'm taking him to the hospital in Peoria at once," she replied.

Olaf studied Christian, who was standing in a menacing silence. Christian's pale color, sunken eyes, and intense stare, frightened him. He watched as Anne moved about, gathering her things, as if nothing were wrong. Olaf wondered if she could see what he was seeing. He thought of questioning Anne, to be sure everything was truly okay, except one look at Christian made him put the safety of his family first. Olaf decided not to get involved; and it was a wise and prudent choice.

Christian could smell Olaf's fear, and found it a very attractive odor. It caused his adrenaline to rise, as well as his level of hunger. It seemed the smell of fear stimulated all of Christian's senses in a very pleasing manner. Olaf could see Christian's eyes begin to change, as if he were looking straight through him.

"Let me help you with your bags, dear Anne," Olaf offered. He couldn't get rid of the both of them fast enough.

Once in the carriage, Christian prodded the horse along the road. "Where are we going? You could be without a clue, for aught I know?" Anne asked.

"You will see, my beautiful Anne," he answered.

As if following some new compulsion, Christian knew he should head north, away from large cities and populations. For some strange reason, Anne went along without a trace of fear. She knew that she had saved his life, and also sensed that he would never harm her. For hours, they rode in complete silence. It was about an hour before dawn that Christian abandoned the carriage. With his new vision, he spotted a cave on the side of a hill. Anne, who was sleeping, awoke with a start.

"Where are you going?" she questioned.

"Come with me. Have no worry," Christian replied, reaching his hand out towards her. "Please, stay close with me. We must hide."

He took her hand, helping her to the ground. Anne responded, as if under a spell. Together, they walked into the wooded area toward the cave on the hill, leaving the empty carriage to disappear into the darkness. He held her hand as they walked through the woods and up the hill. At the mouth of the cave, he squeezed her hand and said, "Follow me." In complete darkness, Christian could now see clearly, leading her through an obstacle course of rocks and boulders. Anne never questioned him as to why. She was now in a world of darkness, and her only link to "life," was holding tightly onto Christian's hand.

Well away from the mouth of the cave, Christian sat down, guiding Anne to do likewise. He put his arm around her and reclined against the wall of the cavern. Christian was driven to his next act as naturally as one

DeathWalker

is driven to eat when hungry. Instinctively, he took his hand and caressed Anne's head in a loving and tender manner. In complete darkness, she could only feel his kind touch and anticipate his next move. She could feel his breath on her neck and was now prepared for his kiss, or so she thought.

To Christian, it was a natural reflex. He kissed her neck and buried his fangs into the artery that carried his nourishment. She relaxed completely as he deeply drank. It was the sweetest taste he had ever experienced. As he drank, Anne experienced complete euphoria, like she had never known. As he drained her blood, he could feel his strength surge to the extent he felt he could fly. For a moment, their hearts beat at the same exact rhythm. He continued to drink until he could hear her heart slow to an almost complete halt. No, he wouldn't kill her, as she was destined to become his mate. With the feeding ritual complete as the sun rose, they would both fall into a deep, deep sleep.

Christian was awakened at sunset. He looked to Anne, who was now in her transformation coma. Out of the cave and into the moonlight Christian walked, breathing the fresh night air. Everything became silent, as if a tribute to his very presence. Without any effort, he raised his arms and rose to the sky, as if no longer a prisoner to the gravity binding him to the earth. As he sailed over the countryside, he could clearly see the warm blooded beings scurrying about below him. He realized that he could merely select his dinner at will. Landing in a field, a cow would become his meal for the night.

Spooked, the cows began mooing and running away. Christian caught up to one quickly on foot, selecting his meal. Jumping on its back, he tore at its neck with his claws until the blood flowed freely. Then, he buried his fangs in its skin and drank as the cow slowly went from running, to walking, until it finally collapsed. Drinking his fill, he instinctively disguised his work by tearing at the carcass in a manner that would dictate that this kill was the work of hungry predators. Though it satisfied his hunger, it did not quite have the "taste" he craved. When finished, he merely lifted his arms and rose sixty feet into the air, taking flight and returning to the cave—and his Anne.

Once there, he would bite into his own vein and let his own blood drip slowly from his wrist to her mouth. Unconscious, Anne would react by automatically licking every drop. He watched as she became more beautiful every night. His second night of searching for food had him

83

searching for the taste he so longed for . . . a human. Gliding across the sky, he could easily identify any living being. It seemed they each had their own unique glow about them. It was near Peoria, on the fringe of the city, that he spotted a solitary being, nestled next to a flickering campfire. He landed some yards away silently, and approached his dinner.

It was a man who looked to be about forty, and he was dressed as a vagrant, in Christian's estimation. His clothes were worn, his belongings wrapped in a blanket, and there was no horse for transportation. This was certainly a man that would never be missed. Christian entered the glow of the campfire, unconcerned of being seen. The man arose instantly, and having no gun, pulled out his hunting knife.

He looked toward Christian and stated in a shaky voice, "You could give a man a fright, sneaking up like that."

Christian did not respond.

The man felt some fear, but tried not to show it. "I don't have much, but I'm happy to share what I have got, kind stranger . . ."

Christian walked forward, and decided to strike immediately. It was a mere instant, and he had the man by the throat. The man hardly saw much but a blur. As he screamed, Christian tore at his throat and began draining the very life from him. It took only seconds until he fell silent. In less than a minute, he was dead. Christian's instinct was to disguise his kill, so after feeding, he slashed at the body with his huge claws and mutilated it to unidentifiable condition, just as he did the killing before. He could hear the sounds of wolves and coyotes, and knew they would be there soon to finish the job. Filled with a new energy, he took to the air. Although his powers and speed were purely intuitive, he was beginning to understand who and what he was. He no longer cared about material things or his family. His new life was only one of guarded pleasures.

Christian never had to face one of the darkest aspects of his being, and that was loneliness. He had his Anne from day one. So he viewed being transformed as a new, free existence. The specter of death was not a factor, and he could only contemplate an eternity with his Anne. He anxiously awaited her awakening. On the third day when she awoke, her metamorphosis was complete. This time it was Anne who stated "We must go . . ." This began their eternity of pleasure.

A vampire lives with the knowledge of its own vulnerability. Completely helpless during the daylight hours, it is driven to solitary places that only wilderness can provide. Much of their human instincts are carried over.

DeathWalker

Not being ruthless in life made Christian and Anne both similar in the world of death. Protecting their very existence caused them to "mix" their kills. Surviving on large game and only partaking in a human when necessary or easily available. Food was plentiful, as their territory covered nearly five states and into Canada. Bear, moose, deer, wolves, and cougar, presented a varied animal diet.

Humans became easy prey in the isolated woods. It was on Christian and Anne's first trip north that their taste for human blood had to be satisfied. It was two Indians, sitting by a campfire, that became their target that night. Christian and Anne descended from the sky, landing near the campfire. Expecting a fight for survival, they were instead both very surprised. The Indians bowed, as if convinced that spirits were upon them. It was the first time Christian heard the Chippewa word "Windigo."

Thus, Indians became one of the easiest of human targets. They often traveled at night in the woods, presenting blatant opportunity. Rarely did anyone ever investigate the disappearance or death of an Indian. The Indians, themselves, never reported it to any authorities, only to their own Chief or medicine man. Ironically, the Indians were equipped with the perfect weapon to defend against vampires—the bow and arrow. Instead, they worshiped the "vampire" as a near-God. He was their "Windigo." In their religious philosophy, a weapon can never be drawn against a spirit, whether good or evil.

The Chippewa Indians tell many stories of the Windigo, who would often appear first as a friend, and then kill you. They tell how the Windigo sits high in the trees, and then descends upon you and carries you off, leaving only an abrupt end to your footprints for others to find. When his presence is detected in their territory, knowing that he cannot be killed, they pray to "KichiManitu", the Great Spirit, for the Windigo to leave and haunt some other tribe. Any Chippewa, to this very day, can tell you tales of the Windigo.

Hunters were always easy prey. They would bait the bears by leaving food on the ground, sitting in trees through the night, waiting for an easy shot. Christian and Anne found it almost amusing to land next to them on the very same limb, and catching them before they could jump to the ground. Drinking their fill, they would leave more human "food" for the bears to eat. When found, it merely appeared as though the hunter fell from the tree, and was then killed and eaten or mutilated by the bears.

Campers, miners, fugitives, and runaways, also became easy meals in the deep, dark woods. Wrapped up in sleeping bags, feeding was never easier. If the bodies were eventually found, they were always written off to being bear, cougar, or wolf attacks. Christian and Anne had the perfect secret existence.

Rarely were they driven to hunt amongst the general population. It was only curiosity that would take them into the smaller towns. Once there, they found it easy to find a meal from the drunks, prostitutes, or homeless.

Christian had much more self control than Anne. Many times he kept Anne from taking great risks to satisfy her hunger for human blood. If Anne was craving, the sight of a human and the scent of blood would drive her to frenzy. It seemed Christian understood their vulnerability to a greater extent than Anne; therefore it would be Christian that would keep Anne in check from risking the exposure of their secret existence.

They traveled about in their territory, rotating their presence by using the moon and its cycle to time their stay. Wisconsin, Minnesota, Canada, and the Dakotas, became their hunting ground. For over one hundred years, the pair satisfied their hunger and enjoyed the freedom of the night. As time passed and roads became paved and cars became common, their lives were not affected. Airplanes were a surprise, and both Christian and Anne had a curiosity that caused them to occasionally fly close to get a better look, but all in all, science and technology had no effect on them. This ended in the summer of 2010, when Anne came upon a curious reporter, Ted Scott. Unable to control her hunger, she ignored the fact that he was carrying the perfect weapon—a crossbow. It was this type of risk that Christian would have saved her from, had he been there at her side.

Christian found Anne's body lying in the clearing. He stared at it in disbelief, for he knew his Anne was gone. For the first time in his vampire existence, he was truly alone. Christian's only love and purpose for existing was now replaced with one dominating emotion—revenge. He could smell the blood of the person that killed Anne under her finger nails. He licked her fingers and tasted the blood, so as to always remember the object of his hatred. He tenderly carried her body deep into the cave they had shared, and sealed the entrance. There, his Anne would rest for all eternity.

Had Christian found Anne's killer at that very moment, he would have torn his heart out in an explosion of rage. But, immersed in anguish,

DeathWalker

he realized that this would be too easy, too kind, and far too quick. He decided to find Anne's killer and study him before taking a revenge that would allow the most pain and suffering. The very thought of it gave Christian a new reason and purpose for existing.

Christian's whole mentality changed. He was now prepared to take risks, regardless of his vulnerability. He was now prepared to expose his very existence, if necessary. He was ready to walk amongst the human population, should it be required. To follow and study his prey, he would have to learn to blend into modern societies "night life." He would do whatever was necessary, to avenge the death of his Anne. Christian was about to reacquaint himself with society, and Ted Scott was about to meet what nightmares are truly made of . . . the vampire!

Chapter Nine

Ted decided to impress Kathy with his cooking skills. In the oven was a Boston roast, carrots, and baked potatoes. On the table, already set romantically with candles, was a tossed salad and a bottle of chilled wine. Although he knew Kathy was likely coming straight from work and would be dressed formally, Ted wore only a pullover sweater and slacks. When the doorbell rang, he buzzed her in.

"Hello," he greeted her as she entered. Brutus was jumping up and down, excited that they had a familiar visitor.

"Hi, my big man!" she said to Brutus, picking him up and kissing him.

"That little shit gets more kisses than I do!" complained Ted.

"Here, Teddy, poor baby," Kathy said, as she kissed Ted hello.

"Are you hungry?" he asked.

"Starved!" she responded.

"Just what I wanted to hear . . ." Ted led her to the table.

"My gosh!" Kathy blurted as she saw the table.

"Just sit back and enjoy!"

As they ate, Ted served and removed the dishes. Kathy found it cute that Ted had gone through so much trouble and was genuinely impressed by his cooking skills. She found the dinner very romantic. Kathy couldn't help but notice Ted was moving a little funny, as if his back was sore. During dinner, they talked business and current events. It wasn't until after dinner that they moved to the living room and the conversation became more personal.

"Ted, did you hurt yourself? You seem to be favoring your back?"

"Well, if you really want to know . . ." he lifted his sweater.

"Jesus Christ! What the hell happened?" Kathy was astonished to view Ted's chest, with ten long lines running downward, each accented by multiple stitches.

DeathWalker

"Kathy, if I tell you the truth, you'll walk out of here thinking that I'm some kind of lunatic, so let's just say a bear did it." Ted responded. "Believe me, it looks a lot better than it did a few days ago. I get the stitches out tomorrow."

"Ted, I'm an attorney. You can't make a statement like that and expect me to accept it without question. If not a bear, then what did this to you? Am I expected to cross examine you?" she asked.

"Do you really want to hear this story?" She nodded yes. "Do you promise not to think that I'm some kind of nut case?" She nodded again.

As he told the story, she was completely engrossed. When he got to the part of where he was caught from behind, he lifted his sweater and again, showing the wounds on his back. She was moved by his wounds and the unemotional, first hand accounting of this unbelievable incident. She never flinched at his story or his theory. She knew Ted had an active imagination, which was necessary for a writer, but his wounds were not imaginary. Though the tale was unbelievable, she wanted to believe, if only for Ted's sake.

"So the ranger we met in that pub is camping out there?" she asked.

"Yeah, John Hall is out there, probably in that very clearing," he answered.

"And you think that it was some kind of human thing that attacked you?" she questioned.

"Vampire, Kathy. I believe I was attacked by a vampire." Ted watched her face as he made his contention.

"Teddy, I'm not one to debate what you saw. After all, the serial killer, Jeffrey Dahmer, was out there eating people, so nothing would surprise me. But . . . don't you think it was a human disguised as a vampire, opposed to the real mythical creature?" She posed a logical question.

"To be honest, I didn't know what to think. I came back here to do my homework on the subject." He arose from the couch, retrieving Professor Steiner's manuscript. "Here, read this." He handed it to her. "Apparently there is someone out there that believes these creatures are not so mythical, after all."

"The name Steiner sounds familiar . . ." Kathy stated, flipping through the pages.

"He's right here at the University," Ted responded.

She thought for a second. "Anthropology?" she asked.

"Yeah," Ted answered.

89

"He was there when I went to school. He's very well respected in his field. I met him many times, he's a sweetie." Kathy was impressed.

"Can I take this to read?" Kathy asked, holding it close to her chest.

"Please do," Ted answered. That question gave Ted the impression that she was leaving. '*Great . . .*' he thought. '*I scared her off. She thinks I'm a nut case.*'

Instead, she set the manuscript on the table. She patted her lap. "Put your head here and lay down," she beckoned. Ted was more than anxious to do so.

"I'm not going to hug you, because it would hurt, so lay down here and let me scratch your head, Teddy." She grabbed the remote and turned the television on. "The early news is on. Is it okay if I watch?" she asked. He smiled, and laid himself across the couch with his head in her lap. Ted had the feeling that he was in heaven. The gentle touch of her hand, combined with the pleasant scent of her body, felt all too comfortable. He closed his eyes and listened as the news played out. It was near the end of the news when Ted was about to nod out, when the bombshell landed.

"OUR FINAL STORY TONIGHT IS THE DISAPPEARANCE OF A STATE FOREST RANGER ATTACKED NEAR ROSEAU, SOUTH OF THE CANADIAN BORDER."

Ted jumped upright, grabbing the remote and turning up the volume.

"TWO RANGERS WERE ATTACKED BY A BEAR WITH ONE OF THEM, A CHIPPEWA NATIVE AMERICAN WHO GOES BY THE NAME JOE THREE FEATHERS, BEING CARRIED OFF. FOREST RANGER JOHN HALL SAID THAT THEY WERE CAUGHT COMPLETELY OFF GUARD. SUFFERING FROM SHOCK, HE WAS TAKEN TO THE ROSEAU CLINIC AND TREATED. HE IS STILL UNDER OBSERVATION AND BEING GUARDED FROM THE PRESS. WE'RE HOPING TO HAVE A STATEMENT SOON. AN INTENSIVE SEARCH WILL BE INITIATED AT DAY BREAK IN AN ATTEMPT TO LOCATE HIS MISSING COMPANION, JOE THREE FEATHERS. WE'LL HAVE MORE ON THIS STORY ON OUR TWELVE NOON REPORT TOMORROW, SO PLEASE TUNE IN."

DeathWalker

"Holy shit! Holy shit!" Ted jumped up and began pacing.

Kathy couldn't believe her ears.

"I've got to talk to Hall," Ted stated. "I've got to talk to Hall. I know this was no bear attack, Kathy. Hall knows for sure what attacked me!" Ted exclaimed.

"Call him," Kathy suggested.

"You're right." He grabbed the phone and began dialing information. He then dialed Roseau Clinic.

"John Hall, please," Ted asked.

The operator put him on hold and returned asking "Who is this?"

"Tell him 'Ted Scott.' It's important." Again, he was put on hold. Obviously, they were screening Hall's calls.

"Ted?" Hall asked. "Is it you?" he whispered, softly.

"John, are you okay?" Ted asked anxiously, as he paced the floor.

"I . . . I can't say much right now. We have to talk, and we have to talk soon. I . . . I can't talk over the phone. I'll get out of here tomorrow. I'll call you when I get out. You stay there. I'll come to you. Give me your number," John asked.

"555-5555. I'm getting my stitches out in the afternoon, but other than that, I should be here. What happened with Joe?" Ted asked.

"He's history. I . . . I can't talk now, but I'll tell you tomorrow. Wait for my call." Hall hung up.

"Holy shit! Kathy, he knows. I know it. He's going to call me tomorrow. He says he needs to meet with me."

"Teddy, I'm going home, but I'm taking this manuscript. I'll call you tomorrow." Kathy kissed him on the cheek and headed out the door, leaving Ted pacing back and forth across the living room.

Ted had completely read the manuscript and analyzed everything it contained. He found what he thought was a contradiction. Professor Steiner stated that vampires could not tolerate holy water, and it actually would burn their skin if they were sprinkled with it. Yet, the Professor did not believe the crucifix provided any protection. Could it be that only a "blessed" crucifix had any effect? Ted reasoned that holy water was merely water that was blessed. Maybe an unblessed crucifix is not a real crucifix at all. He wanted to speak with the Professor about that.

He went to bed and stared at the ceiling, wondering about what exactly happened to John Hall. Was he attacked? Did he see a vampire? How did he escape? Now, would someone believe him? How did Joe Three Feathers

Edwin F. Becker

die? He could hardly sleep, burdened by the anxiety of anticipation of John Hall's visit. He found it hard to believe that only a week ago he was bored and searching for something exciting to write about. Now, he seemed to be the subject of some strange story himself.

* * *

At 9 A.M., his phone rang, and it was John Hall, asking for directions and saying he would be in town by five that evening. Ted gave him directions on how to reach his condo. Aside from getting his stitches removed, he decided to buy himself a crucifix and to have it blessed. He went to a fine jewelry store downtown and selected a crucifix for himself, about one inch in size, with a matching gold chain. He bought a second one for his father. He figured his birthday was coming up, and that would be reason enough to give it to his dad. If he did it in that manner, he knew his dad would wear it. Then, he picked out a third one, for Kathy. He hoped she would accept it as a gift, even though they hadn't known each other but a short time.

After having his stitches removed at Hennepin Medical Center, it was only six blocks over to Eighth Street and St. Olaf's Church, where a priest was more than happy to bless Ted's jewelry purchases. Once blessed, he put his crucifix on immediately. Then he went home to wait anxiously for John Hall. While waiting, Kathy called and asked to stop by, which Ted thought was great. Since she had to work late, she wouldn't get there until about seven. Ted waited in anticipation for Hall's arrival. His mind was filling with questions. What did Hall really know? What did he see? Did it resemble what Ted had told him? How did Hall get away?

His phone rang. It was his dad.

"Teddy, there are cops and rangers all over these woods. I'm told there was a bear attack out here somewhere."

"Dad, I know all about it. Remember John Hall? He's coming over here to talk with me."

"Hall? He was here! He was out there hunting for that renegade bear."

Ted's doorbell rang.

"Dad, I have to go. Remember your promise. I'll call you later tonight, or tomorrow, and fill you in. See you." Ted ran to buzz John Hall in.

92

DeathWalker

John Hall entered, looking much the same as he did in the field, with his three day growth of beard and his face looking dirty. Brutus barked a warning and sniffed his guest, as if deciding whether he was friend or foe. Hall's attire was the familiar hunting outfit, except that the knife on his thigh was missing. He looked serious and intense. After shaking hands, Ted invited him in.

"Ted, you're in big trouble. I saw that thing. There is no way to defend against it. That damn thing is coming here!" Hall stated.

"How? Why?" Ted gasped.

"You are the only person I will tell this to, and I'll deny I ever said it, because it would make me sound like three levels of crazy. I met a vampire." Hall looked at Ted, as if expecting him to disbelieve.

"Where? When?" Ted asked.

"We were camping on that boulder, and it was late at night, when the thing landed there. He specifically wants you. It is really pissed! That damn thing could smell the blood from the sliver of your shirt that I was carrying! He picked up Joe with one hand!" Hall exclaimed.

"He wants me?" Ted asked.

"Yeah. He says you killed his mate. Apparently you were right, you did kill something. She even had a name—Anne. He says he's coming to get you. He's going to kill you. His name is Christian. This thing can turn from a monster to a human in seconds! Ted, I was never so scared in my whole life!" Hall appeared very frightened.

"Christian? An evil vampire named Christian?" Ted asked in disbelief.

"That's what he said," Hall uttered.

"Did you tell the police?" Ted questioned.

"You've got to be kidding. Tell the police that a vampire attacked us? If I did, I would be in a padded cell right now," Hall stated.

"What happened to Indian Joe?" Ted inquired.

Hall put his face in his hands. "He tore Joe's throat apart. He drank his blood before my very eyes. I couldn't do a thing about it. In fact, I thought I was a dead man. The only thing that saved me was the fact that he wanted me as a damned messenger. He took Joe's body and said that when it is found, it will appear that the wolves had at him. I made a story up about a bear. What the hell was I going to say? Vampire? Shit, they would think that I did it or they would lock me up for being crazy. No one would believe it. I couldn't stop shaking for two hours!"

"Now you know exactly what I was going through . . ." Ted replied. "Does he know where I live?"

"No, no! He knows that you are in Minneapolis, but that's all. And I'm sorry, but I gave him your name. I, I had to. If I didn't, I wouldn't be standing here right now. He doesn't know your dad is out there. If he did, I believe he would kill him in a split second. I have never seen anything like this." Hall was shaking. "Shit, Ted, after he did what he did, I couldn't even move until daylight. I was too damned scared!" Hall was embarrassed.

"John, I know what you're going through. Remember, I just got my stitches out. I know a little bit about these creatures now. Obviously they can be killed, because I actually killed one, and it looks as though I may have to kill another one. I don't have a choice. I just wish I could get it over with." Ted said it so casually that Hall was startled.

"He did say that he had all eternity to hunt you down. How would he find you? I have no idea. All I know is that we never had this conversation. This is between you and me. If anything is ever brought up . . . I'll deny it. It was a bear as far as I know, and when they find Joe, his body will likely confirm it. Ted, all I can say is that I have never been afraid of anything in my whole damned life—man, or animal. Now, *I'm* scared to death. There's no way I will ever go back out in the woods at night. My hunting days are over . . . history . . . finito."

"Why don't you help me get him?" Ted asked.

"Shit, I couldn't help myself. I don't know what I'll do." Hall sounded totally defeated.

"Look, it's not that I'm not afraid . . . it's a question of him or me. I don't have a choice. It's either that, or stay locked up in my condo for the rest of my life, never going out at night ever again."

Ted's doorbell rang; it was Kathy. Ted asked Hall not to mention the vampire, or his vendetta, in front of her. He wanted to tell her, but in his own time. Kathy entered, holding the manuscript written by Professor Steiner. After being introduced to Hall, Kathy couldn't hold back her comments.

"Ted, this is unbelievable, I couldn't put it down! I read it in one sitting. If I didn't know Professor Steiner, I would swear this is fiction. It's the most frightening thing that I have ever read. Just to think that these things possibly exist, is scary. Steiner's not saying these are some kind of

DeathWalker

crazy people; he's saying these are the creatures that myths are made of and that they are not human."

"Kathy, I need to talk to the Professor. Come with me?" Ted asked.

"Sure." Kathy answered, setting the manuscript down.

Ted handed the manuscript to Hall. "Here, read this. It may help you cope with your experience. This will tell you what I'm up against." Hall looked at the title and thumbed through it.

"I will," he replied. "I'm staying in town. I'll call you tomorrow. We can talk then." Hall grabbed the manuscript and left, leaving Ted and Kathy alone. The fear began creeping into Ted's mind.

"I'm scared, Kathy." Ted stated "Hall says that he saw a vampire and that it's coming after me. Apparently, I killed its mate. It knows that I'm in Minneapolis and will be coming here."

"What are you going to do?" Kathy asked.

"Prepare. I guess I'll prepare. First thing tomorrow, I'm buying a good crossbow." Ted answered. "I'm going to see Steiner tomorrow as well, and talk it over with him. I'll see if he has any ideas. I'm sure he will be able to help me in some way," Ted said.

"I'll go with you, if I can get away," Kathy stated.

"If Steiner is correct, I have a lot of options. It can't enter into my domain unless invited, so I am safe here. Garlic, holy water, and a crossbow can protect me." He reached for his neck, producing his crucifix. "I bought this today. Steiner doesn't believe it will help, but I don't think it will hurt either. I need to talk to Steiner. In the woods, I would be able to hear the silence and know the vampire was there somewhere. In the city, how will I know he has found me? How will I know he is coming? Where will he hide during the daytime? Can I hunt him before he hunts me?" Ted had nothing but questions.

"Come on, let's go get something to eat." Kathy suggested.

They locked up the condo, and headed for a nice restaurant just down the street and around the corner on Hennepin Street. Once they stepped outside, the sunset seemed more significant than ever before. Ted realized that the beauty of the sunset was gone, and was now replaced by anxiety and fear. Knowing that it would be dark by the time they finished their dinner, Ted thought about turning around and changing his mind. He kept telling himself '*There's no way he could find me this quick.*' Yet, in his mind was the question: '*Could he?*' He held Kathy's hand tightly as they strolled to dinner.

*   *   *

Christian awoke from his rest, prepared for his long journey. This would be his last sleep in the deep, protective woods. He knew he was changing. Since the loss of his Anne, Christian finally realized that he had no one to protect. The wilderness that shielded their existence no longer had meaning. Alone, he was unconcerned about exposure, for he had no reason to exist. He was prepared to move amongst the living. He was ready to take risks. The revenge that filled his total being, made feel him aggressive and powerful. He also realized that he was *very* hungry.

He lifted his arms and rose to the sky, taking flight and heading southeast toward Minneapolis. He decided that on this night, he would make half the journey. As he moved across the sky, he watched the warm blooded beings dart across the cool ground. He hated this time of year, for the summer days were long and the nights were far too short. The only advantage was that food was plentiful. He looked down as he passed over a group of campers enjoying their night in the woods. He smiled as he flew over them, almost enjoying the thought of landing and feeding. But there was no need, for he knew a solitary target would soon present itself.

As he passed over a small town, he watched the cluster of lights and the stream of headlights leading both to and from. At a cross road, he spotted his dinner. He appeared to be a young male, walking along the road, probably hitching a ride. Only a light at the intersection made the crossroad an oasis of light in the darkness. Christian watched the hiker move away from the light, proceeding down the highway and into darkness, before striking. As he landed, he knocked the hiker to the ground. Startled, the hiker jumped up quickly, facing his attacker. Christian looked at him as only a good meal, and nothing more. The hiker put up his fists, as if to defend himself.

"Amusing . . ." Christian muttered.

He walked directly to him. Grabbing him by the throat, he lifted the human into the air. The hiker screamed, "No! I didn't do anything to you! Why are you doing this?"

Christian sank his teeth into the hiker's neck, tearing his flesh and creating a gaping wound. With blood spurting out, the hiker's screams faded as Christian drank the warm, nourishing liquid. He felt his strength surge as he drained the hiker of every bit of life. Finished, Christian shredded the hiker's torso with his long, sharp claws, making it appear

DeathWalker

as if he were attacked by an animal. He then tossed the corpse into the drainage ditch. It was so quick and easy, that it reminded him of the revenge he was seeking—Ted Scott's death would not be that swift and easy. He lifted his arms to the sky and continued his journey, soaring within the cool night air.

*　　*　　*

Finished with dinner, Ted and Kathy made the short walk back to the condo. Ted's eyes looked in all directions as they walked. He watched the doorways and looked to the roof. He looked to the sky and beyond the shadows. He did not enjoy the thought of becoming the prey of the ultimate hunter. He kept his arm around Kathy, and realized how protective he felt of her. Once inside, they retired to the couch and the television. His stitches removed, he felt no discomfort as he made his move and kissed her passionately.

"That was a long time coming," she stated. "I almost thought that this was going to be a platonic relationship," she purred.

"Platonic this!" He kissed her passionately once again.

With Brutus watching intensely, Ted and Kathy explored each other's bodies, kissing and wrestling the length of the couch. As Ted was about to become out of control, Kathy rose to her feet.

"Teddy, I really have to go," she stated.

"You're kidding me?" Ted asked, in disbelief.

"No. This isn't our night. I really do have to leave." She sounded sincere.

"Wait, I have something for you . . ." He retrieved a small velvet box.

Kathy opened it, viewing a beautiful gold cross on a delicate gold chain. She was overwhelmed.

"Teddy, this is very nice. Why?" she asked.

"It's for you. It's blessed . . . I believe it will protect you," he answered.

"Well, whether it does or doesn't, I'm keeping it. Thank you." She leaned over and kissed him. "I'd like to go to the Professor's with you, if I can get away early," she stated.

"Well, I'll call him tomorrow and let you know what time. John Hall might join us, if that's okay," Ted stated.

They kissed and she made her exit. "Call me when you get home?" he asked. She looked behind, smiling. "I mean it!" he yelled.

Ten minutes later, his phone rang. It was Kathy. He whispered, "Goodnight." He walked to the window, looking out across the skyline. He could see every star, along with the full bright moon. "If he is coming for me, will he fly?" Ted wondered as he looked at the sky. "If he does, is it a bat? Or is it a person?" He turned away from the window.

"I wish I had my crossbow . . ." he mumbled as he picked up Brutus."I'm relying on you, big guy. If he shows up, God damn it, you better be barking." Brutus just wagged his tail, and licked Ted's face.

He felt the fear starting to set in. Ted only hoped that the Professor's book was correct, especially the part about a vampire not being able to enter a private domain without being invited. Visions of waking up in the middle of the night to the image of red, glowing eyes and sharp fangs would definitely make sleeping difficult.

Ted reflected on the many stories his mother had told him. As a child, they were mesmerizing . . . but as an adult, he had disregarded those tales as Chippewa fables. He truly thought that his mother had made them up. Now, he was realizing that the description of the "Windigo" was closer to actual reality, than his childhood nightmares. His father never allowed the Chippewa culture to become a part of their lives; therefore, his mother was left to tell them only as bedtime stories. As he remembered the vivid descriptions his mother used, they now sounded all too familiar. Red eyes, flying, and even presenting himself as another human before carrying a person off and killing them, all were appropriate to the vampire, though his mother called it the "Windigo" in her stories. He wondered if his mother actually knew more than what she told him about this old Chippewa myth. Ted did remember his mother calling him urgently to come home a number of times when things became dark and quiet.

As he looked at the sky, he put his free hand to his cross, holding it tightly. *'I'm going to give you more than you bargained for, you bastard,'* he thought. This would be the first of many sleepless nights for Ted Scott. As he lay there, Christian was coming closer . . . and closer.

Chapter Ten

At 2 A.M. on a week night, there is rarely anyone on the streets of the neighborhood north of downtown, west of the Mississippi. Only those that thrive in the darkness can be found scurrying around in the shadows, using the cover of night to shield their activities. So it was unusual when the police cruiser spotted a well dressed white man standing on the corner of First Street North, looking slightly confused. He pulled his cruiser over and rolled down his window.

"Is there any problem?" he yelled through the window of his vehicle.

"No, none at all," was the reply.

"Are you sure you're not lost?" the officer asked.

"No, I am not lost. You can continue with going on command," the man answered. Knowing that the neighborhood was possibly dangerous at this late hour, the police officer felt he should ask just one more time.

"Are you sure that I can't be of some assistance, sir?"

The man smiled and answered. "No, thank you, but I humbly appreciate your concern."

The officer shook his head, as if in disbelief, and drove on. If this was a "John" looking for a hooker, he was certainly risking his life walking around this area on foot at this hour. He pulled his police cruiser to the curb, deciding to record this event in his log book. He wrote

2 A.M., middle class white male, thirties. Dressed in three piece dark business suit, hair brown, 6'2" to 6'3", 200 pounds, corner of 1st Street North and 4th Avenue.

Being less than a block away, he glanced in his rear view mirror and the man was gone. Had the officer turned around, he would have seen the man still standing there, and realized it was only the reflection of the man that was mysteriously missing. Instead, the officer drove on.

Christian had just arrived in Minneapolis and was "sensing" his direction. He had followed the Mississippi traveling south, and landed north of the downtown area. He was feeling the pangs of hunger and as he traveled through the shadows, he scanned the street for a warm blooded meal. Naive of the modern culture, little did he know that the meals would soon be drawn directly to him. He had avoided mixing with the population for a hundred years and was in for some intense culture shock. He had only seen the changes from a safe distance, and now he was in for a much closer look at how his world had changed. He had observed much of the new technology, but was ignorant of changes in the people, as he had never had the desire or need to interact.

"Hey, white bread. Got some green for yo' home boy?" The voice came out of a dark doorway. Christian could smell the presence, just yards ahead of him.

"I am sorry; I do not understand your statement . . ." Christian replied.

Two black men stepped out from a doorway, about twenty feet in front of Christian. To them, he appeared to be an easy mark; a bewildered, middle class white guy, who was obviously out of his element.

"Oh, the chump do' not understand? Green, bread, bucks—what's to understand? You hear what I'm sayin'? Give it up, yo yuppie ass lookin' mutha fucka! Do you hear what I'm saying!" the voice demanded.

"Green? Bread? Bucks? What is that, may I ask? Is this something I might possess?" Christian questioned, confused by their tone. He studied the men, who were moving around and waving their hands, in what appeared to be some ritualistic-type movements. He was amazed at the display of what he considered to be elaborate ritualistic jewelry, not having an understanding of modern "bling." Christian's hunger was put on hold and overtaken by his curiosity of just what these men were up to. He found his mind flooded with questions.

'Why were they waving their hands?'
'Why were they grabbing at their crotches?'
'Why were they wearing these shirts with numbers?'
'Are they escaped prisoners of some sort?'
'Why does one appear to have metal teeth?'
'Why is he walking in such a way, is he crippled?'
'Why do they appear so angry?'
'Why does he repeat "Do you hear what I'm saying?"
Does he think I am mute?'

DeathWalker

"Negroes," he commanded. "Is this your language? If so, I am not adept at communicating with you," Christian answered.

"Negroes? Negroes?" The blacks were livid. Confident, they moved forward, intent on violence. "Why, you white honky mutha fucka, I'll cut your white ass. Do I look like Uncle Tom to you?"

All Christian could do is wonder, *'Who is this Uncle Tom?'*

They both produced knives and were now waving them, menacingly close. Christian held his ground, watching them in complete confusion. He knew that they seemed angry, but did not understand exactly why? One mugger stepped forward, and upon getting close, Christian reached out and grabbed the knife away in a fraction of a second, with his bare hand grabbing the sharp steel blade. The mugger quickly stepped back in disbelief, and in return, produced a large handgun from under his jacket.

Waving the high powered hand gun, the mugger knew he was—once again—in full charge. "What are you, some kind of Kung Fu mutha fucka? Well, Kung Fu this!" As he waved the gun, the other mugger was amused and laughing hysterically, yelling "Blow his ass up! Just cap his ass!"

"Now give me your wallet, mister white honky Kung Fu, or I'll blow you away, right here, right now!"

Christian's curiosity had been satisfied, and regardless of the confusion in language, he now realized his plight. Incredibly, they actually thought him to be a victim! Insulted, he decided it was now time to satisfy his hunger. In a blur, he grabbed the laughing black man by the throat, instantly crushing his windpipe with a single squeeze. Releasing him, he lunged for the other one, who fired the gun at pointblank range into Christian's chest. Christian's eyes were glowing bright red, and pure fear had replaced the mugger's false courage, as Christian didn't flinch when the bullet buried itself in his body. The very thought that he was considered as prey now outraged him. Normally, Christian only killed what he needed to feed, but in this case, he wanted both their lives and was blinded by rage.

A loud "AAAAHHHHH" could be heard echoing the empty streets as Christian tore a chunk of his throat out and drank the blood that was flowing freely in a warm red river. The other mugger watched, choking in horror, as he was suffocating to death. When he finished, Christian threw the body next to the choking victim. With a clean swipe of his claw-like finger nail, he neatly cut the other's mugger's throat. The blood flowed on to the sidewalk, where it would appear there was more than enough blood to attribute to both victims. Knowing he may need currency in moving amongst the population, he emptied their wallets, pocketing a large wad of bills.

After licking his lips clean of blood, he continued on his journey toward the brightly lit downtown. He looked down at his chest as the little bullet hole magically disappeared. Christian was wearing his original clothes. They were actually the same clothes he was killed in, over a hundred years ago. They always appeared clean and pressed, as if never worn, each and every night. This outfit, just as Christian, produced no reflection. Should he need to, he might acquire and wear any clothes that met his fancy, but as it was, these appeared quite expensive and trendy. He looked very much "in vogue" in 2011, as the style appeared custom tailored; much as it did in 1885.

He studied the city in every detail. There were plenty of places to hide from the sunlight. Sewers were everywhere, as well as huge storm drains. From the sky, he saw many large warehouses and deserted buildings, so although out of his element, he did not fear for his survival. He continued his walk in a direction driven by instinct. As he approached the downtown area, the light from the business signs started to eliminate the dark shadows. He needed to observe the people; learn their customs and the nuances of contemporary language. He continued moving south on First street to Hennepin, and soon noticed a number of men going into what appeared to be a modern looking pub within the downtown border. The sign read, "The Gay Millennium." He followed along.

Entering, he made his way to the bar and sat on a stool. The throbbing of loud music was annoying to Christian, for it was offensive to his sensitive hearing. *'Why is the music so loud? Are modern people deaf?'*

As Christian looked about, the bartender approached, asking "What can I get you?"

Christian replied without bothering to make eye contact. "Water, please. Just water."

The bartender smirked, now asking "Evian? Perriere? Colorado Spring? Which one would you prefer?"

Christian looked confused. "I am in need of only plain water. You select one."

The bartender shuffled away, retrieving a stylish bottle and fine crystal goblet, before pouring the water for Christian. Christian watched,

DeathWalker

disbelieving that water was treated as if it were a fine wine. *'Why is water being treated as if it were rare?'* he wondered.

"Four dollars. Plastic or cash?" the bartender asked.

'How is plastic a form of currency?' he thought to himself, as he reached for his newly acquired roll of money, tossing it on the bar, not even knowing the full value of modern currency. The bartender was taken by the fact that Christian had set about $500 down, as casual and nonchalant as a twenty dollar bill. The bartender carefully removed a five dollar bill.

Christian looked around the room, noticing that there were no women in the immediate vicinity. *'Where are the women?'* he wondered. He arose from his stool, looking back toward the dance floor. He was shocked to see only men, who were dancing with other men. As he scanned the room, he could see men hugging and kissing each other while seated at intimate little tables. He fell back onto his stool in shock and disbelief. He had never seen a real homosexual, where now he seemed surrounded by them. This was a subject he had only heard of as a young man, but never witnessed prior to this moment. It his day, homosexuality was considered a mental affliction. His mind whirled in confusion. *'Why are some of these men dressed in odd ways? Why are some so feminine and others overly masculine? Do they suffer from different afflictions?'* As he sat pondering this unusual phenomena, he felt a hand rest gently on his knee.

"Hi, handsome. Would you like some company?" a feminine voice asked.

Christian looked to find a man sitting next to him, but was confused, for he spoke in the voice of a woman.

"Why do you speak this way?" Christian asked.

Not having any idea of what Christian was really asking, the man answered "Because I like your looks!" he flirted.

"You are attracted to me, so it necessitates you to speak in such feminine manner?" Christian asked, raising an eyebrow and turning towards the stranger, completely befuddled.

"Yeah, I like your looks. You look to be the strong, silent type." He smiled as he squeezed Christian's knee.

"What is this place?" Christian asked, thinking he had wandered into an asylum.

"You don't know?" the stranger chuckled, sitting down next to Christian. "To be politically correct, it's an alternative bar, but 'gay bar' is the common term used to describe it," the man answered.

"Gay? Gay? As in happy?" Christian asked, becoming more and more confused.

The man laughed. "Yeah, happy. Really, really happy! Gay is just a nicer term than queer or faggot. Where have you been, in another country? I suppose that would explain your worldly charm. You must admit, the term is far better than being called a queer."

"I have been away. I have been far away," Christian responded. "Are there very many of these places, perchance, in this area?" he asked.

"There are more and more every day. We're out of the closet, you know. We even have our own parade every year!" he bragged.

"You have been kept in a closet?"

The gay laughed. "This persona you wear is funny!"

"Are you not shunned by society, as having a mental illness?" Christian asked. He was surprised, for homosexuality had always been considered a mental illness.

"Shunned? Hell no! We're a political force. It's very popular to be gay. Hell, the government even has a quota to hire us. Almost every program on TV has a gay character," the man stated. "I'm Troy." He extended his hand, giving a soft and gentle handshake.

"Christian is my name." '*What is TV?*' he wondered.

"Oh, Christian. That's sexy," Troy purred, offering a giggle.

"If there are many of these establishments and of your kind, what is of the family life?" Christian asked.

Troy laughed. "Boy, you have been away for a while. Today, we can have our own families. We can adopt children, or even hire a person to have a baby for us. Some states even let us get married."

"Two men? Married? What would be the purpose?" Christian asked in bewilderment.

Troy laughed again, being very amused. "Boy, you are funny. I'll play along. Would you like to go somewhere quieter? Maybe where we could be alone?" Troy offered.

Christian couldn't believe how the opportunity presented itself.

"Yes, I would like that." Christian stated, giving a smile of his own.

"Maybe we can drive a short distance and stroll through Loring Park?" Troy suggested. Christian's smile widened, and he nodded in approval.

"Follow me." Troy held Christian's hand as he led him through the bar and out the back door. The bartender noticed them leaving and called out to them, as Christian had left the huge roll of bills lying on the bar. But

DeathWalker

before he could catch them, they were out the back door and gone. Once outside in the dark alley way, Troy attempted to embrace Christian, who instantly pushed him away. Shocked, Troy asked, "I thought you wanted us to be alone?"

Christian's hunger started to rise, and his eyes started to turn red. "I do . . ." he responded. This time, Christian's voice was deep and threatening. Troy knew something was terribly wrong, and was becoming very frightened.

"Please, don't hurt me. Don't hurt me! I have AIDS!" Troy whimpered, backing up to the alley wall behind him.

"*AIDS?* What is of this AIDS?" Christian asked.

"It's a terrible disease. It's a virus in my blood. It will kill you if you get my blood on you." Troy cried, tears streaming down his face.

"Kill me? It can kill me?" Christian asked mockingly.

Troy was nodding emphatically. "Yes, yes. It will kill you if you make me bleed."

Christian smiled. His fangs were now protruding and gleaming in the faint street light. He looked directly at the cowering Troy and growled "I am already dead."

He grabbed Troy, biting him furiously on the neck. Blood splattered everywhere as Christian gorged himself for the second time this night. When finished, he discarded the body to a dumpster. '*He was quite correct.*' Christian thought. '*Slight after-taste, this AIDS disease. Similar to those who had the Pock some years ago . . .*'

As Christian walked from the alley, close behind followed three men. Christian didn't need to look, for he could hear their footsteps and feel them breathing. He walked slowly along the dark street.

"Hey, sissy boy," one of them called. Christian continued walking, as he didn't recognize they were actually calling to him.

"Hey, faggot . . . queer! We're talking to you!" the men yelled.

They started running toward him, so Christian turned to observe what this was about, not realizing he was actually being regarded as the prey, once again. He whirled around to face his attackers. One of the men had a baseball bat and was intent on doing some gay bashing. He ran up on Christian and without warning, swung the bat full force. Christian merely held out his hand, catching and stopping the bat, with no visible effort. "Cease," he demanded, staring in complete bewilderment at the angry man.

All three men stopped dead in their tracks. "Do not anger me," Christian stated in a calm but demanding tone. His eyes were starting to glow red. "I have no need to kill you on this night," he stated.

Not impressed, the man with the bat swung his free arm in a perfect left hook. Christian grabbed his arm by the wrist, holding on to it tightly. In a flash, he took his free hand, and with a razor sharp claw-like finger nail, slit the man's wrist. Blood started gushing from the wound in spurts two inches high. Christian now released his grip. The man was in shock and crumpled to the ground, staring at the fountain of blood spurting from his wrist.

"I informed you that I have no need to kill you on this night." Christian turned and slowly lifted his arms to the air, rising effortlessly into the sky. Two of the men ran in fright, leaving their companion shivering and bleeding on the ground. Christian would now find a nice, dark storm drain and prepare for his rest. He found his first taste of modern civilization slightly confusing, but most interesting. Most amazing was that no one was alarmed by his normal appearance, and that he was actually mistaken for as prey to these lawless types. He found modern society a bit strange, as he encountered Negroes that seem to speak their own language and saloons that cater to mentally afflicted homosexuals. He began to wonder if he would even have to hunt while visiting this strange city.

As he searched out shelter, he was overwhelmed with sadness from the loss of his Anne. It is said many times that couples that have been married five or six decades, never survive when one is left alone. It's all too common that when the first spouse dies, the remaining spouse dies soon after, not being able to face life alone. Christian was feeling an emptiness created by over a hundred years of companionship. He had never actually been alone since he became a vampire and knew that after he satisfied his revenge, his next priority would be finding a new mate.

Ted awoke with the sunrise. He had slept in one hour intervals, dreaming that the vampire would come crashing through his window and attack him while he slept. His first act was to get the phone book and search for the closest sporting goods store likely to sell crossbows. It

DeathWalker

would be hours before any store would be open, forcing Ted to sit and concentrate on his plight.

He knew the vampire was coming for him, but when? How could he possibly locate Ted in the Twin Cities area with a combined population of a million people? Was this even possible? Ted plodded through his morning routine, eventually sitting down for a cup of coffee. The sound of the telephone ringing pierced his concentration.

"Teddy? This is Mike." It was Ted's detective friend.

"Hey Mike, how are you?" Ted asked.

"Fine, Ted. I've really got something for you. Can you come down here to the station?" Mike asked.

"Sure," Ted answered. "How soon?"

"ASAP. I have a story for you. Get down here." Mike hung up, leaving Ted to hear only a dial tone.

Ted quickly got dressed, patting Brutus goodbye, and was off to the police station. A short drive later, and he was bounding up the stairs to Mike Evans's office. He noticed that there was a different feel to the office as he entered. People were buzzing and scurrying all about quickly. He walked through the field of desks wearing his press pass as he worked his way toward Mike.

"What do you have?" Ted asked, extending his hand.

"Teddy, we've got a real killer out there." He handed Ted copies of his reports. "This white guy was seen in the early hours of the morning over near the Nichollet area on the west bank. In his thirties, sharp dresser, really out of place. Sometime later a block away, two blacks turned up mutilated."

Ted interrupted him. "Why would you associate the crime with the white guy?"

"Let me finish, will you? Okay . . . then a man of the exact same description shows up at a gay bar also on Hennepin a short time later, plunking down a $500 tip for a $4 glass of water, and leaves with a known homosexual, a regular at that bar, whose body is found in the bar's dumpster a few hours later—also mutilated in a similar manner. But, that's not all. Only a few blocks away on 2nd, near Hennepin, three guys are supposedly attacked. The three are known gay bashers by the way, and we get reports on them every now and then. My gut hunch is that it was them that did the attacking. But never the less, one guy has his hand almost amputated at the wrist, supposedly by this guy's fingernail or claw.

107

The guy stopped a full swing with a baseball bat with one hand and when he was done, these drunks swear he flew off into the sky! How's that for a story?" Mike was grinning.

Ted was pacing, with a worried look on his face. Ted knew that Christian was now in Minneapolis.

"Ted? Ted? Earth to Ted!" Mike desperately was trying to get his attention. Ted looked directly at Mike and spoke softly.

"I know who it is, Mike."

Mike was dumbfounded. "You think you know who it is?" he uttered in disbelief.

"Yeah. If I tell you, you'll think I'm completely nuts, so maybe I should leave now." Ted was thinking only of buying his crossbow as soon as possible.

"No way, Sherlock. If you have a clue, lay it on me," Mike beckoned.

"It's a vampire, Mike. He's a damned vampire and he's after me. That's why he's here in Minneapolis." Ted watched Mike's face break out in huge smile.

"Get the hell out of here. A vampire? Are you nuts? What is this? Okay, don't tell me, you're trying to become a Stephen King or something." Mike was now laughing.

"Okay Mike, I'll tell you a little about the killings." Ted started. "Would that convince you? How about the fact that their throats were torn out?"

"Only on two of them." Mike responded, halting his laughter. He raised an eyebrow at Ted. "How did you know that?"

"Let me add that the white guy in question is not only white and in his thirties, but also speaks precise English, as if from the East." Ted said, in a matter-of-fact manner.

"Teddy, what the heck is this about? Talk to me." Mike beckoned, giving Ted his full attention. It was clear that Mike no longer thought Ted was pulling his chain, and was actually being serious.

"Mike, you're going to have this problem until he finds me. That is why he is here. As long as he is in Minneapolis, look for a dead body every night. After he gets me, he will leave. I promise you that. You see, I killed his mate. I was attacked up near the border in the woods, and killed a female vampire. It was a fluke. I had my crossbow equipped with a wooden arrow, and I shot her through the heart when she came at me. Now he seeks revenge. It's that simple. If you really want this killer, I'm

DeathWalker

your bait. But don't think you'll shoot him with that." Ted pointed to Mike's revolver.

"Ted, you've got a few facts correct . . . but a vampire, I just can't believe. I'm sorry." Mike shook his head, reaching his right hand up and ruffling up his own hair. "I think you've been writing a little too much. But, let me tell you, the story is good, real good. You're testing me right?" His eyes searched for Ted's, hoping that he would offer a smirk or something to let him know that he wasn't actually trying to pass this off as being real.

"Yeah, that's what I thought. Remember what I said, Mike. If you really want him, I'm your bait." Ted turned away from Mike, sighing in dismay. "See you. I've got some errands to run." Ted left Mike shaking his head in wonder. Mike wasn't sure whether Ted was making up a story, or just putting him on . . . or perhaps Ted had possibly lost his grip on reality.

Ted made it to his car and was quickly on his way to a large sporting goods store. The crossbow that was at his father's house he had purchased over ten years ago, so he was anxious to learn what new technology had to offer. He was in for a pleasant surprise. Entering the store, he made his way to the archery department, where a huge display of products greeted him. It took Ted only seconds to focus on a crossbow of his liking. It was about 18 inches wide, with a pistol grip. It was light in weight and easily loaded with a power of 150lb pull and 250 feet per second—near that of a slow bullet. He took it off the rack and cradled it as he looked for arrows. This became a problem, for the arrows used in these smaller weapons were now typically made of carbon steel. Ted, however, quickly found a workable solution by finding some arrows made for traditional bows.

Wooden arrows used in traditional bows are typically much longer than those used in crossbows, but Ted decided to buy them anyway and cut them down to correct size. He selected a dozen.

"Can I help you?" a clerk asked.

"Nah, I'm fine," Ted responded.

"Those are the wrong arrows, you know? You need these . . ." The clerk held out the steel arrows.

"That's okay. I need wooden arrows, so I'm cutting these down," Ted replied.

"Wooden arrows? With the force of that bow, if you hit something solid, they might shatter and splinter," the clerk responded.

"I'm only shooting at hay bales, so it's no big deal." Ted was trying to get rid of this unnecessary help.

"Want to see something neat?" the clerk asked. Ted nodded reluctantly. The clerk walked to a display cabinet and produced a hand held, miniature crossbow pistol. Ted was amazed. It was about 12 inches long and 8 inches wide. Before the clerk could even start his sales pitch, Ted blurted, "I'll take two of those."

The clerk looked confused, but offered a smile. "Don't tell me, you want to make your own wooden arrows? I'll get a couple dozen for you."

Four hundred dollars later, Ted was on his way home, well equipped for battle. It would take but a few hours to remove the tips of each arrow and cut it down to a size that could be fired from his new purchases, but Ted only had time to trim a few before calling Professor Steiner to schedule an appointment. The Professor was free at three o'clock. Ted called John Hall, telling him of the meeting. Hall asked to attend, and agreed to join Ted at the University. Ted called Kathy at her office, but was told she was away in court, working on a case. For the first time since he had quit being a reporter, Ted was watching the clock, which seemed to be ticking faster than ever before. He watched the hands speeding forward as he cut each arrow the exact length and sharpened the tips to a fine wooden point. Since the most recent events, everything seemed urgent and time became more valuable than ever before. In late August, the sun set at about 8:30 P.M.. This was one factor that he would always be aware off, for it truly meant life or death.

Chapter Eleven

utside Professor Steiner's office, John Hall was nervously pacing. Under his arm was the Professor's manuscript. Ted greeted him, and knocked politely on the Professor's door.

"Come in!" called a friendly voice.

Ted introduced John Hall as they then sat down, across the desk from Steiner.

"Your vampire is here, Professor," Ted announced.

"What exactly do you mean, Ted?" Steiner asked, setting down a report that he had been reading, and offering Ted his full attention.

"Well, the first time we talked, I wasn't completely honest with you. I actually killed a vampire. It was a female. I wasn't sure how honest I could be with you, until I read your manuscript. Now her mate is here in Minneapolis, searching for me, seeking revenge. He killed a few people last night in a classic vampire style," Ted stated.

Steiner raised an eyebrow at Ted, wondering if this was all a put-on. "There was nothing in the newspaper about such killings," he said. "Here, look . . ." He handed Ted the paper.

On the first page was a story about the victim of a hate crime, found in a dumpster. There was no mention of the mutilation. Ted found the second story on page twelve. It was a short blurb, mentioning that two gang bangers were found murdered, and were likely the victims from a rival gang. Again, not a mention of the manner in which they were killed. He laid the paper down. "This is pure bull shit. I was at the police station this morning and heard about this first hand from a detective. This is a cover up!" Ted exclaimed.

"It wouldn't be the first time, would it Mr. Scott?" the Professor asked.

"Professor, I need to verify certain facts found in your manuscript. Why do you think that a crucifix or cross is ineffective as protection from a vampire?" Ted questioned.

"Well, in two of my studies, the victims died with a cross or crucifix in their hands," Steiner responded.

"Let me ask you this, Professor. Did you know if the crucifixes were blessed? I ask, because a vampire is not afraid of water; only holy water. The difference, of course, is merely the blessing. Could it be the same with the cross?" Ted queried, while nervously grabbing his own crucifix from under his shirt as he spoke.

"It's possible, for I never was able to find out if the crosses were blessed or not. You have to understand that I had to write that precise theory, only knowing two people died holding a cross. I couldn't very well recommend it as protection. But, I agree that you may have a good point. Unfortunately, there is only one way in which to find out, and it would be tragic if one were wrong . . . don't you think?" the Professor asked. Both Ted and Hall nodded an affirmative.

"Professor, how long should it take for a vampire that has tasted my blood to find me here in Minneapolis?" Ted asked.

"Picture the population of Minneapolis as the blades of grass on a football field. Millions of blades of green grass, stretched one hundred yards. Now picture yourself as a big yellow dandelion. You are one dandelion amidst millions of blades of grass. How long would it take for one to find that single, bright yellow dandelion? That's exactly how long it will take the vampire to find you. Not long at all, I'm sorry to say . . ." His voice sounded weak at the very thought.

"Professor, how can I be sure he won't come crashing through my window in the middle of the night? Are you positive that a vampire must be invited, in order to enter a private domain?" Ted asked.

"Ted, I can only tell you as much as I know. There is no record or story that I was ever presented that told of a vampire breaking into a private residence. But then again, this is the first case of a 'vampire seeking revenge' that I have ever heard of. I would sprinkle holy water on your windows and hang garlic around each frame. I would do the same with the entrance doors. Let me ask you this: Assuming that you can protect yourself, how will this ever be resolved?"

"Obviously, Professor, one of us must die. It's that simple. I can't just sit home at sundown, surrounded by holy water and garlic for the rest of my life! At night he will hunt me, and during the day I must hunt him." Ted spoke with conviction. "This brings me to my last question, Professor. How do I find him?"

DeathWalker

"My boy, if I knew that, I would have found one and been famous by now. Logically, he will be in a sewer or storm drain, underground, well protected from the sun. But, he could also be in a basement of a vacant building, or any dark, uninhabited place you might think of. I would start with the sewers and drains within a mile of your residence. Next, locate vacant buildings and basements in your area. Give me your exact address; I believe the University has a blueprint on file of the sewer and drainage system. I'll get a copy and identify your address, giving you a start for our search," the Professor stated.

"You said 'our' search, Professor," Ted pointed out.

"Yes, I did say the word 'our.'" He smiled. "I am an old man, and I won't be much help, but I need to do this. I want to be included, if you will allow me. If you have the space, I would like to stay with you until this is resolved." The Professor had invited himself to Ted's condo.

"Do you have any idea what you are asking? I faced a vampire and will never ever forget it. It paralyzed me with fear, literally. Don't do this, Professor. You are most welcome to stay at my condo, as I have another bedroom, plus a sleeper couch, so I have the space. However, if I were you, I wouldn't get involved. Do me a favor, Professor; think about it for a few days. When you obtain the blueprint, if you still feel the same, pack a bag and bring it along with you." Ted offered.

"What has Mr. Hall to do with all this?" the Professor asked, bringing attention to the silent man sitting beside Ted.

"John's life has been disrupted by this vampire too. It was John that was chosen to bring me the message of revenge. This vampire killed John's companion, just to make his point. John is helping me," Ted stated.

"You actually have seen and spoken with him?" the Professor asked unbelievably, turning his attention to Hall.

Hall watched the Professor become excited. "Yeah, it scared the shit out of me! It isn't something one looks forward to." Hall barked at him, finding it hard to believe that someone could possibly be excited by this.

The Professor couldn't contain himself. "Now that everything is in the open, I have a few questions. Since the both of you have seen a creature that I have only dreamed of seeing, does his face transform from a human likeness, or does it remain that of a beast?" The Professor looked from Ted to Hall, and back to Ted, who answered first.

"I only saw the face of a beast. She had amber eyes that turned to a glowing bright red. That's all I saw."

113

Edwin F. Becker

John opened his mouth and then paused, as if deciding whether to relive his memory. "His face was human at first," he began, looking up, as if envisioning it. "Then it changed. His eyes went from black, to bright red as he became angry. Then he transformed into the face of an animal. His fangs were three or four inches long. His voice went from a deep human voice, to a growl-like voice. And, oh yes, he can hiss. Not like a small cat, more like a big cat or a huge reptile. I watched him go from human to animal, then back to human, in the course of a few minutes. He lifted my friend's body with one hand, as if he were a bag of groceries." As John spoke, the Professor was taking notes.

"His fingers were longer than that of a normal man, and turned claw like. The finger nails were as long, and sharp as a knife! The speed in which he moved was incredible. Fast! Very fast! He landed on this big boulder where we camped, and we never heard him. Not a sound. But Indian Joe smelled him coming. He said it was a foul odor." By the expression on John's face, there was no doubt this was painful to recall. "That's about it, Professor. I never saw him fly. He jumped from the rock into darkness. That's all I remember, and I will never, ever forget it." John paused before baring his soul. "Professor, if you are face to face with a creature that you have no way of defending yourself from, and it intends to kill you in the most horrible manner, it is not something that you will ever want to experience or relive."

The Professor stood, and walked around the room as he talked. "Gentlemen, we have our work cut out for us. I will secure the blueprint and we will start our search. I recommend that you both get yourself some holy water, garlic, and stakes. I guarantee that once we start our search, he will soon sense that he is being hunted. We will all be in danger from that moment on. Ted, I will call you when I have my work complete."

They said their goodbyes and left the Professor pacing about his office. "Ted when you're ready to hunt, call me." John said as he walked away. Ted watched as Hall departed with his head hung low, as a man who had been defeated and spirit shattered.

Ted couldn't get to his car fast enough. He drove directly to the supermarket, where he bought the equivalent of a bushel of garlic cloves, along with a two liter Pepsi. In the parking lot, he poured the Pepsi on the ground. His second stop was St. Olaf's Church, where he would fill the empty two liter bottle with holy water. Taking a paper coffee cup from his car, he scooped the water and filled the bottle, emptying the

DeathWalker

church's receptacle. He glanced at his watch—it was 6:30 P.M.—roughly two hours until sundown. He quickly drove home.

He entered the condo to find Kathy sitting on the couch, watching television and petting Brutus, who was cradled in her arms.

"How did you get in?" Ted asked.

"Oh, the young girl that walks Brutus, Pat, let me in. I hope it was okay?" Kathy asked, taking her eyes off the television screen and lifting Brutus off her lap.

"Sure; I was just surprised," Ted answered.

Kathy watched as Ted carried his purchases to the dining room table and dumped them.

"Planning on starting a new diet? Garlic and Pepsi Clear . . . sounds delicious," Kathy chided.

"Not Pepsi Clear. It's holy water. I'm not taking any chances," Ted stated.

"Teddy, I want to believe you, but my logical mind keeps telling me that this is hoax of some kind, to the extent that it's got to be a human who is doing this. They might think they're a vampire, but I just can't believe this supernatural creature exists . . ." Kathy questioned.

"Professor Steiner believes it," Ted responded.

"Teddy, ask the Professor if he believes in the missing link, Bigfoot, or the Loch Ness monster. I'll bet he believes all of them exist . . ."

"Kathy, believe me. I may be a writer with an overactive imagination, but this is not part of it. We are not dealing on a human level. I found out today that he is here in Minneapolis. Two people had their throats torn out in one night. What are the odds of that happening?"

"I didn't hear about that. Was it in the news?" Kathy asked, being careful not to sound patronizing.

"No, not exactly. The deaths were in the news, but the causes and details of the deaths were not publicized," Ted replied. He decided to change the topic. "This garlic gives me a taste for Italian. I'm ordering a pizza. Cheese, okay?"

"That's fine," Kathy replied, going back to the television screen, unsure what to say.

Ted ordered the food to be delivered, and went about the task of stringing the cloves of garlic. Kathy eventually pitched in, and within an hour, the task was completed and the pizza was delivered. They sat down to the casual dinner.

"Teddy, what are you going to do . . . live like this for the rest of your life?"

"No . . . the Professor, John Hall, and I are going hunting. I believe it's my only option. Get him before he gets me," Ted responded.

Almost compulsively, Ted kept glancing at his watch. It was 8:00 P.M . . . soon it would be dark. Ted was worried for Kathy if she stayed with him past sunset.

"Kathy, you should leave before the nightfall," Ted suggested.

"Look, Teddy. I'm a big girl, and I only live a short block away. Besides that, there are people and doormen everywhere on this block. Who would take that kind of risk? Don't answer that—I know, a vampire. But remember, I have my cross," Kathy responded. She pushed the pizza box away and curled up to him, molding her body against his. She kissed him gently and whispered "Don't worry; I can take care of myself." For the moment, Ted felt removed from his fear and replaced it with feelings of affection. They kissed, and soon were wrapped in each other's arms. At that instant, there was no time; only pleasure. As Ted explored her body, he whispered "Is this okay?"

Kathy responded "Teddy, it's our night." He relaxed, and let his instincts take over.

Christian awoke with the setting sun. As if programmed, he stepped from a storm drain above the Mississippi west bank into the night air, sensing the direction he must follow, toward his prey. He studied a huge dam at St. Anthony Falls, remembering the days before it existed. Realizing he was hungry, he also realized that he likely had no reason to hunt, for food was plentiful in Minneapolis and would soon present itself. Climbing up the wall to street level, he moved toward the downtown area at a fast pace, heading in the direction of the Loring Park area. He could feel he was closer to locating his target. He sniffed the air, and knew Ted Scott was getting closer and closer with each step. It was like a magnet, pulling him into confrontation.

As he walked along, he could see a solitary figure standing just around the corner about a block ahead. The general area appeared to be active and trendy with shaggy, long haired people walking about. He continued his

DeathWalker

pace in the direction he was driven to travel. Christian studied the man as he passed. The man was looking in different directions, as if waiting for someone to arrive. He appeared nervous, for even though he was standing basically in the same place, his hands and feet kept moving. As Christian passed, the man asked, "Want to buy some shit?"

"Shit?" Christian repeated, as he paused.

"Yeah, shit. You know; blow, snow, toot, nose candy, whatever." The man responded as though irritated that he had to explain.

"Nose candy?" Christian stopped and pondered that thought in confusion.

"Look, I thought you wanted to do business," the man stated, looking Christian up and down. "Obviously, I was wrong. So beat it, dick head!" the man ordered, this time in a loud demanding tone.

"Do business? What manner of business, may I ask?" Christian inquired. Again, he was curious of the modern customs.

"What the fuck are you, Forrest Gump? Some kind of moron? Look, I said beat it, you fucking dork. Go on; get the fuck out of here before I kick your ass down the street!" The man moved toward Christian in a threatening manner, as if to strike him with his fist.

Christian's eyes were a dead giveaway that violence was forthcoming, as they started glowing a crimson red. He grabbed the man by the hair, pulling him closer. Grinning, he growled "Dinner is served!"

The man gazed in horror. "Jesus Christ . . ." was all he was able to say before Christian's fangs protruded, preparing for his feeding.

Between the cavernous tall buildings and empty concrete streets, "Hey! No, no, AAAAAHHHHHH!" could be heard echoing across the night. Then, suddenly, complete silence. Christian was no longer hungry, as he had drained the man's blood as thoroughly as one might squeeze the juice from an orange. He left the body lying in the street, with no concern. Checking the pockets, Christian once more confiscated a large wad of bills, and slipped them into his jacket. He continued his journey, moving instinctively toward the direction of Ted's building.

Christian was generally amazed at the abundance and availability of food in this city. His memories of the twin cities were of waiting until the early morning hours to stalk an unsuspecting victim. It was either that, or mingling within the population, and enticing a potential victim into straying away from the rest of the population. Never was it as easy as this. There was no thrill of the hunt, as this was literally a human buffet. A

117

hundred years ago, if a person screamed, others came running to help or investigate. Many vampires were discovered and hunted down because of this human instinct to help one another. Now it seems no one cares, or is even remotely interested if another is in distress. He glanced back and watched in amazement as a few automobiles drove passed the body without even slowing down. *'Maybe I was wrong in avoiding the densely populated cities,'* he thought. *'There are so many people; it seems no one cares about a single death any longer.'*

Within a few minutes, he was passing the downtown area. He smiled as a few homeless beggars called him into dark hallways or alleys, asking for "a buck." *'No one would ever miss these people . . .'* he thought. He never saw so many homeless beggars at one time. He realized that he could survive for years just feeding on the homeless.

Once downtown, a prostitute beckoned "Want to have a good time?" Christian recognized her calling immediately. *'These things don't change, even in a hundred years.'* The clothes were more modern, but the look was the same: painted face, revealing blouse, short skirt, and high heeled shoes. As removed as he had been from civilization, he knew what she was before she spoke. His only astonishment was her age. She appeared so very, very young and tender. "Hey! Want to have a good time?" she called again.

Christian looked upon her deliciously, answering. "No, my dear. I already had one this evening. Maybe we will meet again."

"This is where I hang out, Mister. Remember, you can find me here!" Christian smiled, for certainly he would remember.

Christian made his way to a fashionable area north of Loring Park, just a mile or so outside of downtown. As he surveyed the neighborhood, it was lined with high rise apartments and condominiums. At street level, it was quiet, with few businesses and only foot traffic. This is where he stopped. He sniffed the air and knew his foe was close. His instincts centered on one building, so it would be here that he would wait for a sign. He slowly paced the street, pretending to be only taking a casual walk. He was amused, observing the people passing by, all unaware of his threatening presence.

✳   ✳   ✳

"Why get dressed? Just stay the night," Ted pleaded.

DeathWalker

"Teddy, I have no clothes or anything. I have to go home. I'll tell you what; I'll bring some things over here, so if this ever happens again, I'll be prepared," Kathy offered.

"Ever happens again? How about tomorrow night?" Ted asked.

"We'll see," Kathy stated, looking for her socks.

"Kathy, I'd like to walk you home . . ." Ted offered.

"No way, Teddy. What would you do, bring along your crossbow? No thank you. He doesn't want me, he wants you. It's still early, and there are plenty of people on the street," Kathy answered.

"Do me a favor and call me as soon as you walk in your door?" Ted asked.

"Immediately, if not sooner," Kathy promised. She walked over to Ted to embrace him.

"You're special, Kathy. You know that?" Ted asked, giving her a gentle kiss on her forehead.

"Teddy, you are very special, too. I'm not quite sure if you're crazy or not, but I'm drawn to you," Kathy stated.

"You may be right! I may be crazy! But it just might be a lunatic you're looking for . . . Billy Joel wrote that. I wish I did."

Kathy was laughing. "This is truly insane. Here you are, recovering from a hundred stitches, swearing a vampire did it. We're naked in an apartment that's strung with garlic and I'm looking at a Pepsi bottle filled with holy water, while you're quoting a rock and roll singer. What's wrong with this picture?" Kathy laughed.

"I love your laugh. You're beautiful," Ted said softly.

"I hope you will be hearing my laugh a lot."

"Yeah, as long as it's not when we're in bed," Ted kidded.

Kathy laughed again. She proceeded to finish getting dressed, and gathered her things. While she prepared, Ted wandered to the window, looking down ten floors to the street. Brightly lit, there was plenty of foot traffic moving in both directions. '*It's impossible that he could have found me this quickly . . .*' he thought.

Kathy emerged, ready to leave. "See you, Teddy!" she called.

He realized at that moment that she was not wearing the cross he had given her. "You didn't really like the cross?" he asked.

"Oh Teddy, I loved it, but I change my necklaces day to day. I didn't hurt your feelings, did I?" she asked with concern.

"No, it's not my feelings I am concerned with, it's your welfare," he responded.

She kept walking toward the door. "Teddy, I'll wear it, I promise."

"Hey, wait," he ran to kiss her goodbye. As she walked to the elevator, he wished she wasn't leaving. Not out of fear for her safety, but because he felt wonderful in her presence. Once she disappeared into the elevator, he ran back to the window, to watch as she exited the building and walked down the street to her apartment.

Kathy came out of the elevator and headed toward the lobby and the entrance that led to the street.

Christian walked by as a young woman came out from the entrance of an apartment building. She never gave him a glance as Christian stared her down, as she bore a very familiar scent. Only a few feet away, he knew exactly who she had been with. He followed her, walking a few feet behind. As she stopped to cross the street in the middle of the block, he continued on the same side, passing her quickly. He hustled ahead and swiftly crossed the street further down, so as to walk toward her when she reached the other side.

Crossing the street, Kathy was now walking directly toward Christian, who was coming the opposite way. Pretending to be looking away, he bumped her, causing her to drop her attaché. Swiftly, he picked it up. Kathy also bent down to retrieve it and as the both were bent over, their eyes met.

"I am so very sorry, Miss. I do apologize for my actions. I simply was not looking where I was going." Christian used his most charming voice. As she arose, his lightning fast hand took a gold pen protruding from her breast pocket, whisking it away. Kathy never noticed.

Kathy was busy analyzing him. Well groomed and well dressed, with impeccable English, he was obviously no threat—or so she thought. Christian handed her the case, staring directly into her eyes. She stared back, and found herself blushing slightly. He knew at that moment that he was in the presence of a woman who had been with Ted Scott. Was it his mate? He smiled politely, as he intentionally brushed her hand as he handed the case over to her. Kathy felt there was nothing unusual, and was not threatened, for they were surrounded by people passing them on the sidewalk. Christian studied her beautiful face and intense eyes, bringing back memories of his Anne. With those memories also rose the intense hatred for his foe, the man who had killed her.

DeathWalker

"Once again, I am so very sorry," Christian apologized.

"It is quite all right. It was an accident." She took her attaché from him and moved along, toward her apartment. Christian returned to Ted's building, fondling Kathy's gold pen.

The phone barely rang when Ted picked it up. "You okay?" he asked.

"Sure," she answered.

"I was about to run downstairs when that guy bumped you. What was that about?" Ted asked.

"Nothing. He wasn't looking where he was going, that's all. He was embarrassed and apologized. It was okay, no big deal. By the way, Teddy, did I drop a gold pen at your place?" Kathy asked.

"Not that I have seen, but I'll check around and look between the couch cushions," Ted replied.

"Good night, Teddy," Kathy whispered.

"Sleep well, Hon." Ted hung up.

Ted loaded one of the small crossbow pistols and went to bed with it on one side and Brutus on the other. He was prepared for another night of tossing and turning. Ted was starting to realize the pain of anticipation. He almost wished that the vampire would come crashing through his window and the confrontation would be ended. Every little noise started his adrenaline pumping, and caused him to stir from his half sleep. He kept his hand on the crossbow pistol, as it became almost an extension of his arm. He laid there staring at the ceiling until he could no longer keep his eyes open.

*   *   *

Christian was satisfied, for he had found his prey. He must now find a resting place close by. Unlike Ted, he was savoring the anticipation of what was to come. He looked up at the buildings many floors and windows. Somewhere up there was his enemy. *'I am here, Ted Scott. I'm coming for you . . .'* he thought, as his eyes drifted to the clear night sky. He was starting to realize that he was safe in this urban environment. No one looked at him as being odd, and in fact, it seemed no one noticed his very presence. Christian didn't realize yet that no one even believed in vampires any longer, and that he was safer than he could ever imagine.

121

Chapter Twelve

Detective Mike Evans was shocked to find that another bizarre murder had occurred the previous night. Though it was only a drug dealer, the method of death was curious. This was the third victim who had his throat ripped out. He remembered what Ted had said about it being a vampire, and had predicted a death of this nature would occur every night. Mike thought the very idea of a vampire to be ridiculous, but Ted's prediction was most intriguing. He decided a short drive and a visit to the coroner was in order, to have him study the similarities of these killings.

Coroner Paul Malone was in his office sorting the day's work when Mike walked in.

"Paul, I need your help. We've had three recent killings that have a similar feel about them. I want you to put those cases through the ringer. I want to know if there are any common denominators on these three. I need the lab to analyze every fiber on those bodies to possibly find a common thread, if there is one." Mike sounded very determined.

"So, you think we have a serial killer out there?" Paul asked.

"Serial killer, psychopath, whatever," Mike answered.

"And you want the profile, if there is any?" Paul surmised.

"Well, if my hunch is correct, you'll have a fourth body to analyze tomorrow," Mike predicted.

"I can already tell you about the first two victims. There is a distinct resemblance in the throat wounds. The third I haven't gone over, as of yet. If it is a serial killer, how did he pick his victims? A sickly gay, then an armed gang banger, and finally, a drug pusher? Good luck on nailing this guy," Paul stated.

"Tell me about it. I need your help. That's why I'm here. I'm not quite sure where this one is going, but I feel strongly that this is just the beginning. So far, this has all been kept low profile, and I'd like to keep it

DeathWalker

that way, okay? No press! We have no reason to scare the general public with this."

"No sweat. Come see me tomorrow. If there is something here, we'll find it." Paul sounded confident.

"Thanks buddy," Mike replied, leaving the room.

As Mike walked out of the building, he made a decision to visit his friend Ted. How Ted fit into this, he wasn't sure, but Ted did predict it. It was a short drive to Ted's condo, and Mike was ringing his apartment bell within minutes. He checked his watch; it was 9 A.M..

"Who is it?" Ted asked through the speaker.

"Teddy, it's Mike. Buzz me in." Mike responded, waiting impatiently.

As Mike boarded the elevator, he admired the building. 'Ted has a nice life,' he thought as he exited the elevator. Ted was waiting for him, with the door open to his apartment.

"Teddy, I need some answers," Mike started.

"Hope you have some very simple questions," Ted replied, with humor.

"Well, I have another guy with his throat torn out, and I wondered how you fit into this?" Mike asked.

"I told you yesterday. It's a vampire. He's coming for me. It's that simple." Ted made the statement most seriously, void of any emotion, as he closed his apartment door.

"Teddy, don't give me that vampire shit again. A psychopath is more in my line of thinking. Give me a break and level with me. Who the hell is he? How do you even know him?" Mike asked.

"His name is Christian, as far as I know, and he's been around for over a hundred years. I killed his mate. Now he wants to find me and kill me. It's a simple case of revenge," Ted explained.

"Teddy, do you realize what you are saying? Do you really believe this shit? Level with me. This is no fairy tale story you're writing, is it? Are you making this shit up or what?"

Ted lifted his shirt. "Here! Did I also make this up?"

"And a vampire did that?"

"No, my girlfriend," Ted answered sarcastically.

Mike was losing his patience. As Mike started pacing in frustration, Ted's door bell rang.

"Who is it?" Ted asked.

"Professor Steiner, Mr. Scott."

123

Edwin F. Becker

Ted buzzed him in.

Mike was still pacing as the Professor entered the condo.

"Mr. Scott!" the Professor called anxiously. "I have the plans. We can now begin our search." The Professor sounded excited, as if this were some form of treasure hunt.

"Professor, this is Detective Evans. He thinks I'm losing my marbles. Mike, the Professor here is an expert on the subject of vampires and is here to assist me," Ted stated.

"What kind of professor are you?" Mike asked, turning to the Professor.

"Anthropology, at the University of Minnesota," Steiner answered, setting his papers and things on the kitchen counter before coming back to Mike.

"And you believe in vampires?" Mike asked skeptically.

"Most certainly, young man," The Professor responded.

"You said you have plans. What plans?" Mike questioned, still eyeing the Professor, looking to catch him winking or hiding a smirk.

"These plot the sewer and drainage systems that surround this area. I believe that this is where we will find the vampire during the daylight hours. I believe it is the most logical place to begin searching," The Professor reasoned. "These drains are huge, and feed into the Mississippi. They are large enough to drive a car through in the dry season."

"So the both of you are going vampire hunting? And I suppose you will drive a wooden stake through his heart also?" Mike said sarcastically.

"No," Ted answered, as he retrieved his crossbow. "This is better."

"My God, you're both serious. Look old man, I don't know you, but I do know Ted, and his imagination is obviously taking over his grasp on reality. You're both borderline crazy. People kill people, vampires don't kill people. Vampires are a myth." As he spoke, Ted's door bell rang again.

"Who is it?" Ted asked.

"John Hall," came the answer.

Ted buzzed him in.

Within moments, John Hall entered, looking as scruffy as ever, and carrying a package.

"John, this is Detective Mike Evans," Ted announced. John nodded in acknowledgement.

124

DeathWalker

"Look what I've got," John began, as he pulled a crossbow pistol out of his package. "250 feet per second, 150lb pull. This will waste the blood sucking son of a bitch!"

Mike just held his head, muttering to himself. "Not another one!" He then turned to the newcomer. "I suppose that you believe in vampires, too?"

"You're damned right I do," John replied.

"What is this, the *Twilight Zone*?" Mike asked. "For Christ sake, how many of you are there?"

"Just the three of us, Mike, just the three of us," Ted answered.

"Well, three amigos, you know if we see you out there with those crossbows, we're going to arrest you," Mike stated. "Let me tell you, should you be arrested, don't be telling the judge that you are hunting vampires, or you all will be in the hospital for mental evaluations."

"The only way you'll see us, is if the police department is patrolling the sewers," John replied.

"And you really believe in this shit as well?" Mike asked John.

"Look Mister Detective, it's not a question of belief. I faced this vampire at arm's length. I know he exists. You can go back to writing parking tickets, or whatever you do that makes you happy, if that brings you comfort . . . but believe me, he's out there! And if you try to write him a parking ticket, you're in for a big surprise." It was clear by his response that John didn't enjoy being looked at as some kind of a lunatic.

"Look, I didn't mean to offend you, but put yourself in my shoes. Doesn't this sound just a little bit absurd? What would you believe in my position?" Mike asked.

John answered quickly. "One, I would try to find anyone that spotted a man going into a drainage pipe or manhole or deserted building around dawn, or coming out of one at sun down. Two, I would patrol this block starting at sun down, looking for anyone suspicious, or hanging around with no specific purpose. He cannot enter this condo without being invited, so I imagine he will be hanging around outside. That's what I would do. Or, you can wait around and just let the bodies pile up."

Mike didn't appreciate anyone telling him how to do his job. "Listen Columbo, we have a lot of homeless people in this city. Many of them sleep in those tunnels unfortunately, so if we followed up every report of a man entering a drainage tunnel or sewer, we would need to double the police force. You said that you faced him. What does he look like?"

125

Edwin F. Becker

"6' 2" or 3", brown hair that was shoulder length, dark eyes and an athletic build. He appears about thirty-five, I'd say 220 pounds. When I met him, he had on a loose white shirt and dark pants; neat, tailored. I know he can look like a man, but when I met him he was quite pissed off and had the face of an animal, with four inch fangs. That's about all I can tell you. It was a sight that I hope I never see again . . ." John shuttered.

"Listen to me. That description is not very specific. White men who have long brown hair, dark eyes and are in their thirties, in the range of two hundred pounds, are a dime a dozen. There are a lot of sleeping vagrants down there and if I find one with an arrow stuck in him, I might have to come back and arrest you. I'm warning you; if you fire an arrow, you better be sure it's a vampire you're shooting at. If you harm a citizen, I'm locking you up. Look guys, it's been nice, but I have to go write my parking tickets. Remember what I said about being seen with those toys in public. You'll end up in the slammer." Mike exited the apartment, muttering "Just what I really need, three paranoid lunatics shooting arrows at people!"

Mike had made up his mind to do surveillance at Ted's apartment. If he could get the resource, he would also put a tail on each of these "vampire hunters." He was confused as to what was really happening, but felt that somehow this might lead him to his psychopath. Once he was back at the station, he summoned a rookie officer.

"Rick, you said you wanted in on some action. How would you like to be part of a stake out? We're looking for a serial killer. I need a body or two for surveillance," Mike offered.

The young rookie nodded in excitement, for he was tired of the desk work assigned to him the last six months. So far, his police career was made up of clerical tasks and janitorial work. Lately, he had felt like a glorified pencil pusher with a badge. He jumped at the offer.

"Can you get me two other volunteers?" Mike asked.

The rookie nodded an affirmative.

"Here's the address. It's near Tenth Street and Marquette, by Loring Park. Starting at sundown, I want one of you on the roof and one parked on the street in front of the building. I would like the third officer walking patrol on the rear and sides. I want you in radio contact with each other at all times. We're looking for a white guy, 6' 2", shoulder-length brown hair, 220 pounds, dressed well, in his thirties. Stop anyone hanging around or walking the block that fits that description. Ask for identification. If they don't belong there and have no reason to be in that neighborhood, take

DeathWalker

care, for it might be our guy. If you think for any reason it's our guy, arrest him. Be very careful, he could be very dangerous," Mike ordered.

"Arrest him for what?" the rookie asked.

"Loitering, littering, I don't give a shit. But use your head. If you find a person that fits but is not suspicious, simply record their identification. Don't get us into any lawsuits, for Christ sake!" Mike demanded.

"Yes, sir," the rookie responded.

"If you have anything, call me at once. I don't care what time it is. You understand?"

"Yes, sir." Rick ran from the office, excited that he was now a real cop on his first dangerous assignment. His buddies, Bob and Tom, also rookies, were only too happy to volunteer for the new assignment. At sundown, they would be on the job with their youthful rookie enthusiasm.

*   *   *

Back at Ted's apartment, they spent the afternoon planning their strategy, mapping out their directions by using the schematic of the sewer system. They were not exactly sure how much territory they could cover during daylight hours, and were careful to be sure that they had exits available so as to not be trapped underground at dusk. They would start the very next morning.

They decided to travel together on their hunt, for only John Hall had seen Christian, and could absolutely recognize and identify him. They felt that Detective Mike had a point, and it might be likely that they would encounter homeless people hiding down within these drains. They could not make a mistake of shooting anyone who happened to merely make the unfortunate error of being asleep in the day time.

John Hall had more than enough gear for the three of them. Because the drainage pipes would be completely dark, they would use miners helmets with spot lights attached, the same that Hall would use if searching a cave. They would each have a two-way radio headpiece for communication, should they become separated. With their first days plan being complete, John Hall left. The Professor was prepared to spend the night, and went about unpacking his things.

Ted had showed him the guest bedroom, and watched as the Professor took his things, neatly stacking them on the dresser while humming an

127

old tune. It was obvious that he was enjoying this, as if it was a sleepover party. Fifty years of studying and tracking a creature that he may now finally get to see in the flesh, was exciting to him. Ted couldn't help but feel that Professor Steiner wasn't grasping the danger of this situation. This was not an anthropological field trip; it was a matter of life and death.

"What are we having for dinner, young man?" the Professor asked, acting as though this were some kind of dinner party.

"I . . . I don't know." The very thought of eating hadn't occurred to Ted. His mind was preparing to confront a frightening enemy.

"I'll whip something up. Leave it to me." The Professor continued humming his tune and wandered into the kitchen area. Brutus followed curiously behind, likely wondering what the new visitor was up to. Opening the refrigerator, the Professor quickly found some sliced ham, offering Brutus a piece. Brutus decided he liked this new guest, and would stick close to him.

The door bell rang, and Ted buzzed Kathy in.

"Hi!" She entered with a smile, kissing Ted's cheek politely.

"I have a new roommate," Ted announced.

Before Ted could say another word, Professor Steiner entered.

"Why hello, young lady. My, you do look familiar." The Professor studied her.

"I attended the university and sat in on a number of your lectures, Professor," Kathy stated, offering her hand. "I'm Kathy Baker."

"Ah yes, I never forget a face." Steiner nodded and smiled, as if pleased by his own recall. He took her hand gently, shaking it.

Ted looked at Kathy seriously, and proclaimed, "Tomorrow we are going hunting."

Kathy set her things down and grabbed a seat on the nearest chair. "Really?"

"Yeah," Ted nodded. "The Professor has the blueprints and we spent half the day mapping our route. Along with Hall, the three of us are going together."

"Are you scared?" Kathy asked, her eyebrows coming together and her forehead wrinkling at the thought of the three of them underground, looking for this alleged monster.

"You bet. I don't particularly like the idea of traveling through dark sewers and storm drains, much less thinking about what we might encounter down there. I just have no choice." Ted shook his head, and

DeathWalker

came forward to take her hand. "Kathy, I want my life back. I can't live knowing this thing is out there stalking me. I want this over."

"Are you sure you must do this? How could this creature possibly find you in a city of this size? Why do you think he would be this close?" Kathy asked.

"Trust me Kathy, he's here and he's close. I can feel it."

The Professor reentered, carrying a tray. "Here young lady, have a nice cup of tea. Come on; sit and relax." He led her to the couch, setting the cup of tea on the coffee table. He then quickly scurried out of the room and continued preparing dinner.

"Teddy, why don't you come over to my place for awhile? We could have a little privacy?" Kathy suggested, standing up and looking for her things.

"That sounds good to me." Ted smiled at her before leaning his head back and yelling to the Professor. "Professor, we're going out to dinner, if you don't mind?"

"Oh, you young people do what you like, but you'll never know what you're missing. It's an old German recipe for meat loaf! But it's okay; it will keep and make great sandwiches tomorrow. Go on, don't worry about me, I'm not here to totally interrupt your life. Brutus and I will do fine." Humming a tune, he returned to the kitchen with his new yorkie friend closely trailing behind.

Ted and Kathy quickly gathered their things like two kids going out on a first date. For a change, Ted forgot his problem, and could only think of being with Kathy, alone. As they exited the door, they heard the Professor yell, "I'd be home before dark if I were you, young man." They both laughed. It was an hour or so before sunset, so Ted had plenty of time for them to be together. They walked the short block to Kathy's building, riding the elevator to her sixth floor apartment. In seconds, they were wrapped in each other's arms. Time didn't exist as far they were concerned, and soon only one thought was on their minds. A while later, they were lying on the floor, still embracing. It was Ted that fell asleep first. Secure in Kathy's arms, he fell into a deep sleep, the likes of which he hadn't experienced in days. As Kathy watched Ted sleep, she had the full intention of waking him after a short time, but she, too, soon relaxed. In minutes, they were both out cold, sleeping like babies.

129

* * *

Rick Stanek, the police rookie, had his two volunteers patrolling the street at sunset. He stationed one on the corner in plain clothes, and instructed the one in uniform to patrol the alley behind the building. Rick would assume the roof duty, already having cleared it with the management company that managed the building association. He had already picked up a key to the front entrance, as well as one to the stairwell that led to the roof. After a quick radio check, they assumed their positions with youthful rookie enthusiasm, ready to nail their man.

As Rick watched the beautiful sunset from the roof twelve stories high, he wondered if they had a chance of catching this serial killer. His mind wandered as he imagined his name in the newspaper. "*Rookie Officer Rick Stanek Nails Serial Killer*" is what flashed through his mind. He knew if that truly happened, he would be on his way to detective status, which is where he had set his goal. "Detective Stanek," sounded good to him. He took a position at the corner. Looking down, he could clearly see the activity on the streets and at the intersection. He watched as his partner slowly walked the block below. Using binoculars, he could zero in on anyone pausing for too long or loitering. Combine that with using the radio, he could direct his partners to anyone he suspected. All he was aware of was that this was his opportunity, and he was not going to blow it. If the suspect showed his face on this block, Rick was going to nail him.

Christian awoke promptly at sunset. He had rested in a dark, deserted building. This area, west of the Mississippi and northeast of downtown area, had become an abundant feeding ground. He walked into the cool night air, conscious of his destination and purpose. He only had two thoughts; one, he was hungry, and two, it was time for his revenge. He walked slowly toward Ted's 10th Street building, as this night would bring him another step closer to his foe. Christian understood that Ted's building housed many people, and though he could not enter Ted's apartment without an invitation, the hallways were public domain, so he could freely roam the buildings corridors. Before doing so, he needed to

DeathWalker

establish exactly which apartment Ted lived in. Tonight, that would be his goal—to locate Ted's apartment.

As he traveled past deserted warehouses, he appeared out of place in his pure white shirt and tailored pants, with matching vest. A prostitute surely thought so, and decided there was only one reason a man looking like this might be walking the fringes of the city. She sized him up and decided that he would make a very good customer.

"Hey! Want to have a good time?" she called, as she slid from the doorway. She unbuttoned the next button of her blouse as she looked at him seductively. She had watched him walking in her direction and he looked the perfect image of a 'John'—a quick buck—she thought.

"Yes, young lady. I would very much appreciate having a good time," Christian answered, as he took notice of her bare neckline and soft, delicate white throat. She smiled broadly at his response. After all, the sun had barely gone down and she already had her first paying customer. *'This is going to be a very good night,'* she thought.

She was standing in front of a dark hallway that entered an apartment building. "Come on inside, where we can have a little privacy," she beckoned, as she slid back inside the doorway.

Christian smiled as he followed her into the dark hallway.

"What would you like?" She purred, in a coy manner.

"Dinner," he answered firmly, looking directly into her eyes.

In an instant, her tone changed, for this was business, not pleasure. "Look, I'm serious. What do you like, really?" she snapped.

Christian's eyes began to glow a bright red as his hunger took control of his senses. "Dinnnneerrr . . ." he said in a half hiss, half voice.

The prostitute's eyes filled with fear and she moved backwards in the only direction she could go. It was also the very direction that would take her deeper into the darkness of this empty hallway, further away from anyone that might hear her final screams or witness the pending horror. Christian lunged for her and in an instant, it was over. She never had time to scream. He gorged himself on nourishment and when finished, he smiled at the very thought that he had yet to hunt in this modern city. It seemed his meals were always being delivered. He picked up her body and carried it to the top of the stairs, deep into the building, before dropping it in a heap. Licking his lips clean, he walked from the structure in a relaxed and casual manner. As he stood on the sidewalk, some teenagers passed. They were dressed in the modern Gothic style. They were all in black, wearing pale white makeup with fingernails painted black and dark purple lip gloss. Christian marveled at the metal objects piercing various areas of their faces. He heard them talking about a rave at some deserted warehouse. Christian now knew why his pale complexion never drew anyone's attention. He was actually normal looking in this confusing culture.

A homeless man sleeping in a car awoke to an amazing sight. As he sat up, he noticed a man dressed very well, who was standing only a few feet from his car, lift his arms to the air and rise slowly to the sky. The homeless man rubbed his eyes in total disbelief.

Christian took to the air, and was soon at the 10th Street building. He decided to survey the building, in hopes of possibly sensing his foes whereabouts. As he made his approach in the darkness, he could clearly see a warm blooded being standing at the corner of the roof. For now, he would ignore him, and merely fly in circles around the building, silently observing the occupants, trying to pin point his enemy.

Floating high above, Christian could only contemplate his revenge, knowing his target was within reach. His instincts told him that this was a night for killing.

Chapter Thirteen

The Professor had finished his dinner and was watching television. He noticed it was now dark, and decided to turn out all the lights in the apartment in order to gain better visibility for viewing the night sky. He positioned his chair so he could view the two large picture windows in both directions. It was as if he expected to see a vampire flying around in the night sky. As he sat in total darkness with Brutus in his lap, he was concerned at the fact that it was now after nightfall, and Ted was not yet home.

Floating in the dark sky, Christian noticed a curious sight. He watched as a man turned out all the lights on the tenth floor at this relatively early hour, and was moving about in the darkness. His instincts told him that this was the apartment he was looking for. He watched as the man sat in a chair, staring out at the empty night sky. Christian decided to pay him a visit. As he flew over the roof, he could see a door that led to the inside stairwell. There was only one complication, and it was that solitary man patrolling on the roof.

Christian watched from above as the man looked through binoculars and talked over the two-way radio. He could hear voices coming from that little black box that the man was speaking into. *'Curious,'* he thought. As he approached, he heard the man say "We've got a guy standing around on Marquette, he could fit the description. Check him out, will you?"

Christian then heard a crackling sound and heard another voice respond. "Roger." Christian landed on the roof, directly behind this man. Rick was looking down to the street but felt this strange feeling that he being watched. He looked right, then left, and saw nothing, but the feeling was still there. Finally, he turned completely around. Shocked to see a man standing behind him, he backed himself to the edge of the building's roof before acting.

Immediately, he went for his gun. Drawing it, he swallowed hard and asked, "What are you doing up here?"

133

"Enjoying the night," Christian responded in a deep, soft voice.

Rick quickly realized he was in the presence of the perfect description of the man they were looking for. "*Rookie Officer Nails Serial Killer*" flashed through his mind's eye. '*Sonofabitch, I got the bastard!*' he thought. "Keep your hands in full view and reach very slowly for your identification!" Rick ordered.

Christian smiled. "Why don't you just take your leave, while you are still alive. I have no need to kill you," he stated, as he ignored the startled rookie's order. Having already fed, Christian would allow the rookie to flee.

"Listen to me, asshole. I'm not screwing around with you! Skip the damned identification. Lay down on the ground and put your arms over your head, now!" Rick commanded, keeping his gun pointed at the defiant suspect.

Christian smiled as he raised his arms to the air and rose a few feet off the roof.

"What the hell?!" is all Rick could say as he gazed in awe. Rick relaxed his gun hand and raised the radio to his mouth. He made the mistake of taking his eyes off Christian for only a fraction of a second. "Tom, Bobby, get up here now, over Tom—" Before he could repeat his command, he felt a strong hand on the back of his collar. He felt himself being lifted from the roof and into the air. Stunned, he immediately dropped his gun as he tried to escape this deadly grasp. Rick was in horror, as he was looking down. The roof below his feet disappeared and he was being carried over the hard pavement over a hundred feet down, where people were walking oblivious to his screams, and traffic pushed on as normal.

"Let me go! Put me down! Don't do this, please!" Rick screamed, kicking and flailing his arms.

Christian decided he would create the perfect diversion. He carried his victim higher into the air, and about a block away to the intersection of 10th and 4th street. It was a busier corner, and he hovered directly over the intersection below. "I warned you to take your leave," Christian taunted, as he carried Rick higher and higher. Rick could only scream as Christian carried him straight up above the roof tops, higher into the night sky. Suddenly, Christian released his grasp and let Rick fall freely over 200 feet to the street below. As he fell, he was screaming the whole way down. Christian stood suspended in the air, watching the commotion as Rick's body exploded on the pavement below. The other two rookie

DeathWalker

officers that were running toward the roof could hear the distant scream and the sound of screeching tires over a block away. They now changed in that direction and ran for that intersection. It was chaos at the site, as cars crashed into one another, trying to avoid the body that landed. Random people screamed and cried for help in hysterics. Christian landed on Ted's roof and proceeded entering the building as he had originally planned, briskly walking down a few flights of stairs to the tenth floor, with grim determination.

The Professor didn't see what had happened, but was awakened from his concentration by the sound of sirens coming from the street. He looked directly down from his tenth floor window and could see people gathering at the intersection, walking towards 4th Street. As the flashing lights and sirens multiplied, the Professor thought to himself, *'Must be an accident.'* Then, he heard a knock at the door. Stumbling in the darkness, he made his way to the entrance. Brutus backed away, growling. "It's okay little fellow," the Professor assured Brutus. Without looking through the peep hole, the unsuspecting Professor opened the door and was facing a bright, blinding hallway light.

There Christian stood, glaring directly at him. "Is this the residence of Ted Scott?" Christian asked, in a demanding tone.

With the bright hallway lights blinding him, the Professor did not get a clear view of his visitor immediately. "Yes," he answered.

"May I see him?" Christian asked, as the Professor rubbed his eyes.

"He is out at this time, with his girlfriend. May I help you?" the Professor offered. His eyes were now beginning to adjust to the light.

Ignoring the Professor's offer, Christian asked "When, may I pray, will he return?"

"It is very difficult to predict young lovers, sir. I do not know when he will be back. Whom may I say is calling?" The Professor's eyes were now focused and he began to realize this visitor looked a bit ominous.

Again, Christian ignored the Professor's question. "May I enter the residence?" Christian asked.

"Who are you?" the Professor asked again, this time in a more demanding manner.

"May I enter?" Christian asked again. This time his request came across more as a growl.

The Professor stepped back, as he slowly realized the ominous visitor fit the description that John Hall had given. But having never confronted

135

a vampire, the Professor was filled more with curiosity and caution, than with fear. As his eyes adjusted to the light, he could clearly see Christian's powerful presence.

"Who may I say is calling?" the Professor asked again.

"I am Christian." His eyes were beginning to glow red, as the thought of revenge was close at hand and he couldn't control it.

"My God!" Professor Steiner gasped as he stepped back away from the door. He was feeling his first shock of fear. "You're the vampire . . . ." the old man uttered.

"I have come for Ted," Christian stated dryly, narrowing his eyes.

"He's not here," the Professor replied in a forced tone of confidence.

"May I come in?" Christian asked again. He was hoping the Professor might agree, in a mistake of being ignorant or purely intimidated.

"I cannot invite you in, as I am not the owner."

Christian sneered. "You are resident here, are you not? Invite me in!"

"I know better than to do that," the old professor answered.

"So you know of me?"

"No; I know of your kind," the Professor stated. "And I know you cannot enter a private domain unless invited."

"This is between Ted Scott and me. It would be a great mistake for you to get involved old man, unless you believe you might enjoy a slow and *very* horrible death," Christian growled.

"Yes, I am an old man. I also may fear a horrible death, but I don't fear dying. Do you?" the Professor asked.

"I am already dead, old fool," Christian hissed.

"That is not so. You should fear death more than I. You see, if I die at my age, what do I lose, maybe ten or fifteen years of life? You, my friend, will lose all of eternity, should someone drive a wooden stake through your heart, or separate your head from your body. Isn't that so?" the Professor said, smugly.

The Professor's impudence enraged Christian. His eyes were glowing bright red. If he could only cross the threshold, he would kill this old man in an instant, but he could not enter without being invited. He growled his final words. "We will meet once more, old man." He turned and made his way to the stairwell, where he returned to the roof. The Professor just stood, frozen in silence, and could feel his hands trembling. He had accomplished his dream of confronting a vampire, but for now, he just stood shivering.

DeathWalker

*　　*　　*

The rookie officers made their way to the dead body lying in the middle of the intersection. They did not recognize the body, but they did recognize the uniform. They knew it was Rick Stanek. A call was placed immediately for detective Mike Evans. He was almost on the scene with the first ambulance. Spotting the uniformed rookie, he asked, "What the hell happened?" All the rookies could do was stare at the mess.

"I, I don't know. He must have fallen off a roof?" The rookie stammered, stating it more as a question than an answer.

Mike looked up, and there was nothing. He then examined the distance from the nearest roof to the body splattered in the street, and knew it was an impossible theory.

"If he fell off of that roof, he must have been shot from a cannon, for Christ sake. It's eighty to a hundred feet from here to the closest roof! He was assigned to an address almost two blocks from here! Are there any witnesses?" Mike asked.

The rookie was still obviously in shock and muttered, "I don't know, sir."

"Find out! Look, this is bad, I know that, but swallow it and get any witness you can who may have seen him fall." Mike turned and walked briskly toward Ted's building.

*　　*　　*

Ted and Kathy were awakened to the endless sound of sirens coming directly past her building. He awoke with a start.

"Jesus Christ, what time is it?" he asked.

"Ten thirty, Teddy. Boy, were we out!"

Ted ran to the window and looking out, he could see a large gathering of people and what appeared to be a battalion of police passing by. Police cars and ambulances created a light show, and the cars were still coming as sirens continued to approach.

"What is it, Teddy?" Kathy asked.

"I don't know. It looks like an accident, from here. Except there are far too many cop cars. An officer may be involved, in whatever it is," Ted deducted. "Kathy, I have to go." Ted began gathering his clothes and

137

dressing feverishly. "Stay here. I'll take a look at what happened and if it's anything unusual I'll call you, okay?" Ted asked.

"Fine with me. I'm in the mood for a hot bath," she responded as she walked to the bathroom and started the water running. Meanwhile, Ted continued dressing frantically. He knew it was his reporter's curiosity that was forcing him to the scene of the accident, but noticed Kathy was calm and relaxed as she turned on bath water.

"Aren't lawyers supposed to chase ambulances and sirens?" he yelled, kiddingly.

"I do corporate work, remember?" she replied as she walked toward him.

Ted kissed her goodbye passionately and quickly headed for the street. Once outside, he swiftly jogged two blocks to the corner and pushed his way through the crowd, to the front of the yellow police line barrier that had already been established. The body had been covered with a sheet and not yet removed, and Ted could see an enormous blood stain smack dab in the center of the intersection. He asked a patrolman, "What the hell happened? Was he hit by a car?"

"We don't really know. It appears he fell?" came the answer.

Ted looked up "Fell from what? From where? Who was he?"

"He was a police officer. He was stationed on the roof almost two blocks from here. Down over there, I'm told." The officer pointed toward Ted's building. Ted quickly put two and two together.

"Oh my God!" he said as he took off running. He didn't know how or why, but felt immediately that the vampire was involved with this "accident" and was immediately concerned for the Professor.

Mike Evans rode the elevator to Ted's apartment. Getting off at the tenth floor, he could see Ted's door wide open. He instinctively pulled out his gun. Slowly, he walked to the door and peeked in to find the Professor sitting in darkness, staring at the dark night sky.

"Professor Steiner?" he asked, placing his gun back in its holster. He kept one hand on it, however. "Are you okay?" he visually scanned the room. The Professor sat in silence. Satisfied that no one else was there,

DeathWalker

Mike switched on the light. This time he spoke a bit louder. "Professor, are you okay?"

The Professor turned, as if in a daze. His face was pale; his eyes were fixed in concern. He answered softly, calmly. "Yes, detective, I'm okay." The Professor offered no more information, for he knew Mike Evans did not believe in vampires, thus would never believe his story.

Mike made his way to the front of the apartment and looking out the front window, he realized there was a clear view of the intersection. "An officer died from a fall out there, did you see anything?" Mike asked.

"No. I'm sorry to hear of the officer, detective. But, no, I was busy," Steiner answered.

"Busy? Busy? Doing what, may I ask?" Mike queried, confused.

"Someone came to the door about that time and I was occupied with conversation," the Professor answered.

Mike watched from the window as a fire truck passed on its way to wash down the blood in the intersection. "Where's Ted?" Mike asked.

As if entering on cue, Ted came rushing in. Seeing the Professor sitting calmly holding Brutus, he thought his fears were unfounded. "Mike, what the heck happened?" Ted asked.

"I had a rookie stationed on top of this building." Mike pointed down to the south. "Almost two blocks from here, he hits the ground. Only a large stain is what's left of him. You tell me. There is no way he could have fallen from this roof and landed two blocks away. How could he jump or fall from this roof and travel fifteen hundred feet out?"

"Maybe he was carried and dropped," the Professor stated softly.

"Carried and dropped? By what? A helicopter?" Mike asked.

"No; a vampire, detective. A vampire . . ." the Professor proclaimed.

"Vampire my ass!" Mike blurted, shaking his head and taking a relaxed step back.

"Why do you say that, Professor?" Ted asked.

"Because he was here, Ted. He asked for you, and he also asked to be invited in. We talked and he left by the stairwell," the Professor stated calmly. "He was quite angry."

Mike Evans immediately ran for the stairwell and went directly to the roof. Walking toward the front of the building, he could see something shiny lying on the roof. As he approached, he could make out it was a gun, likely belonging to the deceased officer. He carefully picked it up, so as to preserve any foreign fingerprints and smelled the barrel. It had never been

139

fired. A few feet away, he found Rick's radio. Again, Mike carefully picked it up, placing it in a plastic bag.

"What the hell happened up here?" he asked himself.

Mike looked around and could see nothing else. He made his way back to the door and after going inside, sealed it with the familiar yellow tape. He would wait until morning before going over the roof with a fine tooth comb in the daylight. He could not accept the ridiculous vampire theory, but knew something was extremely unusual about what was happening the last few days. He was sick to his stomach about losing the rookie. He never intended to place the rookie in such danger. It should have been a simple case of picking up a few unarmed suspects, or so he thought. It would become his job to visit Rick Stanek's family and deliver the bad news. How could he explain this? It could only be described as an accident, but who will believe it? Yet if it was a homicide, who would possibly believe that?

Walking down the stairs, he decided to get the tough job over with and inform Rick Stanek's family. He stopped briefly at Ted's, informing him that he would return the next morning.

Ted sat mesmerized, as Professor Steiner described his ordeal in fine detail, from Christian's knock at the door, to his enraged exit. The Professor relived every specific moment, as if savoring his encounter for what it really was—a confrontation of a lifetime. This myth that he had been pursuing, for the first time in Steiner's life, had became reality. Ted could only listen and observe as the Professor related his fear in an almost jubilant fashion. The contradiction of emotion was something Ted understood. Steiner had worked decades studying a creature that he believed existed, but didn't know for sure. He had endured criticism and ridicule from his peers on this subject, but as of this night, as frightening as it was . . . the Professor's theories were finally validated.

"I was correct. I was correct! He could not enter unless invited. You should have seen his eyes, they were mesmerizing. I could almost feel his anger from three feet away. I have no doubt had I invited him in, he would have killed me instantly. I opened the door and there he was, standing right outside the doorway."

They talked into the night and the hours flew past. About the tenth time that the Professor told his story, Ted fell fast asleep on the chair where he was sitting. At about the eleventh time, Steiner did the same.

DeathWalker

*　　*　　*

Christian had traveled back to his hunting grounds north of downtown and was walking the streets trying to shed his rage. He had been so close, that he could almost taste the revenge that he knew would be ever-so-sweet and fulfilling. He walked quickly and determined, as if working off excess energy. He was soon outside the neon lights, into a seedier part of town. His concentration was at its peak, and all sights and sounds were blocked out. Oblivious to his surroundings, Christian didn't hear the peddlers trying to hustle him as he briskly walked by. He didn't hear the beggars pleading for a dollar. Christian could only think of Ted Scott, and how close he had come to revenge.

So it was with great surprise that he felt a firm hand on his shoulder, and he was awakened from his trance by a loud, gruff voice.

"Hey, mother fucker, I'm talking to you!" The man was obviously upset. He was scary looking, compared to Christian. This man was as big as a bear. 6'6", about two hundred and fifty pounds, covered in tattoos and dressed in black leather.

Christian turned to face him, confused for the moment.

"You can't just walk through my block without paying the tax. You don't pay the tax, and you can't walk down here, understand? You don't pay the tax and you walk in here, you'll be lucky if you crawl out," he said, menacingly.

Christian just stared at him in silence, as if he couldn't believe this was happening.

"Are you fucking deaf or something? This is my street and I make the rules," the man stated with arrogance.

"You are wrong my friend, this I warrant. This is now my street," Christian responded.

"Who are you, the mayor or somethin'? Look dude, I could care less about your fancy suit. Understand? You've got about three seconds to empty your pockets, dick head. Now do it!" the mugger demanded.

Christian's mind was no longer on Ted as he became offended at the rudeness and disrespect of his next victim. Not very hungry, Christian decided to toy with him. He reached into his pocket, as he was still carrying the wad of bills he had acquired from the drug pusher the previous night. He slowly pulled out the wad in full view of his assailant and carefully peeled off one bill. He threw it at his feet. "Have your tax," he said, in a mocking tone.

"Pick it up, asshole!" the mugger yelled.

Christian smiled, as if amused, and stood silently.

"Okay, pale face, it's a new deal. You get the bill on the sidewalk and I get the roll in your pocket. Hand it over!" the mugger demanded.

Christian anticipated exactly what would happen next and his adrenaline was pumping. His eyes were starting to glow red and his fangs slowly became visible as they protruded from his mouth. The man reached for Christian's throat and as he did so, Christian grabbed his arm, digging in his long, sharp claws. The man countered by grabbing Christian's throat with his free hand. When he did so, Christian grabbed him by the throat with his other hand, and stared directly into his eyes.

"You have thirty seconds to live," Christian hissed.

The man that was so confident and aggressive, was now filled with fear as he tried to frantically pull away.

"Let me go! What the fuck are you? Let me go!" he yelled.

"Not before you pay my tax . . ." Christian growled.

He lunged forward, biting him on the throat. Not a fatal bite, but one that would only cause more pain, fear, and panic.

"AAAHHHH! Oh shit! What the fuck are you?" the man screamed.

As the blood flowed, Christian only became more excited. When the man tried to run away, Christian pushed him to the concrete.

"What do you want? Please, just tell me what you want?" the man howled.

"Blood! I want your blood!" Christian answered, smiling.

"No! Quit fucking around! Here, take my money," the man screamed, scrambling to his feet.

"In your next life, remember how it feels to be the victim," Christian hissed.

He then pounced upon his victim, biting and tearing at his throat savagely, as the mugger screamed in horror and pain. Soon it was done, and he stood over the dead, mangled body. He left the body as it laid, and continued his journey into the night. He felt justice had been served.

As he walked, he replayed the evening's events in his mind. How close he was to being invited into Ted Scott's apartment bothered him greatly. But it was the Professor's words that kept coming back to him. *"He is out with his girlfriend; you know how unpredictable young lovers are."*

DeathWalker

Christian smiled. '*Young lovers . . . young lovers. Young lovers no more . . .*' he thought. '*I will take Ted Scott's lover, as he has taken mine!*' The very thought of killing Ted's lover brought joy to his dark heart. He knew what she looked like, for his instincts had told him it was the girl he had met on the street. He also knew which building she lived in. He reached into his pocket, pulling out her pen. He smiled again, for he knew it might come in handy the instant he had taken it. He felt a wave of satisfaction as he raised his arms to the air and floated up into the sky.

Gliding through the night air, he was soon over Kathy's building. Long past midnight, the lights were out in all but a few apartments. Christian landed on the roof of the building next door and sat in the darkness, staring at the dark empty windows. '*Where are you, my dear? Where are you?*' he wondered. Thinking about Ted's lover brought back memories of his Anne. He knew she would never have believed how his life had changed and what he had become. He had truly become a predator. For one hundred years Christian had killed for survival and only survival. Now he was killing for the sake of killing, and he enjoyed it.

Christian sat in sad lament and whispered "Oh Anne, dear Anne, look what I've become. Look what I have become . . ."

Chapter Fourteen

Ted awoke abruptly to the constant ringing of the door bell. He had been fast asleep, still sitting in the chair in the living room.

"Who is it?" he asked.

"Ted, it's John. Let's go, buddy," John urged.

Ted buzzed him in. John Hall entered with his adrenaline pumping.

"Jesus Christ, guys, we're losing daylight here!"

The Professor awoke with a start. "Oh my goodness, it's late, isn't it?" he asked.

"Come on, guys. We're losing valuable sun time; let's go!" Hall sounded more like a drill sergeant than a partner in this search.

"Let me at least take a shower and have a cup of coffee, okay?" Ted pleaded. Hall nodded an affirmative.

"I now know what your vampire looks like, Mister Hall," The Professor stated.

"He was here?" Hall gasped.

"He could not enter, but he stood in the hallway. He was looking for Ted."

"Jesus Christ, he's got balls! You should have popped him right then!" Hall exclaimed.

"I mistook him for a visitor and besides, I know nothing of those weapons," the Professor answered.

"Well you best learn and learn quickly. The next time you see him, you just might need to defend yourself."

"He could not enter."

"Come on, Professor, let's get ready and get on with it!" Hall was anxious to proceed with the hunt.

144

DeathWalker

*   *   *

At about the same time, Mike Evans was entering the coroner's office.

"Paul, please say you have something for me?" he begged.

"Sorry, Mike, I can tell you that the three bodies have very similar wounds to the throat. Some of the starting points of those wounds are absolutely identical. Other than that, we found no prints, fibers, or fluids that are common to the three; nor can we absolutely attribute a single attacker common to all three. Of course, we still have to examine the fourth victim," Paul stated.

"Fourth victim? There's a fourth victim?" Mike's voice echoed in the sterile white tile room.

"Yeah. He was brought in last night. A giant guy, 6' 6", and maybe 260 pounds. He was torn apart pretty good. Looked like a bear got a hold of him and chewed on him a bit."

"What do mean, bear?" Mike asked.

"Well, the guy was a big man. I imagine only something bigger than him could have destroyed and mangled him like that. I didn't really confirm it was a bear, I used it as an example, since I have yet to examine him . . ." Paul explained.

"Yeah, a death resembling that would almost always have to be attributed to an animal attack. It *is* the only way to explain it, isn't it?" Mike asked, thinking about the supposed "bear" attacks earlier this year. He was now captured by the same curiosity that had ensnared Ted months ago. "Tell me about Rick Stanek?" Mike asked.

"Well, quite frankly, that one really baffles me," Paul responded.

"Like how?"

"Let me first say that in my time, I've seen a lot of 'jumpers.' I have also examined a few unlucky sky divers whose chutes didn't open. I know the difference from a high fall—let's say, ten stories—and a *very* high fall—let's say, 2000 feet. This one was somewhere in between. The state of the damage to this body tells me it was traveling at terminal velocity, over a hundred miles an hour, when it made contact with the pavement. This is not a guess, it's a fact. I was told he possibly fell from twelve stories. That makes absolutely no sense. Twelve stories equal, what, a hundred, maybe a hundred and twenty-five feet? No way, Jose. He would have had to fall from at least twice that high, judging from the bone damage. How do I explain this condition, unless he jumped from an airplane?" Paul was perplexed.

"How the hell do we explain it?" Mike responded. "Here he is landing in the middle of an intersection, hundreds of feet from any surface he could have fallen from? Then, he hits the ground at terminal velocity? What the hell is that?"

"It seems we are confronted with something that might not fit into the profile of we are normally used to dealing with."

"Thanks Paul, thanks a million. I've got to run . . ." Mike was literally off and running. He didn't buy into this "vampire" thing, but he knew that there was something highly unusual about what was happening in this city. Maybe Ted was on to something, even if his imagination was getting the best of him. He found himself speeding to Ted's condo. Mike now began to believe that possibly they were dealing with something outside the boundaries of what he considered reality.

*   *   *

"Let's go, let's go! Finish the damn coffee, for Christ sake. What is this, the breakfast club? We have got work to do and I don't want any daylight wasted!" John Hall was yelling, as he was anxious to get on with the hunt.

The apartment buzzer sounded, and it was Mike Evans. He entered, and before he could say a word, Ted was quick to tell him that he had no time and would talk with him later, but Mike interrupted.

"I'm going with you on this hunt. Let's not talk about vampires, but let's say that I believe you're on to something. Besides, I have a few things that you may need. One, a badge, in case you get stopped for trespassing, and two, a police radio, in case we have a problem and need support of some type. Where do we start?" Mike asked.

"Are you serious?" Ted asked.

"Very serious," Mike replied.

"Leave your ticket book here, detective, because this may get a little rough. Don't expect him to put his hands up," John Hall chided.

"Look guys, get the damned jokes over with and get down to business, because I'm going with and that is no joke. I viewed a body in the morgue

DeathWalker

of what was a man that was six foot six and built like a cage fighter, lying in a heap, mangled like a rag doll. Yes, I want in on this!"

The Professor spread the blueprint across the table and pointed to a specific area. "Here is where I assumed that a vampire might be hiding if he wanted guaranteed peace and darkness. Here is where it would be. There are three main tributaries in the drainage system; this one is the closest to Ted's building. Right at the beginning there are two drain pipes that feed into this particular tributary. At this point, because gravity drives the water overflow, these are the highest, driest, and darkest, because they are a dead end—one way in and one way out. We can enter at this point, where 394 crosses 10th, about a mile away at the overpass. We should be able to enter and examine this whole section and still be out within daylight hours. This, gentlemen, is where we will start."

As the Professor talked, Ted was loading his crossbow pistols into a gym bag, along with a generous supply of wooden arrows. Locking up, they would all travel together in John Hall's van. Within a few minutes they parked, and the large entrance pipe was in sight, just as the Professor had stated. Hall, who was an expert at hunting, gave the orders.

"This is it, guys. Check the lights on your helmets. I've got a few flares that I will bring along. Professor, you carry the large spotlight. Teddy, take these extra batteries, and stuff them in your pocket. These headpieces are all tuned to the same channel. Put them on. If one of us whispers, everyone will hear it, okay?" Everyone nodded. "Okay, guys, it's party time!"

Together, they walked down the hill to the drainage system entrance. Surveying the opening, it was seven to eight feet in diameter, which was large enough to walk upright down the center, but only in single file. John Hall offered to lead the way.

Even though the screen blocking the entrance was somewhat bent back, as though someone had entered previously, Hall took his wire cutters and started cutting a hole so that they could easily walk through. "Look the other way . . ." he ordered Mike Evans, kiddingly. "I don't want to get a ticket for destroying public property." John laughed and Mike looked away with shrug.

"It will be about half a mile, walking single file, before we reach the main storm drain. Once there, it's large enough for us to walk side by side," Professor announced.

Ted had always avoided going into closed-in, dark places, for fear of becoming claustrophobic. As he stared at the storm drain, he knew this would be his big test. At the end of this day, he would absolutely know whether he was truly claustrophobic or not.

Hall set the marching order. "It will be me, then Ted, followed by the Professor. Mike, you bring up the rear, and remember, everyone, you don't have to yell with those microphones on; if you do, you'll blow our damn eardrums out. Let's do it!"

They walked slowly into the large concrete pipe. At first, the darkness wasn't a factor, as the daylight shined brightly, illuminating the tunnel. However, as they moved further and further away from the opening, it became completely dark. Looking back, only a pinhole of light could be seen behind them. It was about a city block into the drain when John Hall picked up a foul odor in the air.

"Do you smell that?" John whispered.

"Yeah," they answered in unison.

"Sewerage . . ." Ted suggested.

"No sewerage down here, this drain is for rain or storm overflow," the Professor answered.

"Be careful . . ." Ted whispered.

At that moment, all of them were having a different reaction to anticipating an encounter with a vampire. In the lead, John Hall felt the chill of fear as he remembered Indian Joe's words on the night he was killed. "Smells bad . . ." Joe said, before they saw Christian for the first time.

Ted felt his mouth go dry and hands begin to sweat, as he had flashbacks of red eyes and glistening white fangs only a few feet from his face. He clutched his crossbow for dear life as they moved slowly forward.

The Professor felt his heartbeat begin to race with excitement at the prospect of this encounter, while Mike Evans followed along with his police instincts in fine tune, as this was more-or-less a routine search.

John proceeded cautiously and within ten yards, was able to see what looked like a human body wrapped in a filthy blanket lying in the center of the drain, blocking the way.

"I've got something here . . ." he whispered as he raised his crossbow pistol and froze in his tracks.

"Be very careful," Ted said softly. "They move very fast." As he spoke, he realized his mouth was so dry that his voice was cracking.

DeathWalker

Hall walked up cautiously within kicking distance, and kicked at the feet of the body. "Get up. Get up now!" He ordered. The body stirred and moved slowly.

Hall took careful aim as all of them froze in place and held their breath in anticipation. "I said, get up *very* slowly," Hall ordered again.

The body was now moving and beginning to sit up. "What the hell? I didn't do anything. Leave me be. I don't have anything." It was the voice of an old black man. As he spoke, a wave of fear lifted as they all relaxed, at least for the moment.

"We're not here to harm you. It's okay. Just move out of our way and let us pass." Hall continued to watch the man closely, as he didn't uncover himself as he started to stand up. Hall maintained a steady aim, just in case this was some kind of vampire trick.

"I'll move, I'll move," the old man answered as he stood up, squinting at the light shining in his face. He moved to the side, molding his body to the wall of the drain. "Go on, go on by," he urged.

One by one, they crossed his path as they slowly moved by. They held their breath, for his foul odor was overwhelming.

"Jesus Christ! That was awful!" Ted exclaimed.

"Hey, get ready, for God knows what else is down here . . ." Mike warned.

Only John Hall had ever experienced such darkness, so the rest of them found the lightless atmosphere very frightening. They could look beyond the distance of their helmet lights and see nothing but a black wall; black and thick as if it were a solid barrier. Ted wondered if they had made a mistake, for this was not favorable ground in which to do battle with a creature that can see them clearly in the dark. He knew his first shot would have to count, given these circumstances. They continued to travel on further into the darkness and away from civilization. Finally, John Hall spotted the end of this small drain, as well as the drop-off entrance into the main storm tunnel.

"We're at the intersection," Hall whispered. "There is a drop-off, and I'm not sure how many feet down it goes." He shined his helmet light downward and could see the concrete floor of the main drain. "It's only about four feet. I'm going in." With that, he jumped into the darkness. "It's okay, clean and dry. You guys help the Professor." Hall shined his helmet in all directions. He knew from the map that he should guide them to the right. One by one, they dropped into the huge main drain.

"How the hell are we going to find the exit out of here?" Ted asked.

"I'm pretty good at finding my way out, Teddy, but if it really worries you, I can leave a flare. It will burn for hours." John Hall offered.

"I don't know about anyone else, but it would sure make me feel more comfortable," Ted responded, and everyone else agreed.

When Hall lit the flare, the burst of red light blinded them all. Adjusting, it was a pleasant break from the surrounding darkness. They stood there for a few moments to enjoy the light, but John Hall wanted to continue the hunt. "Let's go guys," he ordered and proceeded into the vast concrete tunnel. It was gigantic, measuring some twenty feet across, and it was hard to imagine it being a pipe. It was built to accommodate and contain huge amounts of water and overflow from the whole city area and carry it to the Mississippi. Again, as they walked away from the flare, the light slowly disappeared and left only a glowing red dot to mark their exit in the background as they marched into darkness. The next twenty minutes of walking seemed like hours, as there was no scenery to judge movement. It was like walking a treadmill in a pitch black room.

It wasn't long before they were all struck with a repulsive stench. Again, they stopped dead in their tracks.

"This is awful," Ted whispered.

"Yeah. It's different than that stinky old man back there . . . it's worse . . . a lot worse . . ." Hall answered.

"What the heck is it?" Ted asked.

"I don't see anything yet. I . . . I don't know," Hall answered.

"Guys, don't panic, but I'm familiar with that odor. It's something dead and rotting . . ." Mike sounded sure of the source of this odor, for as a detective, he had encountered it many times before.

John Hall led them slowly and carefully forward. His mouth went dry and palms were now sweating as he raised his crossbow and proceeded with extreme caution. It was only a few yards before he spotted the source of the foul smell. It was a rotting dead body, just as Mike had predicted. John Hall stepped closer and could see it was a woman, only half clothed with her throat torn open. Her skin reflected the helmet light as it was pure white, as if drained of every drop of blood. "Oh shit . . ." he whispered.

As he stepped aside to move around the body, the others all came forward, shining their helmet lights on the macabre rotting sight. As Hall stepped aside and forward, he tripped and stumbled over something else. Maintaining his balance, he shined his helmet light down and could see

DeathWalker

another leg. As he moved the light across the floor, it was clear it was another body, in much the same rotting condition as the first. "Jesus Christ, another one!" Hall gasped.

The stench was overwhelming, and Ted and the Professor were gagging. Everyone was talking at once. "What the hell do we do?" Hall asked.

"Jesus Christ, Jesus Christ!" is all Ted could manage to say, covering his mouth and nose with a hand.

"My God, look at these poor girls!" the Professor cried.

"God, we walked into his damned feeding ground!" Hall exclaimed.

"This could be a vampire's lair," the Professor assumed.

"Yeah, it could also be some kind of serial killing psycho!" Hall muttered.

"I'm calling this in," Mike announced.

Still gagging, the Professor was barely able to say "No, no! Look up! Look up!"

All of them shined their helmet lights upward, and there, hanging from the ceiling of the pipe, was a vampire, hanging upside down. His hands were crossed over his chest and he was in a deep trance. As horrific a sight as it was, there was even a more frightening factor. This vampire was not Christian. This was not the vampire that they were looking for, and a blanket of fear ran through the group. The vampire was hanging and obviously in a deep sleep, for their noise didn't even cause him to stir. He just hung there with his arms folded over his chest, as if resting in a coffin. For an instant, they stood staring at the frightening sight.

"What the hell is that? Jesus Christ, I don't fucking believe it!" Mike blurted. "I'm calling for help!" he whispered.

"No!" the others whispered in unison.

They all were frozen for a second, just staring at the macabre sight. It actually looked dead, yet they all knew it could become alive in an instant. Ted broke the silence.

"There is no help, only us," Ted explained.

"Bullshit! I have never seen anything stand up after being hit with this nine millimeter." Mike replied as he drew his gun.

"Mike, guns won't do shit to this monster. It's up to us. Why do you think we brought crossbows instead of shotguns?" Ted asked. Mike held his weapon anyway and was ready to fire.

Hall asked "Who takes the first shot?"

"Can you hit him in the heart?" Ted asked.

151

"Yeah," Hall stated confidently.

"Professor, get ready to turn on the spotlight. Point it directly at him. Assuming John hits him, follow the fall of his body to the floor. I'll be ready with a second shot." Ted ordered. "Go ahead and aim John." Ted whispered. "Shoot and turn on the light on three. Ready? One . . . two . . . three!"

The click of the crossbow was followed by the blinding blast from the huge spotlight. The arrow hit the vampire solidly in the chest but above the heart. He awoke with a deafening scream, turning a summer-salt in mid-air and landing upright on his feet. Everyone froze in stark terror, as the vampire immediately came forward in attack mode, with fangs glistening in the bright light.

John Hall was shaking uncontrollably, trying to load his weapon as the vampire rushed forward, now within arm's reach. The vampire's screams of anger were interrupted by a solid and sickening "thud." Ted had fired his arrow and hit him directly in the heart with the backup shot. The vampire dropped to his knees and began tearing frantically at the fatal arrow, which was barely sticking out of his chest. Hissing and screaming, the sounds were unearthly. Then suddenly, there was complete silence as he crashed face down on the concrete floor.

"Professor, thank God you kept the light on him," Ted whispered.

"Teddy, thank God you made that shot!" Hall gasped in relief. "I really thought I bought the farm!"

"I don't fucking believe it, I don't fucking believe it, did you see that fucking thing?" is all Mike Evans could say. "A vampire! A fucking vampire! I guess you got your guy, Teddy!" Mike proclaimed.

"No . . ." came the joint answer.

"I don't know how many of these things there are, but this isn't the vampire we expected to find. He's still out here somewhere . . ." Hall explained.

"Give me a break, are you saying there are more of these things flying around at night?" Mike uttered in total disbelief.

"I'm sorry to say, but yes, detective. Yes, there are," the Professor answered.

"I'm calling it in," Mike stated. He grabbed his radio and began calling.

DeathWalker

"This is detective Evans, over." He waited for a response. "I need massive support. We've got a few bodies and a clean-up needing to be done. I also need forensics and an investigating team. Listen to me. We are in the main storm drain that runs under the city. We entered at 394 and 10th. We are deep into the main storm drain tunnel, that's all I know. If there is a service entrance directly into this main drain, you can possibly drive in here. If you do, we're near the very beginning. Over."

"Detective, can you stay at the radio? I'm going to get an expert from the water and sewers, please stay online. Over."

"10-4," Mike responded.

There was dead silence. Then, clearly, movement could be heard directly ahead of them. It sounded like something moving and brushing against the concrete. The sounds gradually faded into a distant echo.

"What the hell was that?" Mike asked.

"I'm sorry to say that we possibly have another vampire. It sounded like it went deeper into the storm drain," Hall guessed.

"If he did, he's going to be at a dead end shortly." the Professor predicted. "There is no way out in that direction for a vampire; only daylight."

"Well, guys, it's either going to sit and wait at that end, or it's going to be coming back this way pretty quick. I'd shine your helmet lights in that direction. Professor, shine the spotlight forward and to the ceiling above," Ted ordered.

"I'm lighting some flares," John Hall stated.

Hall started lighting flares and placed them further up the tunnel, toward the dead end. Soon, they were engulfed in an eerie red glow. John Hall walked back, proclaiming "Now we will at least see the damn thing coming."

"Detective Evans? Over," came from Mike's radio.

"Evans, here," he responded.

"Detective, we found that there is a service ramp that leads into a drain, about three miles from where you're possibly located, at Lowery Hill. It will take a few minutes for the department to get a key to unlock it. Expect to see headlights coming in your direction in about fifteen minutes. We just need to confirm your location as the main storm drain that runs parallel to 4th Avenue South, over."

"Confirmed, over," Mike Evans replied.

"We're on our way, Detective. Over and out."

153

"The calvary is on its way." Mike announced with relief in his voice.

"Yeah? Well, what are you going to tell them when they arrive, Detective?" Hall asked.

"Well, I'm not going to mention this vampire shit. The dead guy over there is a psycho and these bodies are his victims. He attacked, you shot him. That's the story I'm telling," Mike stated.

"What were we doing down here with crossbows?" Ted asked.

"Our hunter friend, Hall, from the Forestry Department, thought a large animal was loose in this drain, which is why you were here in the first place. Sound logical?" Mike asked.

"Okay with me," Hall answered.

"Don't go talking about how he was hanging from the ceiling. He came at us out of the darkness, you understand?" Mike asked.

"Okay."

"Yes."

"Yeah," they all answered in unison.

They were all pacing back and forth frantically, and instead of looking toward the end of the drain where the other vampire had escaped, they found themselves looking toward the opposite direction in anticipation of seeing the headlights of the police cars. Suddenly, they all jumped, as a loud "smash" was heard and screams erupted echoing through the tunnel. The vampire had struck John Hall.

"Aaaahhhh, shit, get her off, get her!" Hall screamed.

It was a female, and she was tearing at Hall's throat with her fangs. Blood was spattering everywhere as she attacked in an uncontrollable frenzy. She was obviously the mate of the vampire they had killed, and was taking her vengeance out on Hall. Her attack lasted a few seconds, as she had caught Hall off guard and vulnerable. She dropped his dead body to the ground. She stood in the glowing red light of the flares with blood dripping from her mouth, and hissed a guttural sound of defiance, facing them.

Mike Evans, in a reflex, drew his nine millimeter and started firing. He watched as her body flinched every time a bullet hit solidly. He fired nine shots and she was still standing there, growling like a wild animal. He froze in shock and disbelief.

"Click, thud," as Ted's arrow hit. But it missed her heart and pierced her shoulder. "Oh shit!" Ted cried, as he fumbled to reload with a trembling hand.

DeathWalker

Mike's automatic pistol held 15 shots and he began firing again watching her body jerk as each bullet found its mark. She continued moving forward and screaming like an animal that was possessed. The sound was deafening, as it was echoing in this huge concrete chamber.

Having finally reloaded, Ted fired once again. This time the arrow found its mark. Her scream changed to one of pure, high pitched agony. She turned to run away, but collapsed, falling into a fetal position. Her last whining gasp brought complete silence.

The Professor ran for John Hall and immediately turned his head away, once at Hall's side. "Oh God, oh God, he's dead. Oh God, he's dead," he kept repeating.

"Oh, Jesus, no!" Ted ran to John's body. One glance at his throat and he knew there would be no pulse. "Son-of-a-bitch, son-of-a-bitch!" Ted cried out.

They all stood silently in the red glow of the flares, amidst five mangled bodies. No one spoke a word as Ted took his jacket and covered John Hall's head. When the head lights of the police cars and rescue vehicles approached, none of them hardly took notice. The tunnel lit up with approaching lights, and they were shocked to see additional bodies in various states of decomposition, lying beyond the area that was lit by their flares. Five police cars and two rescue vehicles soon arrived. Viewing the bodies, some of the officers drew their guns.

Mike's captain could only exclaim, "My God, what happened here?"

Mike took a deep breath and began explaining. "We went hunting for a bear and ran into a couple of psychopaths. We found this burial ground by accident. Looks like we surprised them." Mike pointed to John Hall's body. "Captain, he's one of our group, a Forestry Department employee." He pointed to the vampires. "They are the perpetrators. The rest are their victims."

The captain slowly walked about, covering his mouth and nose with a handkerchief. He turned to Mike. "Arrows?" he asked unbelievably. Lifting the jacket off John Hall's head, he looked quickly and shook his head. "Mike, I will really be anxious to read this report." He walked further down the tunnel, viewing a body that was almost skeletal. "Boy, you really tripped onto something . . ." he then turned and yelled, "Get a photographer down here, before anything is moved. Don't let anyone in the storm drain. Put a guard at that service entrance!" as he yelled, he walked toward Mike. "Looks like you solved a number of missing-persons cases in one giant swoop. If you want to go and start the paperwork, I'll take over from here."

Mike looked toward Ted and the Professor. "Can we take them home? They're my friends. I think they've had enough for one day," Mike asked.

"It's your case, do as you like." The captain responded.

As they rode back to daylight, Mike told them both that he would handle the details and inform them of the report the next morning. Mike had the car drop them at Ted's condo, and he continued on to the station to start filling out the police reports. Silently, they entered the condo and sat staring at each other. Finally, Ted spoke. "Looks like you have a few more chapters for your book, Professor."

"One of them will be very sad, Teddy. Very sad, indeed," Steiner said solemnly.

Chapter Fifteen

As the sun set, Christian awoke sharply. He walked from the deserted building to once again make the journey to Ted's building. He was hungry and wondered how long it would be before a meal would come in his direction. As usual, it wasn't very long. Only a few blocks from his lair, a homeless man approached. He was old, feeble, and barely able to walk. His defeated appearance caused Christian to lose his hunger—if only for a moment.

"Please, mister, can you spare a buck?" the old man asked, looking at Christian with eyes that were heavy with pain and sadness. Christian stopped and studied this pitiful being, and looking at his old, worn appearance, his hunger was quickly forgotten.

Instantly reaching into his pocket, Christian produced the large wad of bills that he had been carrying for two days. This pitiful old man needed a "buck," and Christian was carrying a wad that was meaningless to him. He looked down on the old man, handing him the whole bankroll of hundred dollar bills. Overwhelmed, the old man's eyes began to well up into tears, as he was speechless.

"This is your lucky night, old man. You will never know how fortunate you are."

The old man could only utter in reply, "Thanks! Thank you mister!" Christian continued on his journey, as there was no emotion attached to his spontaneous reaction.

Maybe the old man just wasn't appetizing enough, or maybe Christian felt charitable toward this old soul. Christian didn't think nor analyze his own action, for it was purely instinctive. It was possible that walking amongst humans had awakened shreds of long buried emotions. Christian didn't analyze this action; it was simply what he was driven to do at that particular moment.

Christian quickly became hungry again. As he continued his walk, his eyes scanned the streets in a predatory fashion, looking for signs of a warm blooded meal. Standing a block away was what appeared to be a man looking in Christian's direction. Curiously, Christian did not sense him as being warm blooded. They walked toward each other; their eyes never left each other's body. They each watched the other's specific movements as two gunfighters might before they draw their guns and fire.

They were soon standing five feet apart, staring at each other intensely as if assessing each other's very being. Christian knew what this being was, and felt repulsed by his very presence. To him, it was another male vampire intruding on his territory. They looked each other up and down without speaking. Each mirrored the other's exact movements. Christian's adrenaline started to climb and the red glow began to emanate from his eyes, as though a confrontation was inevitable.

To Christian, this vampire looked to be younger and of this century, with his ponytail and earrings. Christian had seen people dressed like this in the Riverside area on the other side of downtown. A man would not be caught dead wearing such things in Christian's era. He was slight of build and smaller than Christian, but this was not an important factor. In the world of vampires, it is ferocity—not size—that is the determining element of survival. Their eyes mirrored deep hatred, for a vampire's territory is sacred, and each would protect it to the death. They live in secrecy; surviving on human blood without being discovered and hunted takes great skill, strategy, and fineness. Too many vampires in one territory can create too many deaths or a shortage of food—thus, discovery and extermination.

At the same moment that Christian had about made up his mind to become aggressive, the other vampire moved away. He was not conceding anything; he was just continuing on his journey. They watched each other intensely as each walked in opposite directions. Christian knew that if ever they met again, it would be fatal for one of them. This was the first male vampire he had ever encountered in his whole existence, and his reaction was purely instinctive. He had no desire to "socialize" with his own kind, for other than their mates, vampires are solitary creatures. It is this secrecy that allows them to maintain the favorable perception of being a myth, and not a frightful and horrible modern reality.

As he walked on, he regained his composure to the extent that he realized his hunger had yet to be satisfied this night. He walked slowly, assuming his dinner would be forthcoming, as usual. He was quite correct. As he scanned the streets of this urban jungle, a large automobile pulled

DeathWalker

up to the curb and a Latin man jumped from the car. "What's up man? You lost, man?"

Christian could see there were two more Latin men in the car. They appeared strange, for on this pleasant late summer night, their shirts were buttoned up to the collar and they had bandanas wrapped on their heads.

"No, I am not lost."

"Come on, come on, Amigo. You can trust us. Jump in; we'll take wherever you need to go. We can see you are lost or something. Come on, we just want a few bucks for gas," he stated, as he was trying to convince Christian to enter the car with them.

Christian had never ridden in a "horseless carriage," and though he knew the intentions of these men was not to merely give him a ride, he also thought that this might prove interesting.

He responded with, "Why thank you, I think I *will* ride along with you."

The man opened the car door for Christian and winked to his buddies, as if scoring a major victory, thinking he had lured his victim. Once comfortably seated, the littler Latin spoke up. "Where to, Amigo?"

Christian smiled knowingly, for he knew it didn't matter where he said he wanted to go, as these men had their own agenda. "I would like to be taken downtown, if you would be so kind," he replied gently, with an honest smile and excited anticipation.

They were all exchanging glances and smiling when the driver stated, "I need to make one stop before we go downtown. It will just take a minute." He turned the car quickly away from the direction of the downtown area and proceeded to return north, deep into an area of neglect. Christian watched through the car window as the deserted warehouses and factories turned to vast areas of rubble, where buildings had been torn down. It was at one of these lots that contained only debris of what once was, where the car suddenly pulled over.

"Okay, here is where you get out. The only question is whether you are able to walk out, or whether we dump your body here," the little Latin man stated with arrogance. As he did so, the man riding in the front passenger's seat turned around, brandishing a large handgun while grinning from ear to ear. The driver only stared forward and sat motionless, waiting for something to happen before driving off.

159

Christian smiled with joy, as this ride was turning out exactly as expected. "I enjoyed my first ride in an automobile. Now I am hungry and must eat," he stated happily.

"Are you stupid or something?" the little Latin man asked. "Your first ride in a car? Where you been, the funny farm or something? Give me your fucking money you middle-class-majority-looking-white-mother-fucker!" he demanded.

The novelty was over and Christian was hungry. He reached his right hand out, grabbing the little man with the big mouth, and pulled him in front of himself, looking him directly in the eyes. This also acted as a shield and barrier to the man in the front seat with the gun. The little Latin man uttered one word, "You" as Christian bit into his throat and enjoyed the flow of the warm, sweet nourishment.

The driver glanced into the rear view mirror and it looked as though his Latin buddy was being held up in empty space by nothing but air, but the sounds he heard were sickening. Turning around, he could now clearly see their passenger looked to be kissing his buddy's neck.

"What the fuck? Kill that mother fucker, don't be kissing him!" the driver exclaimed. The man in the passenger's seat came over the rear seat, in an attempt to help separate his friend and get a clear close shot with his gun. "Hey, mother fucker!" he yelled.

As he continued feeding, Christian reached out and grabbed the man, pulling him over the seat by the throat. "Let go, you son of a bitch!" he screamed. The driver, so intent on looking forward to a fast getaway, was totally confused by the chaos.

"Kill that fucker and let's get out of here!" he demanded, while still remaining focused directly forward, prepared for a fast getaway.

One look at the damaged state of the little Latin man, and the passenger side man went completely hysterical. He saw the blood and the torn throat and then the red eyes and fangs of a monster the likes of which he had only seen in horror movies. "Oh shit! L-let me go . . . what are you? Help me, God, please help me!" He was screaming, trying to use his force to push himself away from Christian, to no avail. Christian now pushed his first victim to the side, and lunged for his next dinner course, which was still being held by the throat. He bit down with great pleasure. "Aaaahhhhhggg—" is all that was heard.

At that instant, the driver glanced in the rear view mirror and could only gasp, seeing the blood and the remains, while now realizing their

DeathWalker

passenger had no reflection. "Dear Jesus!" he cried as he opened the door and took off running, as fast as his feet could carry him. Christian ignored his escape and continued to drink his fill. Within minutes, he was completely satisfied. Exiting the car, he smiled. "Thank you so much for the ride, it was quite pleasing." There was no response from the two corpses in the back seat, who died with expressions of horror forever recorded on their faces.

It seemed that it was always following a good meal when Christian enjoyed flying the most. He took to the air in ecstasy, looking down at the warm blooded beings scurrying below. He felt invincible; not only did he not need to hunt in this modern culture, he was also beginning to understand that this new society, of which he was once so afraid, now did not even recognize or acknowledge his very presence, or even imagine the possibility of his existence. This was a freedom he had never known in his whole one hundred years. *'If only Anne could be here.'* he thought, as he glided in a dark sky that seemed to embrace his powerful presence.

He landed behind Kathy's building and walked around to the busy street in front. He examined the entrance and noticed a man standing near the street corner. "Excuse me, sir. I watched a young woman walk into this building with a brief case. She had brown hair and is about thirty years old and about this height," he held out his hand to about a five foot high level. "She dropped a very expensive gold pen and I was wondering if you lived here and if you knew of her? I would like to return her pen," Christian explained.

"Sorry man-" he knocked on his sunglasses. "-but I'm blind. Yeah, I live here, but I haven't seen a woman in forty years. I know them by voice, smell, and by touch. I like the touching part!" he kidded. "Sorry, I can't help you."

"Oh, I am sorry. I presumed you had sight," Christian apologized.

"Haven't you ever seen one of these?" the man held out his white cane.

"Yes, it's a cane, but why does that have meaning?" Christian asked.

"Are you color blind or something? It's white. White cane equals blind dude. It goes together," the man snapped.

"I apologize; I do not wish to be disrespectful. I am not from around this area," Christian responded.

"This area?" The blind man laughed. "Listen to me, my man. You sound a little inexperienced, as if you just flew in from another planet. Let

161

me warn you. Don't be taken in by anyone that talks friendly around here. This is the big city. They'll set you up and take you to the cleaners—and that's if you're lucky," the blind man offered.

"How do you survive?" Christian asked.

"Anyone screws around with me and they'll get this white cane over their skull."

Christian enjoyed the spirit of this man. "How is it that you became without sight?"

"Vietnam," he replied.

"I am sorry, I don't understand?" Christian responded.

"Viet . . . Nam. What else is there to say?" he responded again. "You know, that little conflict in the jungle where over fifty thousand of our soldiers died? I guess it's only the wars with Roman numerals after them that most people remember."

"Ah yes, Vietnam. Once more, I apologize." Christian, as well educated as he was on world geography, had no knowledge of what Vietnam was, for that country didn't exist by that name in the 1890's.

"Look, my friend, you sound sincere, and so I'll help you with a bit of advice. On the sixth floor is a woman that's about 5' 2". I can tell that by the sound of her voice when she speaks. Judging by her vocabulary, she's a professional and is likely to carry a briefcase. I'd guess from the energy in her voice that she's in her late twenties or early thirties. She smells very nice but I haven't given her the touch test yet, so I can only guess she's attractive by the way men comment as she walks by. You see, blind men can hear things other people don't pay attention to. I hope this helps you."

"Thank you. This does help me. Should I knock on every door?" Christian asked.

"Jesus Christ, where are you from? Go into the hall and ring each sixth floor doorbell. There's a little speaker and they will ask who you are. If you recognize her voice, you'll know. If you don't, just excuse yourself and try the next one. If and when she does answer, she'll buzz you in," the blind man explained. "One last word, my friend. If you're some kind of deviate and hassle her any, I promise I'll find you and break this cane over your head." The blind man smiled, as if enjoying the very thought.

Christian liked this blind man, as he had courage and spirit. He walked into the lobby of the building. The wall, as the blind man had explained, was a row of names with buttons next to them. As he studied

DeathWalker

those of the sixth floor, only three had names of women. He pressed the first one. "Hello, who is it?" an elderly woman asked.

"I apologize, it seems I pushed this button by mistake," was his response

He waited a second, and then pushed the next button. "Yes, who is it?" a warm voice asked. Christian knew immediately it was her, the one he was looking for, and he made his next move.

* * *

Ted and the Professor took a break and were eating pizza. Both had spent much time writing, having recovered from the morning's ordeal. The reporter in Ted forced him to chronicle the details of the experience. The scholar in Steiner wrote an analysis of the same. Though the lights were turned on, Ted had closed all the drapes and blinds, for they knew it was likely they were being watched, or so they thought. They had no idea that Christian had turned his full attention to Kathy.

* * *

Having finished all his paperwork, Mike Evans was being interrogated by his Lieutenant.

"Mike, tell me the truth. I read your report, but a little voice inside me is saying 'bullshit.' Come on, off the record, level with me. What really happened down there?"

"Look, the report says it all," Mike responded.

"Well, if I believe every word of it, this means we caught the people that tore the heck out of those other victim's throats also. We can stamp a case closed on those bodies too. Likely, we will not have that problem in this city again," The lieutenant surmised.

"I wouldn't say that . . ." Was Mike's response, for he knew that at least one more vampire was in existence.

"Why wouldn't you say that? You killed two freaks that were tearing the throats out of innocent random citizens. Why would you think this isn't the end of those crimes?" the lieutenant asked.

"I . . . I don't know. Call it a hunch," Mike replied.

163

"Hunch? Hunch? Who do you think you are; Omar, the psychic?" the Lieutenant yelled.

At that moment, an officer walked in and interrupted their discussion. "Boss, we've got two guys with their throats torn out, sitting in the back seat of a parked car in the abandoned business district. I mean fresh! When they found the car, the engine was still running." He quickly turned and left.

"Okay, Mr. Psychic, level with me," the Lieutenant pleaded.

"Look, I can't at this time. It's just a hunch, and it's completely bizarre," Mike replied.

"Bizarre? Bizarre? I'll give you bizarre. We now have six fresh deaths caused by a person that enjoys tearing out throats. We have a male suspect that leaves $500 tips in gay bars. We have a bum we picked up tonight trying to cash $100 that some guy gave him—$3000 worth! The man's description happens to fit our $500 gay bar tipper. We have a rookie officer that lands in an intersection, dying from a 200 foot fall, but wasn't in an airplane. We have gay bashers that saw a guy take off and fly away. But wait! I also have a man who lives in his car, who reported the same damned thing. A guy that looked like a businessman took off and flew into the air? Bizarre? Give me a fucking break! Come on, Mike, talk to me!" the lieutenant pleaded. "Look, you're in a dark tunnel, hunting something with crossbows. You kill two people. One is shot full of holes like Swiss cheese. Both have wooden arrows in their hearts and implants in their mouths. Damn it! Tell me what this is!" The Lieutenant pounded his desk.

"It's in the report, that's all I know." Mike stood his ground. He would never say the "V" word.

Exasperated, the Lieutenant dropped his head down and ordered, "Get out of here. Get the fuck out!"

It took only a minute before Mike was speeding, on his way to Ted's condo.

Their pizza party was interrupted by the door bell.

"Who is there?" Ted asked.

DeathWalker

"Mike. Buzz me in, Teddy." Ted could hear that Mike sounded frustrated. He soon entered, talking a mile a minute. "Teddy, I don't know what the hell to do. My lieutenant is putting it together. I believe he has suspicions that we were on a vampire hunt. He knows that I know, and wants me to talk about it. If I do, they'll probably lock me in a loony bin," Mike complained.

"I've got a hunch that he knows already. The fact that he's asking, is proof that he might be thinking the same thing we are, and will believe everything you tell him," Ted assumed logically. "He's probably looking for assurance that he's not the crazy one."

"Well, no damned way am I going to tell him exactly what I witnessed. Just so you both understand, this is what happened. For the record! Hall was hunting a wild animal that he had tracked to the drain system. Being friends and interested, we all went along. I went along because you were going onto city property. We were first attacked by the male. I dropped my gun in the darkness, and Hall and Ted took him out with their crossbows. The female came next, attacking and killing Hall. Assuming I was still without my weapon, you began firing arrows. I eventually added a few bullets, fifteen to be precise. That's what I know. I saw no red eyes, I saw no damned fangs, and I saw no one hanging upside down from the ceiling." Mike collapsed on the couch, covering his face with hands. "Jesus, I'm in deep shit. I'll either lie about this for life, or be branded a nut case."

"I don't think you have a thing to worry about," Ted stated.

"What the hell does that mean, Teddy?" Mike asked.

"I believe to get what he wants this vampire will become bolder and bolder, doing more and more killing. I believe that if you hold out a while, you won't have to be the first to say the word 'vampire'. People will be saying it for you." Ted fixed himself a drink.

"I believe Teddy is right," the Professor agreed. "We will not be the only ones who encounter this vampire, and in fact, we are not. We're just the few that are alive to talk about it. I believe that if this vampire persists in his revenge, the whole city will know and be aware, because they will not be able to attribute these deaths to a mortal man any longer. Mike, you might be worried about being branded a nut, but even so, you'll live through it. Ted here has the real problem; the vampire wants him dead . . . dead. Maybe you should think about that."

Ted shook his head. "One thing I can tell you . . . I won't make it easy on him. He'll remember me. Yes, he'll remember me," he whispered. He

165

walked to the window and opened the drapes, looking out over the dark sky. "Mike, I don't think your lieutenant will think you're crazy if you bring up the possibility of a vampire. In fact, I'd bet on it."

"Why? Why would say that Ted?" Mike asked.

"Look. Look out there." Ted pointed out into the sky.

Gathering at the window, they all witnessed the same sight—a police helicopter. It was flying low, and shining its lights in the sky and on roof tops.

Mike dialed the station. "This is Evans. Can you tell me why one of our birds is patrolling the sky over here near Oak? Yeah . . . yeah . . . okay, thanks." He turned and looked at Ted and the Professor with wonder. "I'll be a sonofabitch."

"What?" came the joint reply.

"They said that Lieutenant assigned it to patrol the sky and look for anything unusual in the area where Officer Rick Stanek died."

"Apparently, it appears that your lieutenant doesn't think the possibility of a vampire is all that insane," the Professor stated.

"Look guys, I'm going home. I really need some sleep. Tomorrow is another busy day. I've got the Captain to deal with, the Coroner, possibly the press. I also may have to call you in for your statements. If so, I'll write them, you sign them. Please stay here . . . don't go out, and don't talk to anybody about what happened," Mike ordered as he turned to leave. "By the way, John Hall's body is being shipped home to California. That's what his family requested." With that, Mike left.

Christian sat on a roof in the dark shadows, observing the helicopter, which was flying large circles in the dark sky. He had never seen a helicopter before, and found it unusual and mysterious. Unlike an airplane, it could hover and quickly change directions. He could see two men inside, and was tempted to fly up and get a better look, but decided not to. He had completed his work for the night and sat in quiet satisfaction, at having struck a blow toward his revenge of Anne. He had hurt Ted, and Ted had yet to know it. He sat, looking at the black sky and twinkling stars. He loved the night, and would spend the balance sitting in peace, absorbing the beautiful darkness.

Chapter Sixteen

ed awoke with only one thought on his mind; ending this stalemate. He realized that they would not be hunting vampires any longer, after the last fatal attempt to locate Christian resulted in the death of John Hall. It was likely that any further attempts would also end in some type of tragedy. They had lost Hall, and were still no closer to finding Christian than they were before they started. Ted liked John Hall, and felt an extreme burden of guilt over his death. There was only one solution that would absolutely bring an end to this nightmare.

Ted realized that living in fear becomes a burden. His condo, which was initially a safe haven, was slowly becoming his personal prison. Thinking about living half a life in the daytime and staying locked up in seclusion by night, was no longer a comforting thought. How long could he continue this? His life had become drawing the drapes at night, lining the windows with garlic, living with the Professor, and cringing every time there was a knock at the door after dark. No, this wouldn't do, and there was only one way out.

Ted decided that he would sit on the roof alone and wait to face Christian. He would take his crossbow pistol and give it his best shot. One confrontation and it would be over, and one of them would walk away, able to live their normal life—whatever that was. The more Ted thought about it, the more it made perfect sense, and he had made up his mind that it was exactly what he would do. It was like his father had once said. "If you can't get out of it, get into it!" He would not tell the Professor until evening, and until then, he would prepare his things in the event that this night was his last.

He was content in his decision, and relaxed for the first time in weeks.

"Good morning, Professor," Ted said as he entered the kitchen.

"Good morning, young man," Steiner replied.

"I've got some phone calls and some business to catch up on today. Is that okay with you?" Ted asked.

"Sure, sure. Just pretend I'm not around," Steiner answered.

Ted took his coffee to his desk and began writing a letter.

Dear Dad,

In the event that you are reading this letter, I am dead. I will leave it to Professor Steiner or Mike Evans to fill you in on the details that led to my death. I could not continue living in fear, and decided to face it and deal with it as you had taught me.

Please take care of Brutus for me. He should be no trouble, as he loves you a lot. Just make sure an eagle or hawk doesn't get him. My last manuscript is finished and is labeled on my desk. Please send it to my agent, Jules Porterfield, in Lincolnwood, Illinois. His address and phone number are both in my file.

When you hear the complete details of my death and what led to it, don't doubt it's the truth, as incredible as it sounds. Dad—never, ever venture out into the night when the woods are silent. I love you very much,

Your son,
Ted

His next letter was to Mike Evans.

Dear Mike

You will find a diary of the last few weeks; it's filed under "vampire." Thanks for all your help and the courage to come to my side at a time when I needed it most. I am asking for one more favor. Should I not survive, Please deliver my things (and Brutus) to my father. His phone number and address are in my files. I need for you to tell him the whole story, from beginning to end, even if it's "off the record."

There is no way I could continue hiding in my condo at night for the rest of my life. I chose to gamble on the fact that my aim would be true,

DeathWalker

should I not have the opportunity of a clear shot. I chronicled the whole story on my laptop computer in great detail. Again, thanks for risking your life.

God Bless you,
Ted

P.S. You can have my crossbow pistols. You might need them someday.

Ted continued writing letters all day. He wrote Kathy a long letter, telling her that she was the first woman in his life he had ever loved, and apologized for meeting her in these awkward circumstances. He wrote friends, relatives, and neighbors, each saying "goodbye." One by one, he neatly stacked them in pile on the desk. He was conflicted, for as sad as he felt writing his letters of farewell, he was also anxious to face his pursuer and end this, once and for all.

He knew this was what he had to do, and whether he survived or not, he hoped that Christian would be dead, or would satisfy his revenge and the killing would stop. It was evident he had no choice, for it was only a matter of time before this vampire would hurt him by connecting him with Kathy, or even his father. He did not want any harm to come to the Professor, who had come to aid, nor to Mike Evans, who stumbled bravely into this vendetta. Ted just wanted it over.

*   *   *

The Professor knew Ted was not his normal self, but reasoned who could be, after the ordeal that they had been through the previous day? As Ted sat as his desk writing, so did the Professor. He was writing a new chapter of his manuscript, and making corrections to his existing chapters, based on his new vampire experience. He learned that vampires could sleep while hanging upside down, and that based on what they had discovered, they would take victims to their lair for feeding purposes. He certainly witnessed that a bullet to a vampire was nothing more than an inconvenience, and also recorded that a wooden arrow was every bit as good as a wooden stake. He was overflowing with firsthand knowledge, and he was compelled to record it in specific detail.

169

The Professor was also having his own ideas about how to deal with this vampire. Why couldn't they just invite Christian in and ambush him? Possibly disable him with garlic and holy water and end his life? At least they would meet him on their conditions, which would certainly be more favorable than what they had experienced in the dark tunnel. He would wait until Ted was finished with his work before offering his idea.

This old professor, that once had a dream of just seeing and studying a vampire, was now thinking of joining the fight and killing one.

Mike Evans was in the coroner's office, contributing to the coroner's inquiry regarding the deaths and bodies found in the storm tunnel. Standing in a cold room with metal slabs filled with bodies, did not make for an enjoyable day. Based on what had happened the past few days, Paul Malone, the coroner, threatened to put up a "no vacancy" sign on the front of the building. He had never had so much work. He was totally confused by the state of two of the bodies. The two alleged murderers that had been killed via the crossbows had aged from the time they were transported to the morgue. When they were placed in body bags, they were described as a male, approximate age 35, and a female, approximate age 30. After opening the body bags, the male—aged 35—appeared more like he was 100, and the female appeared to be at least 80. What the officers suggested to be fang implants, x-rays had proven to be completely natural. Their bodies were in advanced stages of decomposition. Paul was confused, to say the least. Mike Evans could only offer that it was very, very dark in that storm tunnel. He did not say the magic word "vampire."

Besides those two vampire bodies and that of John Hall, there were six other bodies found, with four of the six having been identified. Two were missing-persons cases, two had been considered runaways, and the remaining two were unidentified because their remains were mostly skeletal.

"How do I explain two bodies that aged fifty years in twelve hours?" Paul asked.

"Why do you have to?" Mike responded.

"What do you mean?" Paul asked.

DeathWalker

"Just what I said. They're two psycho nobodies and they are now dead. Who is there to explain to? And why? You know what they did, you know the cause of death. They have no identification and their prints are clean. Just bury them as John and Jane Doe," Mike responded. "So the bodies aged? So what? Who the hell cares anyway?"

"I care! My people bag bodies that go in one age and come out another bothers me, okay?" Paul stated. "What do you know about this Mike? Level with me. What am I dealing with?" Paul asked. "My God! This is Minneapolis for Christ's sake, these things don't happen here! Do you listen to any of the talk radio? Citizens are frightened! What the hell am I dealing with? My superstitious Native American radar is going off!"

"You're the forensic expert, you tell me?" Mike retorted.

Paul walked to a desk and pulled out a clear plastic bag containing three short arrows. "Is there any coincidence that the same bodies that aged so drastically, also died from an arrow in their hearts? If I took these bodies out into the sunlight, would they go up in smoke?" Paul asked.

"Now who's getting crazy, Paul? Go up in smoke? Get serious," Mike responded.

"All I know is that we have way too many corpses with their throats torn out lately, and I've seen vampire movies, too." Paul answered. "Did you see the photographs of the crime scene in that tunnel?" Paul asked.

"No, not yet. Why?" Mike wondered.

"Well apparently, the same two bodies that had arrows sticking out of them also didn't like having their picture taken. They didn't show up on the film!" Paul explained.

"Paul, you say the 'V' word and you won't be coroner very long; you'll be working in the State hospital or locked up there," Mike stated.

"Then you do know!" Paul replied.

"I know that this isn't over yet. So expect a few more bodies in the near future," Mike said. "I'm not saying another damned thing."

"So there are vampires. I'll be God damned!" Paul gasped.

"I didn't say that. I never said it. I'm through here." Mike started to walk away, but then he turned and smiled. "Paul, don't be foolish enough to take one of those two bodies into the sunlight. They will go up in smoke—and I didn't say that either."

Mike felt a small bit of comfort knowing that his lieutenant and the coroner were both starting to believe in vampires. At least he was no longer alone in his stark raving lunacy.

Mike, too, was thinking along the same lines as the Professor. What if they set up a trap? What if they used Ted for bait? If he and Ted had crossbows, they could shoot at the same time. If they each had two crossbow pistols, they could get off four shots. It was risky, but it was better than what they had been through. He was anxious to talk to Ted about it. He was planning the strategy when his radio broke his concentration.

"Detective Evans? Over."

"Mike here," he responded.

"Lieutenant wants you in the office, pronto!"

"I'm on the way. Over and out."

Upon entering the office, he found the Lieutenant bending over a map. Noticing Mike, he called him to have a look.

"Mike, look at this. We just found a prostitute's bloodless body a few hours ago, right here." He placed an "X" on the map. "Now, we have an old homeless man that meets a guy who gives him a bankroll, here." He placed another "X" on the map. "Three Hispanics pick up a guy here, and he kills two of them, here." He marked two more "X's" on the map. "Another guy is sitting in a car, here, and sees a guy fly into the air." Again, he places an "X." "Lastly, a giant mugger gets torn to shreds here." The Lieutenant placed the last "X." He held up the map, which now displayed a hunting ground that was virtually on top of them.

"Our guy is living right within these few blocks of Third Street, north of Hennepin. He's almost living in our backyard, for Pete's sake!" the Lieutenant exclaimed.

"Only a few deserted buildings and store fronts for the most part. Maybe a few vacant lots, but little else." Mike studied the map and clearly saw the pattern. "Jesus Christ, you're probably right."

"I was once a detective you know, before I became a desk jockey and baby sitter. Now get over there and see what you can find first thing in the morning. Take what weapons you need and take a few men with you. I don't want the details, only the body," Lieutenant stated seriously.

Mike nodded. "I understand, sir."

"Mike, I know you're on to something. If you think that I don't understand that this rash of killings is unnatural, you're mistaken. I've read the reports and I know that you're dealing with something that may seem far too absurd to even talk about. So don't talk about it. If you have a method of stopping it, just proceed and take whatever you need."

DeathWalker

Mike understood clearly that his boss believed that possibly something far too frightening to discuss was at the base of these crimes. He answered, smiling knowingly. "Yes, sir."

"Now get the fuck out!" The Lieutenant yelled, and Mike walked out smiling and on his way to purchase two crossbow pistols.

*   *   *

Finished with his letters, Ted started gathering all his important papers and putting them in a box. His insurance policy, his mortgage papers, car title, bank books, copyright certificates, jewelry, and other treasured items. When finished, he scooped up Brutus and held him close while he put his feet up and watched television. He was saying goodbye to Brutus in his own way. Ted knew that this little four pound hair bag would take on this vampire in a second to protect him. He found a tear running down his cheek as he kissed Brutus on his forehead. "Wish me luck, little guy."

Though he had confidence in his ability with a crossbow, he knew that this was not going to be a turkey shoot. He would likely get one shot, and it had to be perfect. As he sat, he held his hand out, as if to check the steadiness. He had killed three vampires—what's one more, is how he tried to think of it. Yet deep in his mind, he knew that this time he would be alone. This time the vampire was stalking him . . . he was watching him . . . waiting for him . . . and he only wanted him and him alone.

The Professor watched as Ted sat there silently, as if in deep thought while the television played. He knew that Ted was not watching, even though he was sitting directly in front of it. Instead of tossing Brutus and chasing him around, Ted was holding him close, stroking him gently. The Professor knew something was surely wrong.

The television blared.

"TWO SERIAL KILLERS WERE CORNERED AND KILLED BY POLICE YESTERDAY. IT IS SAID THAT THEY MAY HAVE BEEN RESPONSIBLE FOR AT LEAST SIX DEATHS IN THE MINNEAPOLIS, SAINT PAUL, AREA. MORE ON THIS STORY AT SIX AND TEN."

Ted just stared with no comment at the obviously distorted news report. Because of his obvious change in behavior, the Professor was really worried.

173

Edwin F. Becker

"Teddy, if it's John Hall that's bothering you, it was not your fault. He wanted to go on that hunt. He offered on his own," the Professor stated.

"No, Professor, that's not it at all. I'm just getting my head together," Ted replied. "I have a few thoughts that I will share with you a bit later."

It was late afternoon, and Ted did not want to tell Steiner of his decision to face Christian alone until dark. He would wait until it would be too late to do anything or call anyone to stop him.

"Very well. I'm here if you wish to talk about it," the Professor responded. "Teddy, I'm going to use the phone in the kitchen, for I have a private call that I must make."

"Sure," Ted mumbled.

Proceeding to the kitchen, Steiner dialed Mike. He was not in his office, and the Professor asked for him to be paged. Within minutes, the phone rang. "It's for me!" yelled the Professor.

"Mike? I think Ted needs some help," Steiner whispered sternly.

"Help? Like how? What's going on?" Mike asked.

"I don't really know, but he's acting funny. It's like he's very depressed," Steiner reported.

"Professor, some depression is predicable. You can't kill anything without a delayed feeling of remorse. It will pass."

"No, I sense he is dealing with more than that."

"Professor, that's not all that unusual. You should be acting the same way. I went through it too. When a person experiences trauma, such as we did yesterday, it's not unusual that the next day it finally sets in. It is a normal post-trauma type of reaction. Normally, this reaction lasts one to three days. Any more than that and maybe I should get the psychologist to talk with him. Professor, remember not only did he lose a friend of sorts in John Hall, but Ted did actually kill two beings. It has to weigh heavy on his mind," Mike reasoned.

"What you say sounds logical, but I think he needs someone to talk with and I'm not that person," said the Professor.

"I'll tell you what, I'll stop by later this evening around ten or so if I can, okay? I've got some things to do tonight. I also have some things to tell you. I believe we may have located the area where Christian might be hiding. I'll be searching there tomorrow morning," Mike said.

"Oh my goodness. How did you find him?" Steiner asked.

"I'll tell you tonight. See you later." Mike hung up.

174

DeathWalker

*   *   *

At sundown, Christian left Kathy's apartment, where he had rested throughout the day. It was easy for him to take her, for he explained to her that he had found her gold pen, as it had fallen into the cuff of his pants. He told her he had traveled across town especially to return it to her. Being polite and excited to have recovered her lost pen, she invited him in for coffee, as gratitude for him taking the trouble of locating her and returning such a valuable item.

Kathy remembered Christian, as he had left her with the strong impression of being handsome, well mannered, and appeared a man of means, judging by his expensive, well tailored clothes. She had very little personal concern, and no fear. This was her fatal mistake. Once invited in, they sat and chatted. Christian directed the conversation to more of a philosophical one, avoiding current affairs, of which he had absolutely no knowledge. He liked the manner in which Kathy held her cup, so proper, *'As if she was raised in the east,'* he thought. Kathy thought Christian was ever-so-kind and thoughtful; plus, very European in his manners and etiquette.

"May I ask if you enjoy your profession?" Christian queried.

"Oh, I would enjoy it more if it was a hundred years ago," she stated.

Her comment struck him like a lightning bolt. "What precisely do you mean?" Christian asked.

"Being an attorney today is all about money. Working for a large law firm is almost like working for a bank. We evaluate each case and if we find it worthwhile in dollars and cents, we represent the client. I hate that aspect . . . but, if I opened my own practice, I would likely starve. So there I sit, in a corporate law firm, doing production law. A hundred years ago, we had ideals. It was about justice, not money." Kathy explained.

He watched closely as she spoke, and recognized the tone of dissatisfaction in her voice. "What is it that you enjoy in your free time?" he wondered.

"Solitude," she answered quickly. "Mostly solitude. I love the North Woods; I could sit in the wilderness for hours, just looking at the sky and enjoying the sounds and the smells of the woods." As Kathy spoke, there was a pleasure in her voice that was put there by the very thought of being away in the wild. Christian knew that feeling all too well, and could easily identify it. As she continued, he nodded, as if he understood her references to the technology that creates the stress she dreads so much, but actually had no clue. He was left with the impression she would enjoy being 'removed' from this society.

"And you? What do you enjoy?" she asked.

"I take pleasure in the night. I love the wilderness, also, but I find the night most alluring. The sounds of the night are a symphony to my ears. I find the glow of the full moon illuminating the woods beautiful and mysterious. Each and every night is a unique, pleasurable experience."

As he spoke, Kathy watched his enthusiasm and began to wonder '*Could it be?*' She began to realize that her guest fit the description that Ted had spoken of. Now, when he begins to speak of the night, his voice changed to one of such affection. It was as if he were speaking of his own private world. Strangely, Kathy didn't feel threatened, but thought it best that he leave.

"I'm sorry, but I must prepare for my date this evening," she explained as she rose from the table.

He rose, thanking her, and reached out to shake her hand. She responded in kind, and they touched. At first, he leaned toward her gently, as if to kiss her politely on the cheek, in a type of continental formality. When she turned her head to offer her cheek, he made his move. Embracing her, he found her neck was exposed and held her firmly as he bit down, sinking his fangs into her soft skin. For an instant, she struggled, but as her life's blood was drained, she succumbed to the inevitable and relaxed. Christian would not kill her . . . he decided she would become his new mate. It seemed fate had sent him the perfect replacement for his Anne.

She reminded him of Anne, with her strong spirit and intelligence. The fact that she could compete in a field dominated by men, told Christian that this was no ordinary woman. Plus, he found her beautiful, with dark hair and piercing eyes. He had fully intended to kill her until they sat and talked of love, life, and the future. She longed for a life of freedom, and seemed tired of the "rat race" as she called it, and the society that was obsessed with material things. She seemed to enjoy the beauty of life and the simple but magnificent gifts that nature provided. Her enthusiastic response about enjoying the night and stars captured his own feelings. And yes, she loved to fly, if only in an airplane or hot air balloon. In the end, he found he could not destroy her, and would keep her as his own. He decided to give her a freedom as she had never known existed. She

DeathWalker

would no longer enjoy the night—she would blend with it and soar like she had never imagined.

Taking her to brink of death, he bit into his own wrist and fed her gently as she "slept." It would only be a few days, and she would wake and they would leave this city forever. As he left the apartment this night, he only had one thought—he was hungry. The overwhelming feeling of revenge had subsided, and having taken Kathy, Ted was no longer a concern. Exiting the building, he walked down the first street toward the Mississippi, and would continue walking until his meal came to him as was his usual experience.

He did not worry about leaving Kathy, as he knew she would not awake this night. From talking with her, he knew she had few friends and also that she had a mind of her own. Anyone who knew her was used to her unpredictability. He saw her answering machine speak in her voice and record messages, so he was comfortable knowing people would think she was gone for a day or two, which, according to Kathy, was normal and routine. He needed to feed and to supply her with his blood, which would forever run through her veins. He walked slowly and scanned the streets for his dinner.

Christian's intent was only to feed and return to Kathy, guarding her until the metamorphosis was complete. He observed three young men watching him as he walked alone, moving north away from the downtown area. They followed him, lagging behind and talking softly to each other, as if planning the strategy of their attack. As he walked slowly, he could sense their presence getting closer and closer as their courage grew, and the street became darker and more deserted. His adrenaline began to rise in anticipation of gorging himself on warm, sweet, human blood. They could not see his face, for if they could, they would have run for their very lives. His eyes were glowing bright red and his fangs protruded four full inches from his mouth. Walking slowly, he waited for them to make their move and attack from behind, as he knew they would. Three against one, attacking from behind, Christian relished what he was about to do to these cowards. He not only wanted to taste their blood; he wanted to enjoy the pure scent of their fear.

They were so close he could almost feel their hot breath on his neck and hear their hearts pounding. Then it happened. He felt a strong blow to the back of his head. Christian turned quickly.

"Arrraaagggghhhh!!!" he roared as he grasped his first victim.

As quick as one could swat a fly, Christian clutched him in one hand, by the throat and bit down, tearing away a large piece of flesh and slamming him to pavement. The other two men had about enough time to stop dead in their tracks in fear and surprise. He quickly pounced on the second one, dealing him the same manner of death as the first. The third man turned to run, screaming. "Help me! Help!"

Christian was not content to just stop and feed—he also wanted all three men dead. As the third man ran, weaving between parked cars and screaming for help, Christian took to the air and landed directly in his path, blocking his way.

"No! No!" the man yelled as he turned to change direction. "Get the fuck away from me! Help! Help!" he screamed in terror.

Grabbing him from behind, Christian roared, "What is wrong? You do not wish your victims to fight back?"

He held the man from behind and bit off a chunk of the back of his neck, spitting over the man's shoulder so that it landed on the pavement, in full view of his victim. The man screeched in agony. "Oh God, no, help me!" Christian spun him around and buried his fangs in his throat, and for the first time this evening, drank deeply. He drank until all life was gone, leaving the body in the street. He turned to attend to the other two victims. One was already dead; the other clung to life, if only by a thread. Christian picked him up and finished him, drinking all that he could hold.

As his features began to change and he once-again appeared normal, he stood, holding the last body and staring at it. He wondered why so many warm blooded predators existed in this society. They had no respect for life, which to Christian, was a nightly celebration. He took lives because he needed to for his very existence. But why did they? He realized that since he entered this city, he had yet to really hunt for a meal, and that he could probably exist for years just feeding on these urban predators. As he dropped the body, a blinding spotlight beamed directly on him. "Put your hands up and don't move a muscle!" a loud, strong voice demanded.

Christian smiled to himself as his raised his arms and took flight, leaving the police car below and the officer staring upward in awe. "Jesus Christ!" Christian could hear the officer talk as he rose higher and higher into the dark night sky.

Chapter Seventeen

The sun had set, and Ted had finished all his work, writing his goodbyes and organizing important papers. He sat in the kitchen, calmly eating a sandwich, feeding small pieces to Brutus. "Well, this is it, Brutus. Wish me luck." Brutus just cocked his head and looked into Ted's eyes sadly, as if sensing something was wrong, very wrong.

"Professor?" Ted called.

Steiner entered with concern in his eyes, as Ted had been silent for most of the day.

"Yes, Ted. How can I help you?" he asked.

"I'm taking my crossbow pistol and going to the roof," Ted announced.

"Why?" Steiner asked.

"I'm going to stay there all night, or until that vampire shows up. Then we will settle it, for better or worse," Ted said with determination.

"No, no, no. I have an idea. Invite him in and we can ambush him. If Mike will help us, we can each take one shot at him. Certainly one of us will not miss," the Professor reasoned.

"No! One man has already died in my place. I won't take any more chances with other people's lives. Mike is married. I won't have it. It's him and I, and we'll settle it alone. I've wasted three of these creatures already and I can do it again. Promise me that you won't get involved. Promise me, Professor," Ted pleaded.

Steiner shook his head. "Teddy, no, you can't do this. It's the depression of what we experienced. Post-trauma, is what Mike called it. Wait a few days. If you still feel the same, then I will promise you," the Professor reasoned.

"No! Promise me now! Please, do this for me. Look; I will go to the roof and take two crossbow pistols with me. I'll take a favorable position so if he faces me, as I imagine he will, the light will be in my favor. I will

179

kill him, Professor, I will. Then it will finally be over. Please, be strong enough to do this for me," Ted begged.

"Teddy, you've almost become like the son I never had. What you are thinking of doing takes great courage, but it's not the most intelligent plan. In fact, it's suicide. Let me go with you and at least take a shot. I can hide behind the door. He'll never even see me, and even if I miss, it will take the attention off of you and you can take your best shot," the Professor offered.

"Professor, I must do this. I can't live another day like this. You stay here. I will face him alone, just as I faced his mate." His eyes bore into the Professor's.

"If this is truly what you need to do, I will not stand in your way . . ." the Professor unhappily conceded.

"Professor, should I not come back . . . there are letters I will need distributed and mailed, stacked on my desk. Would you do that for me?"

The Professor nodded sadly, as Ted left to prepare for his confrontation. Wanting to be seen in the dark, Ted put on beige summer pants and a bright white shirt. He then went to his gym bag and produced the two crossbow pistols. He pulled the draw strings back and fired them a few times without arrows, testing that they functioned perfectly. He loaded each one and walked to the front room with one crossbow in each hand hanging at his side, where the Professor was sitting.

"Wish me luck," Ted said softly, looking at the floor.

"Are you sure you must do this, Ted?" the Professor asked one final time.

"Yes, Professor, I need for this to end," Ted stated.

"Then go with God at your side, Ted Scott."

The Professor turned and stared out the open window into the clear night sky as Ted left, walking the stairs slowly to the roof entrance. Taking a deep breath, he opened the door to the gust of cool night wind. He looked in all directions before choosing to sit with his back to the busy street side. This allowed a slight glow of light to illuminate the area he was facing. As he rehearsed the situation in his mind, he assumed the vampire would land and immediately attack. He pictured the vampire landing and at that time, he would fire his first shot, slowing Christian down. He would then quickly drop the crossbow in his right hand and switch to the one in his left, taking his final shot. He assumed there would be no conversation, only violence. He played and replayed the scenario in his

DeathWalker

mind. One quick shot, change the second crossbow to his right hand and then another shot. He sat thinking about it, over and over and over. He could see the vampire drop in agony and almost feel the anxiety lift. He sat alone in the dark, waiting patiently.

*　　*　　*

Christian watched from above as the flashing lights sped toward the area where he had dispatched his last three victims. He was flying higher than the spotlight could shine and felt safe. Returning a few miles to Kathy's building, he scanned the rooftops instinctively. In the midst of the dark rooftops, he spotted one solitary warm blooded being sitting on a roof alone. It was Ted's roof, and Christian knew who this was immediately. He circled twice from high in the sky, thinking that maybe this was a trap, but he could sense no other being in the vicinity. He was compelled to land.

Ted had been sitting for hours and was almost in a trance-like state when Christian landed silently, beyond the glow of lights. Christian stood in the dark, watching Ted just sitting there, cross legged like an Indian on this deserted roof top. Seeing the crossbows in his hands and the glow of light surrounding Ted, Christian knew exactly what Ted's intention was instantly. One of them must die.

He spoke from the darkness. "Ted. Ted Scott?" His voice was deep and commanding.

Ted jumped to his feet, looking with squinted eyes in the direction of the voice. He could see Christian as a dark shadow beyond the faint glow of street lights. He was ready to raise his hand and fire, but he did not have a clear target. Ted's mouth went dry as the beads of perspiration formed on his forehead.

"Yes, I'm Ted Scott. I killed your mate. If it matters, she attacked me. It was an accident, as I was protecting myself, but it was I that killed her," Ted explained, his voice cracking with dryness.

"Life and death are not accidental, Mister Scott," Christian stated with hostility seething.

"Then let's get on with it," Ted demanded. His eyes were focused on the target, waiting for Christian to step into the faint glow of light so he could see his target clearly. His finger itched for the chance to fire. He pictured an imaginary three inch circle prominent on Christian's chest.

"On with what, may I ask, Mister Scott?" Christian replied, knowing exactly what Ted intended.

"Your revenge. You said you wanted revenge," Ted stated.

"You are wearing a blessed cross, Mr. Scott." Christian could feel it repelling him.

"Yes, yes I am," Ted answered.

"Am I to stand here and allow you to shoot arrows at me, while you hide behind the protection of a blessed crucifix? Is that what you mean by 'getting on' with it?" Christian asked.

"No. This will be the end of this. It's either you or I that walk away this night, and I want this over with." Ted ripped his crucifix from his neck, tossing it as far as he could.

Christian not only watched the crucifix as it flew through the air, he could also feel its blessed power drift away into the darkness.

"Well then, it seems that this has become an eye for an eye situation, so to speak, as according to your Bible. You are familiar with The Bible, Mister Scott?" Christian questioned arrogantly.

"What? What do you mean, eye for an eye?" Ted asked.

"I have taken your comely Katherine, Mister Scott, in exchange for my beloved Anne. So in effect, at this point, we're even," Christian replied defiantly.

"You fucking bastard! You're lying!" Ted screamed. In an instant, his blood began to boil and a rage like none other that he had felt before began to fill his entire body.

As they spoke, Christian kept pacing back and forth, just beyond the glow of light that ended at his feet. He could see that Ted's trigger finger had tensed and was prepared to fire, and realized there was only one ending to this confrontation. He knew he had to disrupt Ted's concentration as he continued taunting him.

"Have you talked to your Katherine in the last twenty-four hours, Mister Scott?" Christian asked dryly.

"You killed her?" Ted asked, disbelieving.

"No . . ." Christian stated with a sly smile. "I have taken her as my mate. She will be a vampire, as I am."

"That's bullshit!" Ted screamed again, careful not to move. He knew Christian was playing him like a game, but couldn't shake the feeling that he wasn't lying about Kathy.

DeathWalker

"Well, if I told you she failed to wear the blessed token you gave her, would that convince you?" Christian taunted.

"Well then, if I do kill you, she will return to normal," Ted assumed. He watched the shadow move back and forth at the edge of his vision. *'Take two steps forward, you bastard . . .'* Ted was thinking.

"Hahaha, what is that, some human fairy tale?" Christian said with amusement.

"Isn't it true that if the head vampire is killed the ones the he created will return to normal?" Ted asked.

"No, Mister Scott. Once a vampire, always a vampire. There is no way to return to your world. My blood runs through her veins now and she's mine. She will always be mine. This is funny Mister Scott, for if you kill me, you must kill her too; because as my mate, she will hunt you down as I did! Hahaha!" Christian was amused with the whole situation. He was feeling his full revenge without even harming a hair on Ted's head.

"You fucking evil bastard, I'll kill you!" Ted screamed.

"Ha! Have you forgotten so easily, Ted Scott? I'm already dead!" Christian mocked.

*   *   *

Mike Evans had responded to a call on the three killings, and viewing the state of the bodies and hearing the officer babble on about a flying man, he fled to Ted's with lights flashing. Racing down Hennepin Street, he drove to Ted's building with siren blaring. Arriving, he frantically rang the buzzer.

"Hello, who is it?" asked the Professor.

"Buzz me in, it's Mike."

Mike felt that if the vampire had killed so close to Ted's building, he would either have been there, or would soon be on the way. Entering the apartment, he could see only the Professor sitting somberly. "Where's Teddy?" Mike asked.

"He wanted to end this," the Professor responded.

"Where is he?" Mike asked again.

"Alone. He is alone on the roof, awaiting the vampire," the Professor answered.

"Shit!" Mike yelled as he turned to run up the stairway to the roof entrance.

"Come on you fucking bastard. Come and get me," Ted pleaded.

Christian knew what Ted's strategy had to be. He figured Ted would fire one shot immediately and a final shot as he charged, should he have missed. As Christian stepped forward into the faint glow of light, he watched Ted raise his right hand, as if it were in slow motion. He watched the trigger finger tense up and tighten on the trigger. At that specific instant, he stepped to the right, with lightning speed, and the first arrow disappeared into the darkness. Christian watched as Ted dropped the crossbow in his right hand and switched over to the loaded one in his left hand.

"Come on, you bastard!" Ted yelled.

Christian sensed no fear as Ted stared directly into his face in defiance. His was now a face transformed to that of a hideous monster. Christian opened his mouth wide as he ran forward, driven to end Ted's life. As Ted raised his right hand to fire, his adrenaline was pumping full blast. It was this reaction that likely caused him to pull the trigger a fraction of a second too soon. The final arrow was released and it pierced Christian's midsection, at least five inches from its intended target—his heart. Ted just stared in disbelief, and knew exactly what was next to come.

"This will be swift, Ted Scott," Christian growled.

Ted stood, frozen in his place, and before he could utter, "Oh Shi—" Christian had torn his throat open. He did not drink a single drop; he just watched as Ted's life oozed out, covering the roof top. At that very moment, the door behind him flew open, and Christian whirled to confront another opponent. As Mike came barreling through, he stopped on a dime upon witnessing the carnage. There, in the glow of the light, stood a hideous creature with his good friend, Ted, lying at his feet in a huge pool of blood. Despite this horrific image, Mike's rage was instant.

As Mike reached for his gun, Christian smiled. Mike realized that he had blown it completely and had made a fatal mistake. He had two new crossbow pistols in the back seat of the car, yet there he stood with only this useless gun in his trembling hand. A weapon that he already knew

DeathWalker

was completely powerless the second he pulled it out in a reflex action. He stood with gun drawn, staring at the vampire who was only ten feet away. Mike could only watch as Christian moved closer with cat like speed. Standing only a few feet apart, Mike could see the red eyes, the huge white fangs, and feel the evil focused on him.

"Put that weapon away, it is useless." Christian stated as he pulled the arrow from his midsection, tossing it aside.

"Oh, Teddy," Mike grieved, looking past Christian and at Ted's body lying lifeless, staring up at the stars.

Mike kept the gun aimed at Christian's heart. "I'm going to nail you for this, you fucking monster!" Mike threatened.

"I can smell your fear strongly from here, my friend. Put that weapon away," Christian demanded.

"Why, so it will be easier to kill me?" Mike asked.

"I have no quarrel with you," Christian responded. "I try only to kill what I need to eat."

"There are bodies all over this city. Did you quarrel with all of them?" Mike asked.

"They are worth nothing! Most are better off being dead. It is better for them, and better for the living, I warrant," Christian replied defiantly.

"You know I will find you and kill you," Mike threatened.

"I don't think you will dare, for the smell of your fear is very strong." Christian raised his arms and elevated about six feet in the air. "I have no quarrel with you." These were his final words as he rose higher and higher, until completely out of sight.

Mike ran to Ted's body and checked, but there was no pulse.

"Shit! Teddy why? Why didn't you wait for help? Damn it, Teddy!" Mike yelled as he took his jacket and covered Ted's face. Some men have a difficult time with crying. Mike felt his lower lip quiver and his eyes became blurry. His tight jaw and clenched teeth began to weaken. Mike stood just staring, and observed a glimmer some feet away. He walked over and picked up the golden cross and clutched it tightly in his hand. He knew this was Ted's fatal mistake. *'God, why did he take this off?'*

As many men do, he swallowed hard and turned the emotion inward, churning it and churning it, until it resurfaced as blinding rage. Then he proceeded down the two flights of stairs to Ted's apartment. The Professor didn't ask, for seeing Mike's face, he knew Ted was surely dead. He watched as Mike dialed the phone.

185

"This is Evans. We have a death at 10th Street. It's on the roof. I need someone to take over at the scene." Mike explained. "I'm going to pursue the killer," he continued. "I'll call in later."

"You're going after him?" the Professor asked.

"Yeah, I have a hunch on where he'll be," Mike answered. "Do you know where Ted kept his wooden arrows?" Mike asked.

"Yes, look for a gym bag in his room," Steiner answered.

Mike grabbed six arrows, stuffing them in his pocket. "Stay here, Professor. I'll see you in the morning." With that, Mike ran for his car, which was still sitting with the engine running. He took off driving toward the Mississippi and Third Street intersection of the deserted buildings. He picked a spot, midway between the three-block area that his lieutenant had circled. There, he parked his car and had a clear view one block North and one block South. He would sit in the darkness waiting for anything that moved within his range of vision. He reached in the back seat for the crossbow pistols and loaded both. All he could think of was Ted. "Damn you, Teddy. Damn you. Why didn't you wait for help?" He sat, anticipating in silence, looking from front to rear; waiting for anything to move in the shadows.

All Mike could think of was killing this vampire. He wondered, '*How could these monsters exist?*' As a detective, he thought he had seen it all but now that he knew what was lurking in the shadows, his everyday job seemed trivial. Sworn to serve and protect, he questioned how one could defend the public from these monsters? He knew he could not even talk about this to anyone without them questioning his sanity. He knew that even if he killed Christian, he would always be obsessed with searching for these beasts. As he watched for any movement, he knew his life was forever changed.

Chapter Eighteen

Only minutes after Ted's death, at the Indian reservation in Manitoba, Canada, the old Indian elder, Gray Wolf, awoke. Bothered and unable to sleep, he wandered outside and lit a fire. Then he sat in the traditional manner to meditate. Normally he slept soundly, but this night he was bothered. He was struck by sadness, and began to chant softly. "Heyya hah, heyya hah," he chanted. It was a chant reserved for a death in the family.

It was almost dawn when one of his grandchildren looked out the window. There, he saw a fire in the darkness, and his grandfather sitting alone. The twelve year old boy snuck from his house and walked slowly to where his grandfather sat, still chanting softly.

"Grandfather? Ogiima? Why are you sitting alone?" he asked.

"I am grieving, my son. I am grieving," the old man answered.

"For who, Grandfather?" The boy became concerned that someone close had died, or at least was deathly ill.

"One of our clan has passed on, little one," the old man answered.

"Who, OgiiMa? Who?" the boy asked, softly.

"No one you know, little one. He was a good man and of our blood."

"Was he from here?" the boy questioned. "Do I know him?"

"No, little one. He was from far away," Gray Wolf replied.

"Then how do you know he died, Grandfather?" The boy looked perplexed.

"When one of us dies, little one, there is a great pain in my heart. Tonight, my heart is in great pain . . . great pain."

"May I sit with you, OgiiMa?" the boy inquired, to which Gray Wolf nodded.

The boy sat next to his grandfather, silently staring at the flames.

"Do you know the story of the Windigo?" Gray Wolf asked.

187

"Yes, Grandfather. I know the many, many stories. Why? The woods are full of sound, Grandfather. There is no sign of the Windigo?" the boy responded.

"I know, little one. I want you to remember those stories and never forget them," Gray Wolf replied slowly.

Confused but respectful, the boy remarked, "I won't, Grandfather. I won't."

Gray Wolf put his arm around the boy and they sat and watched the fire in silence.

Hours had passed and it was just before sunrise when Mike finally spotted a man walking quickly across the street, about a block away. He watched as the man entered into a deserted building. 'I've got him . . .' he thought. Mike watched as the sun slowly rose, knowing that it would provide protection, in the event he had to make a hasty retreat. Mike also knew that the sunlight might also become his ultimate weapon.

He sat for a minute, contemplating his alternatives. If he called for backup, he would only be taking "unarmed" men in with him, as their guns would offer no protection. In effect, he would only be risking lives. He took a deep breath and stepped from the car. A crossbow pistol in each hand, he walked slowly to the deserted building. He looked up at the morning sky before walking in. The warehouse was completely empty, with the few windows it had painted black, making the building dark as night on the inside. Mike propped the door open, giving himself a path of light as he walked further into the empty structure. Being an old building, it had unusually high ceilings. He looked up, and could see a window glowing faintly, as it, too, was painted over in black. Setting down the crossbows, he looked for—and found—something to throw. It was a large, heavy bolt. He pitched it through the window. It shattered, allowing beams of light to come filtering through, illuminating a vast area.

He looked around the building and saw nothing but boxes and debris. At the far end of the building was an open stairway to the second floor. Picking up his crossbows, Mike walked slowly to the stairs. "Am I fucking nuts?" he mumbled under his breath as he scaled them, one step at a time, to the second floor. The stairs kept going up, so Mike traveled into

DeathWalker

another level of complete and utter darkness. He stared at the outer walls, looking for a painted window. He eventually saw a soft gray glow about midway in, but high on the wall.

Walking back down stairs, Mike searched for items to throw, finding a few more bolts and stuffing them into his pocket. Again, Mike slowly scaled the stairs, proceeding cautiously toward the painted-over window. Setting his crossbows down, he pitched a bolt through the glass. Instead of the window shattering, only a bolt sized hole was made, and a solitary, thin beam of light rushed in. As he reached into his pocket for another to try again, his peripheral vision glimpsed something dark moving in his direction, and he heard the sound of footsteps shuffling. He quickly picked up a crossbow pistol, facing the shadow that was rapidly approaching. "Stop where you are!" Mike ordered, as if he was speaking to a common criminal. At this point, he was reluctant to fire, because his police training had instilled caution in his actions. In the back of his mind, he still felt that this could merely be a homeless person or a crack head, and he didn't want to overreact.

The shadow continued to slowly move closer, and Mike carefully aimed the crossbow at the center of its chest. "I said stop where you are or I'll fire!" he yelled. A deep, loud "Arrrrhhhhhggggg!" was all that was returned. It was a sound that Mike had heard once before and now he was absolutely certain of what he was dealing with. Ten yards away, Mike yelled out, "You bastard I told you I'd find you!" and fired his first arrow after taking careful aim. He heard the sickening "Thud!" and as quickly as he fired, he dropped the empty crossbow, picking up the second loaded one.

He stood and aimed again, as the figure continued coming forward. Grabbing the crossbow pistol with two hands and aiming carefully, he fired again. Once more he heard the familiar "Thud!" of an arrow sinking in flesh. With that shot came a piercing scream, and Mike quickly produced another arrow from his pocket, trying to reload as the figure was still moving forward and was becoming visible in the faint glow of light. His hands began to tremble and shake; he found he couldn't look down to accurately reload successfully. "Shit, shit!" he mumbled, as the vampire was upon him.

He grasped the arrow in his right hand tightly and dropping the crossbow, he prepared to meet his attacker in hand to hand combat. He had never felt this much anger in his whole life, nor did Mike feel the three inch claws run across his shoulder and down his left arm, for his adrenaline was surging and he concentrated on one thing—plunging that arrow into this vampire's heart. With all his strength, he slammed the arrow into the center of the vampire's chest, screaming "Die, you fucking bastard!" He knew he had punctured his target when the vampire released his grip, and he heard the high pitched screech of surprise and agony. The vampire moved away and slowly sank to its knees, finally collapsing. Mike stood in shock, for he had thought surely, only a second ago, he was doomed to die. Slowly, he walked over to examine the body, finding that it was not Christian. This vampire was smaller, and had a pony tail and a silver earring in his ear. It was an eerie sight, as one of Mike's arrows had struck the vampire directly in the center of the forehead; the second, through the throat. "Sonofabitch!" is all Mike could mutter, as he felt the warm blood running down his arm, which was now aching in pain. Leaving the crossbows where they laid, he walked slowly to his car in shock, saying the same thing over and over. "Sonofabitch!"

On the radio, he placed an 'officer needs assistance' call and within minutes, the place was crawling with police and Mike was on his way to Hennepin Medical Center. One hundred and forty stitches later, he was lying heavily sedated in a hospital bed. Under sedation, all he could repeat over and over was "Sonofabitch, I'll get you, you sonofabitch!"

Chapter Nineteen

hristian sat in the darkness, watching Kathy sleep, knowing she would soon awake, her metamorphosis complete. At sunset she began to stir and had opened her eyes. She looked around the room, clearly confused.

"Kathy?" Christian said softly.

She looked to him and smiled. "Katherine. I prefer being called Katherine."

"We must leave now," he stated.

"Yes, I know," she responded.

She arose and gazed around the room, as if it were a strange and foreign place. As her new eyes scanned the room, what were once her most coveted objects now went ignored, as if they held no meaning at all. As far as her new life was concerned, she instinctively needed to be without walls or boundaries. She longed for the night. It was as if she had been reborn, as she examined her hands and looked down at herself, as though she was seeing this body for the very first time.

Christian offered his hand and she grasped it, smiling, as if knowing the pleasures this new life would bring. As they walked to the door, she paused, glancing at a velvet box lying on a table, as if it alone held some forgotten meaning. She took one final look at her apartment, knowing that she would never again return. Then, she turned, following Christian to the hallway. Her eyes were fixed on the little velvet box as she closed the door. It was as if she sensed that the velvet box contained the blessed crucifix that Ted hoped would save her from Christian.

As they boarded the elevator and pressed the button to the first floor, an old woman studied them both before speaking and saying "Hello Miss Baker." Katherine smiled, but didn't speak and only nodded.

As they walked from the lobby into the street, the blind man stood near the entrance, waiting for his ride. "Good evening," Christian offered to him as they passed. The blind man instantly recognized his voice.

Edwin F. Becker

"How did it work out for you, with that girl?" the blind man asked.

"It turned out fine," Katherine responded.

The blind man smiled. "He's not a deviate is he? If he is, I'll smack him one!" He was kidding with her.

"No, he is a real gentleman," Katherine replied.

The blind man smiled, but noticed that her scent had changed dramatically and he picked up a musty odor as they passed. '*Strange . . .*' he thought, as he had never smelled anything like it.

As they turned the corner, Katherine stated "I hunger . . ."

"Soon." Christian replied. "Believe me, your hunger will be satisfied soon."

They walked a busy street, further and further away from the apartment that she once called home. The lights of the densely populated downtown area came and went as they walked the streets of west bank, going north. Soon, they were strolling in an area that one would not normally go without a badge or a weapon at that time of night.

"Hey, baby," came a rough voice. "Hey, you lost or something?" a man asked, as he stepped directly in their path.

"No, we're searching," Christian responded.

"Searching for what?" the man asked gruffly.

"Food!" Christian answered, as he quickly grabbed the man by the collar and pulled him close, immediately biting his throat and tearing out a bite-sized piece.

The man tried to scream, but all he managed to do was produce a sickening, gurgling gasp. His blood flowed freely and Christian moved his head away and held out the offering to Katherine, who, without hesitating, drank willingly and anxiously of this new, warm, sweet nourishment. When she finished, she licked her lips, simply stating "Divine!"

"Now let us go home," Christian stated. Lifting his arms, he rose from the ground only a few feet. Watching him closely, Katherine did the same, defying gravity and rising toward the stars.

"Where are we going?" Katherine asked.

"We're on our way home . . ." Christian answered.

"Where is home?" she questioned with wonder.

"Look around. It is all ours! The world is our home," he stated, proudly.

DeathWalker

* * *

It was the next morning that Mike Evans awoke in his hospital bed. His wife, Marnie, was at his side.

"How long have I been out?" he asked her.

"Almost twenty-four hours," she answered, tears streaming down her face.

As he tried to sit up, he felt the awful pain across his left shoulder and arm. "Jesus Christ!" he exclaimed.

"Over one hundred stitches . . ." Marnie stated. "The doctor says that you're a very lucky man. You came very close to losing the use of that arm," she explained, as she offered him a cup of water. "Your Lieutenant called and said to tell you that the case is closed. He called Ted's father and gave him the bad news of Ted's death. The body is being sent up to Roseau. And, oh yes, Kathy Baker has been reported as a missing person as of yesterday morning."

"How soon can I leave, Marnie?"

"As soon as you like, but you'll be in a sling for some time."

"I need to bring Ted's things to his father, and I also need to investigate Kathy Baker's apartment," Mike rambled.

"Mike, you need a few days rest. Why don't you let someone else handle this?" she pleaded.

"No; I promised Teddy. Call me a nurse, I'm checking out . . ." Mike stated with conviction. Marnie knew that there was no reasoning with Mike once he had made his mind up.

"I'll get your clothes . . ."

As Mike watched her retrieve his clothes, he knew a barrier would exist in their marriage that he would never remove. Never, ever, would he be able to share the horror that he now knew existed in this world. This would become something that he must hold inside. He had opened a door to a world that he knew could never be closed.

Thirty minutes later, Mike was on his way to Ted's condo. Upon arriving, he soon found the Professor, upset that Kathy had disappeared.

"I believe that he took Kathy!" the Professor announced. "Her parents called and Ted's dad called, both looking for her. They said her office called and she hadn't been to work for three days!" Professor Steiner explained. "Are you okay?"

193

"It was nothing that a couple hundred stitches couldn't fix," Mike replied.

"I take it that you found one?"

"Yeah, but not the right one. Christian escaped us. Probably forever . . ." Mike muttered, sadly. "I need to call Teddy's father," he stated, as he dialed the phone.

"Mister Scott?" Mike asked. "This is detective Mike Evans, Minneapolis P.D . . . . I was also a close friend of Ted's," he explained. "Listen, Mister Scott, we need to talk. I will handle everything here, so don't worry about Brutus or Ted's things . . . but I would rather talk about this in person, if you would be so kind to accommodate me. I can be up there by tomorrow evening, if that's okay with you . . . great, I'll see you tomorrow night then. Goodbye." Mike hung up. "Professor, come with me," Mike ordered.

Exiting Ted's condo, they made their way down the block to Kathy's apartment building. In the lobby, her mail box was clearly marked **Kathy Baker 622**. Up the elevator to the sixth floor, Mike knocked on the door. There was no answer. He tried the door, finding it unlocked.

"Wait here, Professor," Mike ordered, assuming that he might just possibly encounter a body. Instinctively, he drew his gun and entered cautiously.

Mike walked about the apartment, finding everything in its proper place. But sniffing the air, he could smell a foul, musty odor. "Professor?" he called. The Professor entered. "Do you smell that?" Mike asked.

"Yes, I do. The odor is very strong," Steiner answered.

"He must have been here for at least a few days," Mike reasoned.

"My God, he must have taken her!" Steiner gasped.

"I'm afraid so," Mike answered. "Looks like I have another very unpleasant call to make. We can only officially determine that she has been abducted, but we both know she will never be found . . ." Mike said woefully.

"Do you think he turned her into a vampire?" Professor Steiner wondered aloud.

"I can only assume that if there's no body and no signs of struggle, then it's likely she went with him as a willing participant. If she did, we both know why that might happen," Mike deducted. "Let's go."

Mike and the Professor boarded the elevator and stood in the lobby. The blind man was getting his mail as he heard Mike say "I wonder if anyone saw anything?" The Blind man turned and faced them.

DeathWalker

"Saw what?" asked the blind man.

Mike immediately noticed the white cane, and knew this conversation was futile, but decided to be polite. "We have a missing woman," he stated.

The blind man responded immediately. "Don't tell me—sixth floor."

"How did you know?" Mike asked.

"I sensed something was wrong, I just couldn't put my finger on it. Her perfume changed. She didn't smell very good. Musty, is what I would call it. A little funky, and definitely musty," the blind man stated.

"When did you last encounter her?" Mike asked.

"Last night. They left last night," he replied.

"They? Who are they?" Mike queried.

"A man. A big man, maybe 6" 2", or so. He spoke very proper English, as if he was well educated. By his voice, I'd say he was in his thirties. They left together."

"What was her demeanor?" Mike asked.

"She sounded calm and happy. No, not happy-" he corrected himself. "-but satisfied. That's how I'd describe it. She acted as though she was happy to be in his company. Why? Did something happen?" he asked.

"Yes. As of today, she's officially a missing person," Mike responded.

"Christ! She seemed so at ease. Could it be that she just ran away with this guy?" The blind man seemed genuinely shocked.

"Yeah, and that's my biggest fear," Mike stated.

"You don't think he did something to her, do you?" the blind man asked.

"Unfortunately, he may have." Mike glanced at the Professor, who was looking on, in torment.

"Shit! I should have smacked that mother fucker when he was snooping around here. He said he only wanted to return her pen," the blind man replied.

"What is your name? And where can I find you, if I need to talk with you?" Mike asked.

"Charles Herman is my name. Penthouse, tenth floor. Anytime, my friend. Glad to help you." The blind man turned and walked away, tapping his cane as he moved.

Mike looked to the Professor. "Kathy is gone. We'll never find her. Worse yet is if we do, assuming *he* didn't kill her, *we* might be forced to, assuming she's now one of them."

195

"I know . . ." the Professor answered. They slowly walked back to Ted's condo.

"Professor, I'll be back in a little while. I have some police business," Mike stated.

"You go right ahead. I'll be packing my things."

Mike's next stop was at the coroner's office, in the basement of the Medical Center that he was just released from hours ago. Paul Malone was anxious to display the photograph of the man that Mike had killed in the deserted building. Polaroid after Polaroid, completely blank.

"Mike, here! Look at these." Paul tossed them on his desk.

"I don't see much," Mike responded, glancing at photo after photo.

"The body is in the other room. Take a photo yourself, if you like. The body won't show up. Now what do you say? Do I hear the word vampire?" Paul asked.

"It's over," Mike stated dryly.

"What?" Paul asked.

"I said it's over. No more killings, no more mutilated bodies."

"You sure? So that was your guy?" Paul asked.

Mike knew that Christian had gone and that the killings were likely finished, so he lied. "Yeah, that was the guy."

"He was a vampire, wasn't he?" Paul asked.

"Come on . . ." Mike said as he walked into the autopsy room. "Where is one?" he asked.

"Drawer three," Paul answered.

Mike opened it to find the body of the female vampire they had killed in the storm drain. "Bring me that cart," he ordered.

He lifted the body onto the cart and pushed it down the hall toward a window. "Watch this . . ." he stated, as he pushed the cart into the beam of sunlight. Immediately it started smoking, like a smoke bomb had gone off. They both stepped back as the body quickly turned into a hideous skeleton, and the air turned foul with a sickening odor.

"Jesus Christ!" Paul exclaimed.

"No. Just a damned vampire," Mike replied. "Now you know for sure, Paul. But it should never leave this room. Yes, I was hunting vampires. I killed them all and now it's over; I hope for forever. I know, you know, and the Lieutenant knows. Nobody would ever believe it, so don't even think about telling the story."

DeathWalker

"Don't worry, I know what people would think. That I had been sniffing a little too much embalming fluid . . ." Paul responded.

"Ted Scott's body? Did it go to Roseau? He'll be buried there. Did you handle it?" Mike asked.

"Not a problem, it's already on its way," Paul answered.

"See you . . ." Mike left, hoping this was the last visit to the coroner's office for a long time. It was time to return to Ted's apartment to load his car with the things he would be taking to Ted's father. Once finished, he would attempt to get a good night's sleep before making the long drive north.

Chapter Twenty

At sunset, Christian awoke swiftly. No longer being driven by revenge, he enjoyed the pleasant concern that he now had for Katherine. They had so much to do and he had so much to show her. He woke her gently. "Welcome to the night," he whispered.

A soft smile graced her face, as she realized it was time to enjoy the darkness once again. They had slept in a cave and were still heading north to a more secluded territory. Outside, they raised their arms and took flight. They were both hungry, but didn't have to say it, as it was understood. Gliding across the night sky and looking down, they watched for a feeding opportunity.

Flying parallel near the highway, two motorcycles could be seen speeding north in the darkness. Katherine could see clearly that the motorcycles were driven by two warm blooded beings. For the first time, she noticed their "glow," and how easy they were to spot. Christian started to descend, so as to get a closer look. He glimpsed toward Katherine, who just smiled. He hovered only ten feet above one of the bikers, and began reading his jacket. "Devil's Bikers," it stated boldly. Amused, Christian decided to go along for a ride and landed on the back of the motorcycle.

"What the fuck? What is this?" the biker yelled, his bike swerving.

"Dinner," Christian whispered in his ear. He grabbed the biker around the neck and viciously bit down. The biker was screaming and applying the brakes. The motorcycle began to tumble as Christian lifted his dinner into the air and continued feeding. As the motorcycle crashed into a ditch, Christian had finished feeding and tossed the body atop the wreckage. The biker riding in front never saw what happened and didn't hear a thing, due to the loud roar of the engine. He never looked back.

Katherine, who was carefully observing, took Christian's example and did the same. She landed on the first biker's rear seat.

"God, what is this?" he screamed.

DeathWalker

"It's what I call 'meals on wheels'!" she replied, laughing. Traveling at sixty miles per hour, he attempted to jump from the bike, only to find himself suspended in midair. "Jesus help me! God no, no!" he yelled.

"Some Devil's Biker you are!" she mocked as she bit into his neck and gently landed him to the ground. She found feeding to be a glorious experience, and savored every drop. When finished, she dumped the body in a roadside ditch, giving it a few good slashes before flying off to meet Christian.

"Is our life only made of pleasures?" she asked.

"Yes, it can be, but we must protect it and never risk exposure," he answered.

Katherine smiled as she rose to the sky in a euphoric rapture. "I love the night!" she exclaimed.

This was a freedom she had never experienced. Once her hunger was satisfied, it seemed the night embraced her with its beauty. The full moon illuminated the countryside, creating images never seen by the human eye. Katherine realized that it was all hers to enjoy forever. Christian watched her wide eyes as they absorbed everything in sight. It pleased him that he had made the right decision and kept her as his mate. Together, they could live a simple existence, away from the dangers of the highly populated urban areas. Christian was content to assume his former lifestyle, as he was tired of the useless killing. Flying into the night, he understood that eternity was his, once more.

As he looked at Katherine, he basked in her joy at becoming a Vampire. He knew she had much to learn and would teach her over time. Christian also knew the she would become a wealth of knowledge in teaching him about all the world history of the past 100 years and of modern technology of which he knew little. He was satisfied, as he had filled the emptiness in his being and had found a mate for eternity. He would immediately begin schooling her in protecting the knowledge of their very existence. He wished to return to being an unknown. He wished to return to being regarded as a mythical creature.

*   *   *

The next morning, Mike's car was loaded with all of Ted's personal items. The Professor was packing his things and preparing to leave.

Edwin F. Becker

"I guess it's over?" the Professor stated in a quizzical manner.

"Yeah, I guess so. There's no chance of tracking him down. Don't you think?" Mike asked.

"Detective, I don't see how we could ever find him. It would be easier to find a needle in haystack," Steiner replied. "It's time I went home." Packing his manuscript in his suitcase, Professor Steiner looked to Mike and replied "I'll publish this, you know? Even if I have to say it's novelized. It will be dedicated to Teddy," he stated.

"That's nice, Professor Steiner, real nice. I'll come visit you at the university sometime?" Mike offered.

"I'd like that. We have a special bond, you know." Steiner placed his hand on Mike's shoulder.

"Yes, I do know." Mike replied, patting Steiner's hand with his. "We are the only two people alive that faced a vampire and lived to talk about it. Maybe you should write that story."

"Yes, we faced him. Indeed we did," the Professor stated proudly. "You know, we will eventually search for him. I hope your realize that. Neither of us can live with this. I will do what I can. Eventually, I will organize a search party to travel to the northwest corner of the state and search for the remains of that vampire's mate that Ted had killed. Should we find them, it will become an indicator of his presence and domain. I assume that where ever she is hidden, he will not be far away. Should I be successful, you will be hearing from me. As you know, I have failed at confrontations."

"Well, I won't. Should you have any evidence of where that vampire is, you call me. I will be doing nothing but practicing with these crossbows and I will look forward to that day. Don't you dare try facing him on your own."

"I am not that brave, Michael. I lack the courage."

Mike just smiled knowingly. "Say goodbye to Brutus, Professor," Mike asked.

Steiner hugged the little Yorkie and handed him gently to Mike, who ordered, "Don't forget to lock this place up." Mike and Brutus were soon traveling northwest toward Roseau.

Four hours into the trip, he came upon State police and a tow truck, pulling a motorcycle out of a ditch. Glancing at the condition of the bike, he knew it was likely a fatal accident. '*Stupid damned bikers . . .*' he thought. He slowed his vehicle and rolled down his window. Flashing his badge, he

DeathWalker

asked the state trooper "What do you have?" The patrolman responded "Just two bikers that crashed. Both are dead and tore to pieces pretty good. They must have been really flying. Probably drunk as skunks."

"Thanks," Mike responded and drove on. He sat back, relaxed, and enjoyed the scenery. He knew why Ted loved the northwest so much, for it was a beautiful country. As Mike drove on, Brutus was fast asleep on the front seat. It was a short six hours and Mike pulled into the dirt road that led to Ted's father's house. He parked his car and let Brutus out. Brutus immediately took off running for the front door and jumped into the arms of Ted's father, who lovingly scooped him up. Brutus proceeded to adoringly clean the old man's face, licking at it gently.

"Hi, I'm Ray Scott," he said as he extended his hand.

"I'm Mike Evans. We have an awful lot to talk about. I brought some of Ted's things and a letter addressed to you, from Ted. I also brought you this . . ." Mike handed Ray Ted's gold crucifix. It was the one the Ted had taken off before his final confrontation.

Ray held it with a tear in his eye. "He bought me one. He told me never to take it off. Here, you should have this." He handed it to Mike.

Ted's dad read the letter and cried in anguish. Then, Mike explained to him that he had a story to tell; a true story of what had transpired that led to the death. They sat for hours with Mike talking and Ray listening. Mike told of the hunting trip and how John Hall was killed. He told of how Christian had visited Ted's condo and how Ted decided to face him in a final battle for life. Sadly, he told of Kathy likely becoming a creature of the night. Mike warned Ray never to invite a stranger into his house at night, and more important, should he see Kathy, it will not be the Kathy he once knew.

Ray was concerned for the Bakers living down the road, as they think their daughter is a missing person. What if she shows up at their door some night? Shouldn't they be warned, he wondered?

Mike assured Ray that prayer might be the only answer, for they would never believe the truth of what had transpired. How could you possibly face them as parents and try to explain that their only daughter was now a vampire? It was far kinder to leave her as a missing person. They could only hope that with Kathy's change, her memories might also have faded. They both knew the precarious situation that the unknowing Bakers' were in. Both agreed they were helpless, as far as informing them.

As night fell, Ray invited Mike to stay the night, and they moved to the front porch to watch the magnificent sunset, never knowing that they were sitting in Christian's backyard.

*   *   *

Christian and Katherine awoke to the sounds of the night. "Come with me," Christian said as he took her hand. Rising to the dark sky, they floated over the tree tops to a clearing in the dense woods, landing softly on a large boulder. It was the same huge piece of stone that his Anne had loved so very much.

Katherine looked up at moon and whispered "What a wonderful place!" It seemed so familiar to her. Christian knew she would enjoy it, for it was Anne's favorite place. Anne would sit for hours, just gazing at the moon. Katherine never remembered lying on this same boulder while enjoying the sun the day she had met Ted, for all her memories of past life were beginning to fade.

"I feel at home here," Katherine stated.

"You are home, Katherine." Christian cooed. "Will you miss the modern life?"

"No. This is as if I stepped into a dream."

"I shun the big cities and the population," he replied.

"We will live in the wilderness?"

"I have for over 100 years."

"What of our food?"

"I have never experienced true hunger."

"Will you tell me of your 100 years?" Katherine asked.

"Will you acquaint me with your modern ways and speech?"

Katherine reached for his hand as they basked in the glow of the night sky. As far as they were concerned, they were in eternal paradise. A paradise they would protect to the death from anyone that posed a threat.

DeathWalker

* * *

As Ray and Mike talked, the woods suddenly became dark and silent. Even Mike, who had no knowledge of the phenomena, took immediate notice. "Whoa, it got quiet all of a sudden," Mike replied.

"Let's go inside," Ray suggested, standing up. "I promised Teddy I would never go outside when the woods become quiet like this."

Walking inside, Mike noticed the gun cabinet with the crossbow hanging alongside. He took it off the holder and examined it. It was larger than the hand held model he was familiar with, and much more powerful.

Ray watched Mike admire the weapon. "It was Ted's favorite. I would like you to have it. Seeing as what you went through, I am sure he would have liked you to have it, too."

"Thanks Mr. Scott. Thanks." Mike could only wonder if he would ever have occasion to need one again. As he handled the crossbow, he imagined Christian standing directly in his sights, and he pulled the trigger. *'I wish I had one more crack at him, that bastard . . .'* Mike thought *'Someday . . . . maybe someday.'*

Mike handed it back to Ray. "I could not leave you defenseless. Believe me; everything in the gun cabinet is useless, should a vampire come knocking at your door. I will return and bring you the handheld version, and then I will take this with pride. I promise you this, Ray; I will always be searching. I know what he looks like, and I will never give up. I will kill every single one of these monsters I can find."

* * *

About a mile away, a little Indian boy was playing outside of his house. His father came to door and noticing the silence, yelled to him, "Ingozis? Ingozis? Tommy, come in the house, come in right now!"

"Why father?" the young boy asked.

"You must not be outside! Geyaabi, Windigo! Geyaabi, Windigo! Windigo!" his father yelled.

The young Indian boy gathered his toys and ran for the house. Once inside, he looked to his father and asked, "Father, what is Windigo? Why does he bring such goshi—such fear?"

203

His father swallowed hard, and sternly looked the little boy in the eyes.

"The animals and life that are controlled by KichiManitu—the Great Spirit—are helping us by sending us a warning. It is up to us to pay attention and listen to them. Understand?" he asked.

"Yes, father . . ." the boy answered, hesitantly.

"When the woods are gayaabi—dead silent—**he** is there, hunting for our souls. **He** will suck the life from you, if you do not respect his presence. **He** is the NibookeBimosa—The Death Mover. **He** is Windigo. We must respect his presence and pray, my son, that he moves on. **He** is the Windigo, the **DeathWalker!**"

*This tale will continue in, **Death Walker II; A Vampire's Domain**.*

Edwin F. Becker